TRACK & ELIMINATE

Track & Eliminate

Copyright 2018 Barry Lees.

All rights reserved. No part of this publication may be produced, in whole or in part, or transmitted in any form or by any means without the permission of the owner. This book is licensed for your personal enjoyment only.

Barry Lees has asserted his right under the Copyright, Designs and Patents Act 1988 to be identified as the author of this work.

ISBN   978-1-9997928-7-9

All of the characters in this book are fictitious. Although reference is made to some real events, any similarity to any persons, living or dead, is purely coincidental.

Cover design by Lidia Ranns

I wish to express my gratitude to officers from the British Transport Police for their assistance in my research for this book.

This book is dedicated to the memory of my grandfather, Edward Lees, who was killed in a rail accident whilst maintaining the line near Kirkham, Lancashire in 1947.

Also by Barry Lees and available on Kindle Books.

This City of Lies

The Governor's Man

By Sword and Feather

Exiles from a Torn Province

Wasps Among the Ivy

The Blue, the Green and the Dead

PROLOGUE

Station to station, lifeblood of the nation,

rends the air through field and town.

Three hundred tons, over rails it runs

before setting its passengers down.

Loved ones reunited and children excited,

the sleek iron horse brings all in.

Overhead cables and old luggage labels

for the vast snake of glass and tin.

Commuters returning, adventurers yearning

for worlds whipping by in a blur.

Most villagers sleep through rumblings deep

and not a soul near it should stir.

All hope lives aboard the powerful lord
of the parallel lines through your nation.
but what of the fool who defies the rule
and brings forth the beast's devastation?

On the track it must stay, the innocents pray,
for St Christopher's travelling masses.
They hold silent breath and think only of death,
'til the red and white Lucifer passes.

CHAPTER ONE

"The train now standing at Platform Eight is the 17.46 for London Euston, calling at Motherwell, Carstairs, Lockerbie . . . "

The announcer continued with the list of stops, monotone and impersonally reciting the same familiar places in a firm yet clear Scottish accent. The passengers ambled, shuffled and perambulated along the numerous platforms, laid out like a marina with jetties for accessing boats. It was the terminus for the main arterial route between two major cities. Those intending to remain for the full five-hour trip, all the way to London, were preparing themselves in their own individual ways. Bulky luggage was wheeled, rucksacks were swung across one or both shoulders, pushchairs were being skilfully steered by stressed parents. The electric engines hummed their readiness to proceed.

In the cab, unseen by his passengers, sat Simon Butters. Twelve years of train-driving experience, and another ten as a ticket clerk before that, had given him the recognised degree of seniority among his colleagues to have his judgement respected and unquestioned. He had dealt with numerous minor incidents and one major one, whereby a man hell-bent on self-annihilation had run out in front of Butters' inter-city to end his life. Simon Butters took the requisite period of inactivity and underwent counselling for his trauma. He had returned to work, firstly with another driver and, within a few trips, he was back at the helm and had remained there ever since.

Squeezed together yet managing to maintain anonymity, Butters' passengers took their places in the carriages, of which there were twelve. Tickets were scrutinised and meticulously matched to seat numbers and polite reminders and low-level challenges brought about civil responses and prompt relocations. Rail company staff worked the platform and helped those who they perceived as having a need for it, whilst the on-board staff wheeled on supplies and wheeled off the remnants of the previous journey. Ramps were utilised to allow trolleys, wheelchairs and prams to ascend the steps. Suitcases were raised, with some exertion, onto the racks by the doors, passengers making themselves comfortable by taking off outdoor clothing and packing it onto overhead shelves. Drinks, snacks, paperback books, newspapers and came out and were suitably positioned.

Mrs Barbara Hunter considered herself to be a seasoned traveller. By rail, vessel or aeroplane, she had learned the unwritten rules of shared transport. How to conduct oneself, how to cater for those who were less experienced in such things, and when to express a complaint. Before taking early retirement from her role as head-teacher of a Glasgow comprehensive school, she had enjoyed a level of compliance in her professional life, which had been enhanced by her elevation to the role of OFSTED Inspector, bringing her years of experience to the less-effective elements of the Scottish education system.

Barbara had her ticket ready for the guard and her luggage was prepared and stowed with consummate efficiency. She folded the skirt of her grey suit beneath her, took out her Daily Telegraph and waited for departure. Feeling slightly peeved at the reduction in status forced upon her by the cost-saving measures from on high, Barbara lamented the withdrawal of first-class travel for OFSTED staff. It was all coming out of the public purse after all.

Ideally, she would have the entire carriage to herself. If she was lucky, she would be spared from the torture of noisy and badly-behaved kids, preferring those who were willing to respect the quiet-zone rules of mainstream rail usage. The ban on smoking in enclosed public places was well-established in Scotland and was soon to come into force in England too. That was welcome news for Barbara, who detested such behaviour. Her urges to treat transgressors as she would the schoolchildren in her charge, were difficult to control, and she regularly did express those views to strangers.

So far, so good. Nobody appeared to be drunk or otherwise anti-social. Seats were filling but some remained unoccupied. She silently hoped for that to be the case all the way to London, city of her birth, where she was to check in to a hotel and prepare for her departmental refresher training event along with officials from the Department of Education.

As the train strained to shift its colossal weight and embark on its journey along the length of the country, over a hundred miles to the South, Imran

Bhatta was steeling himself for a very different challenge. It was the arrival of his wife's parents, and their luggage, which posed him discomfort. They were due to stay for a week, a very long week, in his opinion.

He had mixed feelings about their stay. His mother in law, Lania, was particularly likeable. The problem was Ali, his domineering father-in-law. Ali was a shining example of how an immigrant can thrive by hard work and persistence. His medical achievements were second-to-none, and he continued to practice, albeit in a consultancy capacity. This had been a heavy influence on his daughter Sunila, who had followed him into the medical profession. This was not enough to appease her father, who blamed Imran for what he saw as his daughter's career impediments.

Although he had been brought-up in the North, Imran had been a law student in London, where he had been introduced, in the traditional family custom, to Sunila. She was a medical student and the prospects of two high-earning professions of equal family status was an agreeable one for their respective families. They were married the week after Imran's graduation, although Sunila's education continued for three more years. Imran was expected to take a position in a prominent law firm in London and he began his articles with good intentions of doing that.

His epiphany had come shortly after he became fully qualified, when he made the decision not to remain a lawyer. It was that revelation which had altered Ali's opinion of his son-in-law. This unpleasant atmosphere deteriorated further when he chose to join the police, worse still the police in a Northern wasteland, which could not be further, both socially as well as geographically, from the rich seam of opportunity to be found in the capital.

Sunila had continued with her studies, and, when qualified, began her career at the main hospital in Pendale. This was not by choice. It was the only hospital in the proximity of her husband's work. She was, undoubtedly a woman of intelligence, and she had the ability to express it. But centuries of cultural formality weighed heavily on her. Her husband's decisions, as her father's had been, were not to be questioned. Ali believed that London was the appropriate place for her talents to flourish. Imran, as her husband, had a stronger influence, which Ali resented acutely.

The presence of the Jaguar car on the double driveway of the Bhatta house felt like a grey cloud moving overhead. Ali and Lania emerged and were greeted on the doorstep by Sunila. Imran took up a position a few feet behind her. Embraces and handshakes completed, they were taken inside. Imran carried in their designer luggage and deposited it upstairs. He found solace in the splendid excuse of having to go to work for a night shift. He could leave in an hour.

Since their last visit, several rooms had been redecorated. Imran had done it himself, a practice considered by Ali as beneath anyone with an education. Lania praised the décor with enthusiasm. Ali was not going to be impressed by anything there.

"Of course, a partner in a city law firm would be able to afford to pay a tradesman to do such things," announced Ali whilst gazing out of the window at the distant hills.

"That's hardly fair," said his wife, "Imran has done a lovely job." She hoped that the tension would reduce by some conciliatory words. She had hoped in vain.

"A degree in law and he decorates his own house. Hah!"

Ali seemed to have no filter. Imran looked at the clock. Only fifty-five minutes until he could leave. He made no response to the provocation. Sunila changed the subject and, hopefully, the tone.

"Imran has been promoted to Inspector now. He's the youngest in the force, aren't you Imran?"

Ali held views on the status of police officers, which had originated in old India, where the role was carried out by those of low caste. He nodded and looked away then he spotted another opportunity to attack.

"Inspector is it? You could have been a partner by now. Instead you persist on this silly whim."

"A police career is not a silly whim," he answered, unable to maintain his earlier resolve. "It is an important role and needs to be done for the good of the community."

"Community?" exclaimed Ali in sardonic laughter. "You have left our community to live in this backwater. Don't tell me you are doing any good for anyone but yourself."

"Ali, please," appealed Lania, "I know that I should not disagree with you but think how you would like to be spoken to like that in your own house." Ali shrugged.

Sunila tried again to get the visit back onto the footing she had hoped for. Imran was boiling up inside. He was not prepared to see out the time before he could go to work. He went upstairs to change. He emerged in his uniform albeit without the protective equipment which he donned at the station. A legacy from his time in a city law office was his attention to detail in his appearance. His trouser creases were razor-sharp and his shoes shone like a soldier's on parade. His return to the lounge was brief and abrupt. He excused himself, mainly to Lania, and headed off.

CHAPTER TWO

The entry in the Domesday Book of the eleventh century, describes the hamlet of Akscaf as having three farms and a total population of seventy-eight. It had a Squire who had rather wisely made his allegiance with King William and had therefore averted the starvation and decimation of that tiny community. The name was modified by time, religion and dialectical influences and by the time the keeping of parish records had come, the name was settled as Eckscarfe.

Nestled on a flat plain dividing the steep slopes of a natural gorge, the village had grown into a population of eight hundred, whilst keeping the number of farms down to its medieval norm. Branching out from agriculture, it had played host to a sizable quarry, providing building stone for centuries and highlighting what the area had in abundance. What it also had was the flattest path through the undulating, Northern fells and the most had been made of that. A major arterial route for both a single-carriageway road and a motorway as well as a main rail line linking England and Scotland, Eckscarfe sat passively overseeing the rapid travellers passing through its valley gorge at blink-only speed.

The village contained a quaint array of architecture. The centre, which housed an ancient stone obelisk, erroneously referred-to as the village cross, was surrounded on all four sides by sandstone cottages, all charm and hanging baskets. From there a main street where more modern interpretations of dwellings had emerged, provided several shops, a village pub and a library which had been closed and was awaiting a new function. The main church was an early Georgian, stone monolith with stained glass depictions of biblical events and a brass lectern in the style of an eagle. Anyone preferring to worship in any alternative to the Church of England had to go to another village or the main town some four and a half miles away.

That town was Pendale, population 20,000 and not mentioned at all in the Domesday Book. Its emergence and growth could be attributed to its location at the junction of an ancient road going North to South and another going East to West. Established as a market town by a charter in the fifteenth century, Pendale had developed as a trading point for the wool trade and for the sale and distribution of building stone.

The West-coast mainline passed through Pendale Station but many of them did not stop there. Collectively, the town considered itself important enough to constitute a compulsory stop on the intercity route, but the commercial considerations of the train operators afforded them a different opinion. Every third train actually stopped at Pendale Station. A seemingly permanent chill wind whistled through the place, even in warm weather. Only two of the six platforms built were in use as all except two branch lines had closed down years before. It resulted in a gloom of inadequacy, which could render any visitor in an understandable hurry to leave.

Eckscarfe was officially in an area of outstanding natural beauty. The dramatic, sloping fells, part green and part weathered, stone scree, served as giant and prehistoric city walls, enveloping the village and the picturesque lake at its edge. Many of the residents had moved to Eckscarfe to appreciate the lovely, rural setting, whilst some chose to live there because of the old-world charm and the low crime rate. Maintaining that feature for the past seven years was Police Constable Peter Keld.

Keld had first joined the force in Newcastle-Upon-Tyne and had transferred across the Pennines in mid-service. He had, he believed, done the hard stuff and he wished to spend the last stage of his thirty-year career in a more peaceful and less demanding role. He had earned it, as his wife Helen regularly reminded him. It had initially been her idea to move. It was a straight choice: do they bring up their two children in an urban sprawl or in idyllic rural setting? His early experiences in a large city had provided him with certain resilience and a range of skills rarely called upon in the tiny village he had come to patrol. He had seen his share and more of the violence, greed and vandalism prevalent in the city. He wanted to live and work in a place where people had a better appreciation of their environment. After a brief familiarisation period in Pendale, he was posted to the village to take up residence in the police-owned house with its own tiny police office attached.

That day, Thursday the fourth, began as any other. He commenced duty at 4pm and anticipated that he would finish at midnight. The only unpredictable element was that he may be called to attend a neighbouring village where his colleague was off duty. That mutual cover arrangement suited all concerned. If not so deployed, he would stay in Eckscarfe and attend to the needs of the villagers as best he could.

At 6pm he was called to go to the home of one of his Parish Councillors where they believed that someone had tried to break in during the day. The Councillor was a retired commercial estate agent called Leonard Hurlington. Upon receiving the call, Keld went straight away to Hurlington's house to investigate. Whilst he was not directly accountable to the Parish Council, Keld knew that they made good allies and bad enemies. Keeping their support was, in the long game, good for his retention of the post and the home that went with it.

Hurlington's house had not been entered, although a significant effort had been made by someone to do so. A tool had been forced into the door frame of the conservatory at the rear and damage had occurred to the door and frame. The unseen inner bolts had kept the door closed throughout the attempt and therefore no trespass had taken place, nor property stolen.

Keld was not keen on calling out a Crime Scene Investigation officer for such an occurrence. Instead, and largely to demonstrate some gesture of effort, he took photographs of the damage and carried out a token house-to-house exercise with the neighbours. He was relieved to hear that Len Hurlington had to go out to a meeting of the Parish Council later that evening. It gave him a dignified reason to leave.

*

Glasgow was ready to send the 17.46 off to London and all points between. Doors were closed and shrill, whistled signals from platform staff heralded its departure. Flags waved, the engine adopted a deeper, grating tone and the engine dragged its ten, unhelpful disciples away from the terminus and out into the deep orange of the evening sunshine. The red, white and blue of the nose split open the light as it gathered speed at a laboured rate out past the maintenance sheds. The overhead power cables dipped and rose beneath the gantries. Shuffling pace became walking pace, became jogging pace, then running pace, became sprinting pace then cycling pace then something which befits a magnificent and powerful machine such as that.

"Welcome aboard this inter-city service to London Euston."

The man's voice, although polished and clear, still had the foghorns of the Clyde shipyards running through its core. He reeled off the scheduled stops along the route and reminded all where refreshments could be purchased. When he mentioned that there was room in first class carriages for anyone wishing to purchase an upgrade, Barbara Hunter curled a lip in distaste at the suggestion that she should travel in style at her own expense.

Progressing through the warehouses and housing estates of Scotland's industrial heartland, the train eased into its cycle of acceleration as the scenery became a series of blurred and momentary flashes. Cuttings and embankments, bridges and tunnels, the inter-city topped a hundred miles per hour before leaving the city and the souls aboard eased into their comfortable seats at a reciprocal yet similar rate.

*

The Village Hall at Eckscarfe, built only two years before and part-funded by the Heritage Lottery Fund, was the only gesture toward modern architecture in the village. Reclaimed, grey stone made up the lower part of the exterior, whilst magnolia render interspersed with smoked glass panels formed the upper strata. Natural, oak window-frames and open roof-beams comparable to old churches had provided the building with an earthy warmth inside. The old-fashioned, wooden roof shingles served as a link to the crafts of yesteryear.

Activities in the Village Hall were numerous and increasing all the time. The main room housed a pre-school playgroup on weekday mornings, a Badminton club on a Wednesday evening and an Over 60s indoor bowling club on Monday and Friday afternoons. Off the main room was a small bar, which was only used for occasional functions, Ladies and Gents toilets with changing facilities, a Committee Room, a Snooker Room and an equipment store. At the end of the main room was a stage made up of modular, black blocks. Assembled on the stage was all of the necessary apparatus for an evening of Rock'n'Roll.

"It's no good having all this gear, it's what you do with it that counts," declared Adrian Hallimond, the sixteen-year-old bass guitarist of Eckscarfe's only indie-rock ensemble, The Proles.

"Profound, Adie, real profound." Drummer Freddie Parr aired his tendency toward sarcasm at every opportunity.

Although Adrian and Freddie had been friends since before they had started school, later recruits to the band were guitarist, Neil Debicki and vocalist Charmian Vallasarias. Neil said little and instead allowed his musical talent, which was not in doubt, to express his world view. Charmian had initially been a controversial choice. She was a competent singer, a free-spirit and a publicity godsend with an eye-catching mane of untidy, white-blonde hair.

The controversy stemmed from the unceremonious dismissal of her predecessor, Perry Vanaugh. Perry was wont to belt out his lyrics in a rasping, punk fashion and whilst he was a big character, it had been democratically decided that the band had to pursue a different direction. All of this fell into the realm of the unrealistic, considering that although The Proles had recorded several songs at a real recording studio, at the expense of their parents, they were yet to deliver the goods in a live concert.

Progress in the current wave of practice sessions was slow. With only two weeks until their first concert, they were not ready. Having a new lead singer had been a setback but the renewed enthusiasm more than made up for that. Adrian had taken a lead in motivating the others to step up. He had asked to use the Village Hall at the weekends, and to extend that to include any evening that the facilities were not otherwise allocated. The previous Thursday had been fine, at least until Perry had arrived and made a scene. Not to be put off, the current line-up of The Proles was working hard to get ready for their inaugural public performance. They had arrived at 6pm and had quickly begun their rehearsal. Four songs later, the smoked-glass front door swung open and Councillor Graham Posner entered the room.

Posner had been the village shopkeeper until his retirement some ten years before. He was a bulbous, sweaty man with rolls of fat spilling over his collar and his belt. His custom, as it had been when he was serving customers in his shop, was to wear a tie which was comically short, reaching only half-way down his oversized shirt.

The song drew to a distracted close as the average age in the room suddenly shot up. When the music ended, Posner told the band how their evening was going to be from then on.

"You will have to leave that for now," announced the voice of authority. "The Parish Council meeting starts at Seven O'clock and we can't do our work with that din going on."

The Proles were less than pleased at hearing that their music was being dismissed as a 'din.' Adrian aired their point of view.

"But we need to practice."

"Aye, I've heard you play and yes, you do need to practice." Posner made himself laugh. He was laughing alone.

"We were told we could have the hall on Thursdays. We were here last week," said Adrian without much confidence in his voice.

"Ah, that was last Thursday. This Thursday is the Parish Council meeting and you have to leave."

"Can't we rehearse after the meeting?" suggested Freddie, still holding his drumsticks in either hand.

"No. It will be too late by then," said Cllr Posner abruptly. "Anyway, that's enough talking. Be off with you now."

The band heaved a collective sigh and began unplugging their equipment. They left it all where it was, intending to come back the following day, after the indoor bowling.

Posner went into the Committee Room and arranged the chairs around the oval table. Once he was happy with the layout, he peered out into the hall to check that the youngsters had left.

"Excellent!" he beamed. His mood was upbeat and for good reason. Matters to be discussed at the meeting of the Eckscarfe Parish Council included good news, which he was looking forward to celebrating.

*

"Emergency, which service, please?" said the operator at the national 999 call centre.

"Ambulance and erm, police, I think?" answered the caller with evident indecision.

The call was relayed through to Ambulance Control, standard practice. The police would get it too in due course.

"Ambulance Service, can I help you?" said the soft Newcastle accent of the female call taker.

"Erm, yeah. Someone was on the railway bridge. I think he's jumped off." The caller sounded young, a teenager perhaps. Some reassurance was called for. Without it, the quality of the information would be impaired, which could mean a higher risk of loss of life.

"Okay, what's your name please?"

"Please hurry, Oh God! I saw him there, on the bridge, then he was gone. He must have jumped."

"Okay, I will pass this on to the police who will make a search. Now, can I have your name?" The caller was too distracted to listen to the question.

"I don't know why he's done it."

"Okay, calm down please." The operator's tone changed slightly, a rise in pitch to cut through the caller's bewilderment. "Tell me which bridge he was on." It had an immediate effect.

"Shipley Road,"

"Where exactly is Shipley Road?"

"What? It's Eckscarfe, sort of."

The operator quickly typed in Shipley Road and the computerised location system narrowed the range instantly. Shipley Road, Eckscarfe near Pendale. She saw on a mapping page that it crossed over the main West-coast mainline. Got it!

"Can you describe the man?" but the conversation had been curtailed at the other end.

Messages were sent via priority channels and within twelve seconds it arrived at County Police Headquarters, Control Room. Once digested, a radio call was made.

"Report from the emergency operator. A witness says that someone has jumped off the Shipley Road railway bridge. No description available. Patrol to attend."

"Four nine double eight, I'll go," was the first voice to respond.

"Thank you, four nine double eight. I will try and get hold of B.T.P."

PC Peter Keld released the transmit button and uttered "Fat chance." He knew that his colleagues in the British Transport Police tended to be an unassailable distance from him whenever an emergency call came in which was railway related. He had nothing against the BTP officers, he counted several as his friends, but he had learned to expect little in the way of response from them. He reached for his car keys and headed to Shipley Road.

Parking his patrol car in a layby on the approach to the bridge, Keld put his cap back on his head and walked up to the bridge. The sides of the parapet were of blue-painted metal and reached to five feet from the ground. He could see along the track as it ran straight toward the right-hand curve at Eckscarfe. He scanned the line and the edges for any sign of human activity. There was nothing to see. He crossed the road, which was devoid of traffic, and peered over the north side. Again, there was nothing. He reached for his radio and waited for a gap in the airwave. When it came, he said.

"Four nine double eight, I'm on the bridge on Shipley Road now. There is nothing on the track North or South. I'll have a look from the field to make sure, but it's looking like a hoax."

The Controller acknowledged then the duty Inspector chipped in from his office in Pendale Police Station.

"Erm Four nine double eight, do not go on the track, is that clear?" Keld had no intention of straying onto a live railway line. He knew the rules.

"Understood," he said, trying not to sound flippant.

He came down from the bridge and climbed a low fence allowing access to the field, which ran along the North side of the line. Bushes obscured his view of the line as it disappeared under the Shipley Road bridge. Walking, then repeatedly turning around to look, he had walked about fifty yards before he could get a clear view of the aperture. As he had thought, there was nothing out of the ordinary.

He returned to Shipley Road and headed for his car. He stopped and looked back at the bridge. What struck him was that he had not yet had a view of the South side of the bridge. He could never see the merits of cutting corners when there was time to do a thing properly, so he looked for a point of access to the South side. The bushes were more overgrown than on the North side and he had to look further to find a way through. When he did, he climbed over a wire fence and landed in a patch of mud.

A curt curse and an air of acceptance allowed him to continue with his visual checks. He crossed the field to the fence lining the mainline. The evening sun was setting and a warming glow gave subtle lighting to the scene. He glanced at the bridge and saw something. He shook his head, rubbed his eyes and refocussed. Something was under the bridge. He leaned over the fence and pulled the peak of his cap lower to reduce the obscuring effects of the evening sunlight. A shiver ran through him. He grabbed his radio and interrupted the current conversation.

"Four nine double eight to Control, there's someone hanging from the railway bridge."

Other uniformed officers set off from Pendale to Eckscarfe to assist. The tragedy of a suicide bought a sombre mood to everyone who had heard Keld's radio transmission. The operator announced that all trains had been halted and that the line was now clear for patrols to approach. By the time the back-up had arrived, Keld had climbed onto the bridge and, leaning over the parapet, he had located the point where the rope had been tied to the metal structure.

He worked at the knot and sent his colleagues down to the track below to ease the corpse down. He anticipated some difficulty in untying the knot due to the weight of the human form hanging from the other end, but the knot came undone with surprising ease. He called to the officers beneath the bridge to be ready to catch it as he lowered the rope. It was much lighter than he had expected it to be.

"Letting it down now!" he called.

"We're ready," came the reply. A few second passed then, "Got it!"

Keld climbed back to the road and hurried down to the track. His colleagues were not so sombre anymore. A different form of disappointment was etched on the faces of his peers.

The suicide victim was lying on the stones by the track. Keld crouched to examine it. He turned it around and saw that it was not human. It was a mere effigy made from a faded, blue, workman's overall and the head, hands and shoes were carrier bags stuck on with carpet tape. It was a hoax; a mean-spirited, small-minded, cruel hoax.

Keld wrestled with the conflict within him. He was annoyed and embarrassed at having been taken in and he had called out other officers from the town to witness it. He was livid that the train services, and all of their passengers, had been held up because of it. On balance, at least nobody had died. However, the prank was likely to have been carried out by someone nearby, someone from his own village. It was that thought which gave him the more lasting discomfort. There were not many people capable of pulling such a stunt. Finding the culprits would bring Keld a new series of challenges.

He took the dummy and threw it in to the boot of his car along with the rope. After thanking the supporting officers for their help, he set off to dispose of the thing. There was no receptacle in the village which could accommodate the dummy, so he set off to drive out to the quarry. The winding lane climbed steadily away from Shipley Road, through the tree-lined meadows and out onto the exposed scree of the fells. A few turns designed to make the ascent easier for heavy traffic, and the road reached the entrance to Wilson's Aggregates.

Keld went straight to the row of industrial refuse containers and threw the dummy, and the rope, inside. He paused to admire the sunset over the Western side of the valley. His previous annoyance was abated momentarily. He was living and working in a beautiful part of the world and he should always remember that.

*

In the Committee Room in Eckscarfe Village Hall, the Parish Council were in meaningful discussion, albeit in a formal and structured way. The chairman was Graham Posner who had placed himself in a high-backed, upholstered seat giving him an overseeing authority to the assembly. At his side, but in a lower chair, was Hilda White, a mouse of a woman who rarely spoke other than to repeat back the contents of her shorthand notes of the meetings. Hilda's role was administrative. She was officially titled Parish Clerk, and had been for longer than anyone could remember.

Seated around the table were the remaining community representatives. There was Jonathan Ullenorth, dressed as a golfer in pastel shades. His lime-green jumper, pale blue slacks and beige suede loafers shouted 'well-off and proud of it.' He had made his living as an insurance broker, selling his self-built business to a national giant just before the onset of internet finance. Fred McAulden, a retired farm manager had the look of an outdoor type but without the calloused hands of a real farmer. Loretta Rokestone was subtly attired, articulate and classy. She did not give away anything of her past life, but, having lived in Eckscarfe for longer than most present, she held an unspoken seniority and there was never a need to discuss it. She had kept a slim figure an unlined face into her early sixties by, horse-riding, fell-walking and yoga. Len Hurlington appeared to have overcome the shock of finding that someone had tried to forcibly enter his house whilst he was out. He beamed a winning smile, showing his dentures to all.

"We shall begin with apologies for absence," announced Graham Posner. There was a snort of derisory laughter from two of the other members.

"Surprise, surprise," sneered Ullenorth.

"Ahem, order please, we are not a rabble," said Graham Posner. "Councillor Hazeldene is away at present. We shall say no more about it. Are the minutes from the last meeting agreed?"

"Proposed," said Len Hurlington.

"Seconded," added Loretta Rokestone.

"That's that then," concluded Posner. "Now, I call upon Councillor Rokestone, our County representative to tell us about what we really want to hear."

"I realise," she began, "that you already know the result, but I shall report how the decision was reached at County. The main issue before us is the recent County Council decision to refuse planning for the proposed Eckscarfe housing development. I can tell you that our opposition to that abomination was the main reason for the County's rejection of that plan."

Ullenorth, Hurlington and McAulden burst into self-congratulatory applause. Posner, although equally pleased about it, urged a higher degree of civic dignity.

"Erm, Councillors, thank you. Go on please, Loretta."

"County have written to Maxlow to inform him of the decision. He wasn't happy about it, but all avenues of appeal have been exhausted now."

"What if he makes another application?" asked Hurlington.

"If he makes significant changes to it, he could submit again. As long as we on the Parish Council stand firm, he will hit the same brick wall as he has this time."

"Excellent," said Posner. "Who ever said the local councils have no clout, eh?"

"Hear hear!" assented Fred McAulden.

The remaining discussions included the frequency of refuse-bin emptying, disappointingly late postal deliveries and the ongoing youth nuisance problems in the village. This raised the uncomfortably incompatible issue of one of the wayward youths being the son of the village police officer. Some of the members wanted to usurp PC Keld and get other officers from Pendale to come to Eckscarfe to deal with the problem. Others were reluctant to cause offence to their policeman, who, in all other respects, enjoyed the confidence and support of the Parish Council, and therefore the village. It was agreed that no action be taken for the time being but reports of such behaviour should be noted for future Council meetings.

As the meeting drew to a close, the participants took two distinct actions which separated them in both gender and leisure pursuits. Whilst Loretta Rokestone and Hilda White returned to their respective homes, the men adjourned to the Snooker Room on the other side of the building. They crossed the main floor of the hall beneath the black stage-blocks where a drum-kit, guitars and amplifiers sat silently. Comments were made about being thankful not to be present when the instruments were to be played. When the Snooker Room was illuminated by the overhead lights, a cupboard was unlocked and a new bottle of whisky was produced along with four heavy-bottomed, drinking glasses.

It was never openly discussed that this was the domain of the men but there was an acceptance among the female Councillors that this practice took place. Loretta Rokestone held the belief that more of the Council's business and decision-making took place behind the closed door of the Snooker Room than in the official Council meetings. What the men did when the meetings ended was up to them. There was nothing any of the women could do about it, nor were any of them inclined to. They left them to it.

*

"The problem on the line has been cleared and the delayed Inter-City service to London Euston will depart in three minutes. That's the train bound for London, Euston will depart in three minutes. Thank you for your patience."

The relief in the voice of the platform announcer was undisguised. It was felt equally by the passengers. Mrs Barbara Hunter made a mental note of the content of a letter of complaint she was to send to the rail operator. The other passengers returned to their seats, settled down and hoped for a smooth journey to their destinations. Driver, Simon Butters waved acknowledgement to the platform crewman. Whistles sounded at either end, doors were closed and the engine's tone changed in intensity. It pulled away from the platform at which it had been forced to linger and gathered speed. Phones were deployed to update those at the end of the journeys. No more impediments please, no more hold-ups, just get us to where we want to go. The evening light had faded and the sun was concealed behind, firstly houses, then rolling hills, distant fells and clouds way out to sea in the distance. Mrs Barbara Hunter adjusted the light above her seat and resumed her reading.

CHAPTER THREE

The train from Glasgow had arrived and departed from all designated stations with precision and efficiency, until it had reached Pendale of course. The ninety stationary minutes had largely been absorbed in a spirit of inevitability by those affected. Seats had been vacated, then filled by new people. Only the long-distance travellers remained in their original places. At Pendale, a woman had boarded with three small children, two of which were under school age. She bustled in a disorganised way as she shepherded the children and their various accessories. The process seemed to affect or involve everyone in the carriage.

Barbara Hunter's entire life had been dominated by other people's children. She thought herself to be a caring soul but at that moment she resented the withdrawal of her first-class travel more acutely than she had before. Her experiences had informed her that children rarely made an appearance in first-class and those who did were invariably better behaved than those in standard.

The flustered mother had tried to remain calm and use encouragement to get her brood settled into their seats for the journey. It was having little effect. Only when she erupted into an angry, shouting volume did the three comply and sit on their seats.

Barbara noticed that the older boy, who was about seven, was wearing a Manchester United shirt, which she considered detestably common. It represented consumerism of the gaudiest sort. 'She hasn't even booked!' thought Barbara, as she tried to shut their presence out of her thoughts.

The unplanned and stationery hour-and-a-half caused by the dummy hoax was a period of intense irritation for Barbara. It would have been bearable but for other people. As the train recommenced its movement, normality seemed nearer, although the mother of three still had her work cut out. Barbara, through the power of her mind alone, managed to shut them out of her peripheral vision and hearing.

The delay at Pendale had set the schedule back by ninety minutes. For those who had mobile phones to hand, more messages were sent to forewarn people of their late arrivals. The train had accelerated as before but this time there was a collective sense of urgency among the passengers about its rate of progress. Simon Butters had sufficient experience to know how these things could happen, and what to do, and what not to do, when they did occur. He had records to keep, both electronic and written, and the period of inactivity had afforded him the opportunity to complete some of it.

Barbara Hunter was of a generation brought up to believe that the use of the toilet facilities on a train was not permitted whilst standing at the station platform. Her need to visit the ladies' room was managed with unseen discomfort during the unscheduled stop but within two minutes of recommencing the journey, Barbara had risen from her seat and made her way out of the carriage.

Finding the *Engaged* sign illuminated, Barbara had no choice but to wait. When the light changed from a restrictive red to a facilitative green, the cubicle door did open and a young woman, presumably from another carriage, emerged to a frosty reception. Barely giving the occupant sufficient time to vacate the tiny room, Barbara entered and banged the door shut, a pointed and largely pointless gesture of impatience, which went unnoticed by anyone.

In the carriage, the young mother of three had taken Barbara's absence as her chance to speak to her children. She warned them to stop annoying the other passengers, although this directive was for the sole benefit of the lady in the grey suit, who was making the 'tutting' sounds, when she returned to her seat.

Simon Butters knew the track very well. Under normal circumstances, he would bring the speed down where there was a designated need to do so. A built-up area, a signal change or as was the case at Eckscarfe, a long right-hand curve.

The Eckscarfe curve had been imposed on the original railway engineers due to a natural feature making a straight line impossible at that point. There was the lake, which was simply too wide for a train to pass over it and too deep for it to be drained and filled in. From a railway engineer's perspective, the Eckscarfe curve was a challenge, which had to be overcome. However, as trains travelled increasingly faster, it became an inconvenience to have to slow down slightly in order to maximise safety.

As the church spire of St Gerard's in the village of Eckscarfe came into Simon's view, he eased the lever to begin the process of deceleration. Slowing a three-hundred-ton train could be a tricky manoeuvre but the key, as Simon saw it, was to do everything in good time and his cue to act was the sight of the village ahead.

It was five hundred yards away at that moment. The village was nestled in the gorge to the left of the line. He applied the brake gradually, leaving the passengers wholly unaware of his skill. The train was at optimum speed as the straight line of the track began to deviate to the right at the beginning of the curve.

It was like a dream, a weird, bad dream. It was as though it was not really happening. Everything that gives a person their orientation was about to be taken from them. All of Simon's years of driving trains had not prepared him to be able to take in what was unfolding in his sight. Instinctively, he reached for the brakes – but brakes only work when the wheels are still in contact with the rails. The illuminated view from the front of the engine gave the optical illusion that the rails were leaving the train and not the other way around. The passengers were, at that moment, unaware. They were about to have their lives irreparably ripped apart.

The overhead power lines on the roof of the engine bowed and straightened with a jolt. They pulled in unplanned directions and soon tore away from the frame, creating a blinding explosion of sparks both outside and inside the driver's cab. Simon fell to the floor among the rain of sparks. The interior lighting in the cab flashed on and off and the lamps of the front of the engine went out altogether. Some of the passengers, whose carriages were, at that moment, still attached to the track, knew that something was wrong, but nobody could have imagined the extent of the impending danger. It became evident to more people when the carriage lights flicked on and off with strobe-like rapidity, before going out altogether. Hoping that it would all be corrected momentarily, everyone apart from the three small children who had been annoying Barbara, anticipated a resumption of the carriage lights without delay. But the lights did not come back on.

The travellers began to feel a bewildering sense of floating. Pulled from their seats by unseen and unfathomable forces, the carriages, which had been designed to tilt in transit, lunged violently as each one left the track and thumped the ground it was never meant to touch. The sparks from the roof-frame quickly became flames, burning an oily mass and sending an acrid pall through the open windows of the carriages behind.

Inside the cubicle of the ladies' toilet, Barbara cursed under her breath. First she had put up with somebody's unruly offspring, then a delay at Pendale, then having to wait for the loo. This really was too much. She fumbled in her Modalu handbag for her mobile phone in order to shed some light. As she leaned over, still seated, she felt her body float off the seat and hang in the air. Disorientation overcame her. The darkness, the temporary suspension of gravity and the feeling of exposure from undress made Barbara's skin run cold.

Simon Butters had been knocked unconscious in his cab but there was nothing he could have done if he had remained compos mentis. He lay, curled like a baby, on the tiny, metal, floor-plate. Barbara was thrown against the door of the loo, banging her head. She too lost consciousness.

In the carriages, the only light came from the sunset through far-off broken cloud and the menacing flashes from continuous sparks of the electrical equipment over the train. As each carriage in turn left the track on the same trajectory as the leading engine, the people, already lifted from their seats, were thrown against the window-panes and across the top of the seats. Some were initially floating like spacemen, frozen in disbelief before clashing against other people screaming in abject terror. Half-hearted and breathless grunts of pain were drowned out by the terrified, many whom had found their voice. Ear-damaging shrieks resounded through the coaches. Arms were raised to defend heads from being dashed against the luggage racks. Hands snatched at anything which could be used as an anchor in that maelstrom of erratic movement. The bright, red, white and blue engine and grey carriages tore over the stone chippings at the side of the track igniting ever-more violent sparks. It ploughed through the flimsy, trackside fencing, buckling the aluminium laths as though they were made of cooked spaghetti. The engine was as out of place as a whale on land. It had come into contact with the ground with a deep and heart-stopping thump, but its journey was far from over.

In a field occupied by sheep, the gravity returned to the passengers with alarming force. Amid the screams of panic, people were thrown against the rooves and floors of the carriages. Bones were broken on impact, blood sprayed across the seats and glass window panels. The engine hurtled toward the village, annihilating the livestock as it ploughed its course of destruction. Mature trees in that field were flattened. The monstrous mass of metal was bending at its links but still defiantly remained in one piece. The engine remained true to its trajectory, but the carriages concertinaed to right angles and found their breaking points. Taking out a section of dry-stone wall, which had stood firm for over a century, the engine ploughed its devastating furrow on through the field, its steel wheels carving deep lines as it neared the wall bordering the Village Hall.

The deafening squeal of grating metal abated as the last carriage left the track. Instead the air was filled with the screams of the terrified, blood-soaked travellers shaken around in tubes of metal and glass. After leaving the rails, the first three carriages had tipped onto their left sides, with most of the windows miraculously remaining intact. Internal debris peppered the interiors with passenger-borne items and the contents of catering trolleys. With the jack-knifing of the carriages, the linkages between them reached their optimum points of tolerance before snapping, sending the carriages on a different trajectory to their engine.

The twin threat spread the destruction across a wider area. The carriages, being lighter, lost speed but continued across the field changing direction at the point of collision with trees. The roof of the second carriage slid into a hundred-year-old oak, which creased it to the extent that the roof was pressed to the top of the seats, crushing everything within that space. Only the seats and tables restricted the total compression of the carriage.

Coach B turned onto its roof and broke its coupling at the front - but not the back, causing the carriages behind to turn over too. The now unaccompanied engine, being by far the heaviest part, kept its momentum longer. It carved its destructive path to the edge of the field and beyond. The brick wall bordering the Village Hall car park fell like a house of cards, and the engine ploughed on, flattening a wooden tool shed and a bin store as though they were made of fresh air. Its wheels grated across the gravelled car park toward the solitary and vulnerable building.

Inside, the elected few of Eckscarfe were going about their post-meeting custom. The gentlemen of the Parish Council played snooker, drank whisky and praised themselves for their collective achievements. There was no way of comprehending what was happening to the building or anyone in it.

The walls caved in, the lights went out and everything that could be understood simply ceased to be. The roof timbers collapsed, masonry formed clouds of dust and although the steel frame of the building had slowed down the already decelerated railway engine, it had been bent double by the impact. Half of the Village Hall was destroyed but the remaining half had managed to bring the train's engine to a stop. The screaming continued for some time yet.

Those living nearby were the first to become aware of the disaster. People ran with torches to the Village Hall whilst others made calls to the emergency services. PC Peter Keld was driving back from Wilson's Aggregates. He was too far from Eckscarfe to have heard or seen the crash. The Control Room radio operator's voice cracked with incredulity.

"Getting several reports of an, erm, 'incident' at Eckscarfe."

Eckscarfe was not only his beat, it was his home and that of his family. His spine stiffened in anticipation. What did she mean by 'incident?' Come on! Say something. Her voice had gathered more purpose as she said,

"The Village Hall has collapsed, some sort of explosion. I'll get more information. Patrols to attend?"

Keld was unable to transmit due to every other person in possession of a police radio hurriedly confirming their attendance. He shifted gear and sped to the village, hoping that the messages were in some way exaggerated. The next update killed off that hope on which his theory was based.

"It's the train, the train has come off the track at Eckscarfe, believed to be numerous casualties."

"Shit!" exclaimed Keld. A wash of conflicting thoughts and emotions came over him making him physically sweat whilst shivering with cold. He fought back a tear at the thought of what suffering was being endured there and he desperately craved knowing if any of his family were involved. It was irrational, considering how far his house was from the railway line, but the more he thought about it, his wife, son and daughter could just as easily be at or near the Village Hall.

He drove his car over the brow of the hill and caught sight of Eckscarfe in the valley below. In the last light of the setting sun, he spotted smoke rising over the rooftops from the far side. He was likely to be the first of the emergency services personnel to arrive, but what could he do?

The Village Hall scene was still but not silent. Wails and shrieks emanated from the combined wreckage. Neighbours were stunned and immobile. The horror before them was real and life-changing - and they all knew it. The utilities servicing the building, however, were not as inert as the people involved. In its catastrophic final movement, the giant railway engine had ripped open the gas supply pipe as well as exposing the electrical and water supplies. Unseen and incompatible substances were heading for a coming together. At the moment that they did, it was a minor miracle that those coming to the aid of those involved had hung back and kept their distance.

The flames licking the edges of the engine had little to accelerate their destructive capabilities. That was until the seeping gas fumes flowed within range of the fire.

The bang was more frightening than it was harmful. The noise drove back the first wave of willing but clueless rescuers. They realised that there may be more explosions, maybe even bigger. The sounds of agonised, human suffering had to be endured. Monotone wailing and low, mournful groaning played a background rhythm to the shrieks and pleas for help. Attempts by willing rescuers, risking their own lives and, noble as their intentions were, could not be sensibly contemplated - and the screaming continued.

Keld stopped his car and dashed toward the scene, witnessing the gas blast and recoiling involuntarily as he ran. He was not quite knocked off his feet but he was stopped forcefully by the wave of hot air and burning dust. As the movement of displaced debris subsided, of the twenty people present, not one of them spoke or otherwise acknowledged his arrival. He shook himself to gather his reorientation and his priorities. His home being number one.

The police radio transmissions summoning resources to the scene did not allow for Keld to communicate what he was seeing. He had to back off before transmitting a situation update to the Control Room, but before he did so, and with a desperation in his wavering voice, he warned the people to stay back and await the Fire and Ambulance services. He returned to his car and phoned his home. Once assured that his wife and daughter were home and safe and his teenaged son was at a school-friend's house in Pendale, he managed to gain sufficient composure to enable him to report to the Control Room what he had seen.

He returned to the scene of the crash and saw several of the villagers helping wounded people to get clear. They had begun to emerge from the carriages under their own exertions and climbed clear of the mangled form through the windows, which were intact but kicked out by those who remained capable of doing so. The fuselage, as with the windows, was still intact, at least from the outsider's view. The door-opening mechanisms had been rendered inoperable, so emergency opening levers were frantically clawed by the fingernails of desperate people who had gone from passengers to prisoners in a matter of seconds.

A straggle of zombie-like beings lumbered, some on hands and knees, toward the light of the village's streetlamps. Many with bedraggled and blood-stained clothing. Steering people away from the ruined building, Keld directed them to be taken to any house, but to let the Ambulance crews know who was where when they arrived. All Keld could do was to establish a safe rendezvous point for the emergency services. He identified the car park of the Barley Mow pub, which would be big enough to begin the aid mission.

Radio messages, largely directed by the duty Sergeant, included a request that an urgent call be made to again stop all trains, both Northbound and Southbound, from approaching Eckscarfe. Fire and Rescue sirens could be heard and the Ambulance services, both on the road and in the air, were also due to arrive. Police emergency contingencies were to be implemented, along with their local authority counterparts. A double-manned car from the British Transport Police arrived and Keld found himself taking directions from them on how to preserve the scene and everyone in it. The priority was to facilitate the safe access for paramedics and fire crews. The police helicopter was authorised to take to the air in order to view the scene and help to establish a plan of action. The senior staff of the force and high-level investigators were also on the list of those to be notified.

Keld sought to keep onlookers and willing rescuers away from the scene until those better prepared could go to work. Many were unable to take in the simple instructions they were being given, mesmerised by the spectacle of human tragedy unfolding before their eyes. Stunned into a stupor, they were ill-prepared to comprehend such sights, sounds and smells. The wailing, moaning and sporadic screaming coming from the train carriages was abated by degrees. People were still being brought out and those who could move were in stark contrast to the lack of any human activity coming from the rubble of the building or the electric railway engine embedded in it. In the darkness of the field beyond the flattened wall of the car park, the carriages hatched more and more of the fortunate from the gaps made by others.

A slowly swirling cloud of mist and smoke rose in the windless dusk air. Darkness was upon them and visibility was negligible. People came into the view afforded by the limited light, walking like castaways, washed ashore on a desert island, falling in tearful exhaustion, some crawling and spattered with blood, mud and sheep-droppings. Willing helpers dashed to help them, supporting their movement and carrying some to the lights of the main road. Reassuring but mindless mantras were uttered but went largely unabsorbed by the traumatised.

"We've got you."

"You're safe now."

"It's going to be alright."

"It's all over, you're okay."

Keld saw the survivors being led to the road and he recognised the need to identify a central place in which they could be housed. The rescuers had already begun to gravitate toward the nearest dwellings. A double garage, lit up like an aircraft hangar, became the first-aid station. People produced blankets, towels and bandages from what they had in their houses and made poor token gestures of care to the wounded. Keld knew that the ones who could walk and speak were less of a priority to those who were not able to do so. He was satisfied that nobody was going to endanger themselves so, after speaking to the BTP officers who remained at the crash site, he headed for the rendezvous point on the pub carpark.

Arriving at the rendezvous point was a marked police car followed by a van. The duty inspector, Imran Bhatta, emerged from the passenger side of the car and placed his cap on before approaching Keld who was colourless in his face and wide-eyed with shock. Keld gabbled out a summary of what he had seen, and the measures he and others had taken. He gave basic facts of what he had established so far. Bhatta listened and whilst giving his best impression of a confident manager of emergency incidents, inside he was a jumbled mess in both mind and body.

He summoned sufficient self-control to give praise to PC Keld for his initial response and encouraged his continued efforts. He gave the order for the village to be sealed off from through traffic and he sent the van crew to place diversion signs in appropriate turning places either side of the village, and for one officer to remain to allow emergency teams in. As he was doing so, the first of a fleet of ambulances arrived in a renewed cacophony of sirens and blue lights.

The ambulance crews spoke to Inspector Bhatta and they agreed to go together to look at the scene some one hundred metres away at the edge of the village. Keld walked with them, talking animatedly, although in part incoherently, about the situation as he went. Bhatta saw some of the survivors being treated and cared-for by the residents. Blankets were being liberally distributed and soothing words filled the air. In the doorway of a house, there was a tearful, young mother holding three small children as though their lives depended on it. One child sported a Manchester United shirt.

Bhatta turned the corner and saw the destroyed Village Hall. The back end of the giant railway engine came into view. Pained moaning could be heard from unseen places but, thanks to the efforts of the BTP team, there was nobody standing near the building. It was a minor miracle, not lost on Bhatta, that the train had not reached the buildings on the main road and the people inside them.

The sparks emanating from the train and those flicking on and off from the electricity main serving the Village Hall had seemed to be the last throes of energy in the static scene of destruction. However, when the leaking gas main seeped its invisible contents across the site it was inevitable that the two incompatible forces would collide – with terrifying consequences.

CHAPTER FOUR

The second explosion shook the ground and the air with far greater power than the first had. From fifty metres away, Keld, Bhatta and the paramedics all dropped to the ground, taken off their feet by both the shock and the blast of hot and dusty air. When they were able to look up, they saw flames shooting up from the rubble. Still unaware whether or not there had been anyone inside the building, it was clear that their chances of surviving had taken a downward turn.

More approaching siren activity could be heard above the human noise. Keld got back to his feet and, shaking dust from his eyes and clothing, headed back to see that a pair of fire engines were being prepared for action. They were accompanied by the Fire Chief, who had arrived in a Volvo with a blue lamp on it. Despite the volume and proximity of their sirens, they had heard the explosion and were braced for further threats.

Bhatta left the Village Hall to the Fire crew to render it safe whilst he deployed his officers and the paramedics to attend to the disengaged carriages across the field. Arc lamps were erected and the police helicopter spread its light across the field. Several of the carriages were laid on their sides and many were still attached at the couplings. The creased roof of the carriage which had collided with the tree made it look like a popped balloon in a line of inflated ones. Intact and damaged panels of glass, forced out by the escaping passengers, lay strewn across the rough grass. Items of luggage and segments of the tables and chairs also peppered the landscape. The disturbed bleating of sheep provided background sound. Several of them lay dead and decimated in the wake of the carriages. The scuttering of the helicopter overhead provided the baseline rhythm to the orchestral piece.

The smell of burning materials stuck in the throats of the rescuers, although none of them could identify what it was that was ablaze. The half-destroyed Village Hall showed no flames and neither did the head section of the errant train, which lay across the site like a fallen redwood from a forest of giants.

Bhatta assessed the potential dangers and gave the order for a close, visual examination of the carriages to be carried out. The aim was to identify survivors, those possibly trapped and in need of help. More police officers arrived along with a medical team from the Accident and Emergency Dept at the main hospital in Pendale. Calls of "Over here," and "There's someone alive in this one," rang out and could be heard above the noise. Hurried pairings of helmeted men and women carrying stretchers and defibrillators criss-crossed the ground. The wounded souls not able to walk or crawl, were dragged from the wreckage and re-domiciled back in the land of the living.

After what seemed to be lull in the chaotic series of events, the Fire Chief reported to Bhatta that the Village Hall was safe enough to be examined for bodies. As a search party was being organised, two women could be heard angrily screaming at the police officers deployed to keep people away. Inspector Bhatta, who was running on pure adrenaline and lurching from one life-altering decision to the next, saw the commotion and headed to find out the cause. He found it momentarily refreshing to see people who were alive and uninjured, albeit physically anyway.

"He's in there, my husband is in there!" screeched a woman in her sixties wearing a cardigan and beige slacks.

With her was a woman of a similar age who was crying loudly but not saying anything coherent. The cordon-keeper tried to calm the situation, but he was losing control of it. Bhatta intervened and his authoritative voice did bring some communicative effect on the frantic pair.

"Madam, please. We are trying to help you. Please take a breath and tell us what you can." When the woman paused for a moment, he continued. "You mentioned your husband?" She turned her full attention, or as much as she could afford in her frantic state.

"He's in the Hall, they're all in there."

"Hold on." appealed Bhatta, "Who do you mean by 'they?'"

"The men, the men on the Parish Council. They are in the hall, under all that." She glanced with a pained expression toward the rubble without actually looking directly at it.

"How many?" asked Bhatta, impassively.

"What?" she spat out at him.

"How many people were, I mean are, in the Village Hall?"

"All of the men, the men on the Council, they were in there, it's Thursday."

Her lucidity came and went in waves. When panic came back, she abandoned speaking and recommenced wailing. Bhatta tried to speak to the woman accompanying her in the hope of gaining more information.

"Madam, please listen to me. What's your name?" she responded to the clarity of his tone of voice.

"Mary Ullenorth, my husband . . . is Jonathan . . . Ullenorth."

"Thank you. Please tell me who else is in the Village Hall this evening." Mary turned toward the hysterical woman and then back to Bhatta.

"Her husband is Graham Posner. There should be Len Hurlington, Fred McAulden and, oh I don't know."

"Thank you Mary, that helps. We will find out for you as soon as we can. Where in the building would they be?"

"In the Snooker Room by now. They have the meeting then they play snooker."

Mary was beginning to lose control again. Bhatta thanked her again before noting the names then reporting what she had told him over the radio.

"At least four members of the Parish Council were in the building when it was hit; Graham Posner, Len Hurlington, Fred McAulden and Jonathan Ullenorth, maybe more. Consider them missing persons at present. I will pass this to the Fire Chief myself."

Police Crime Scene Examiners arrived at the Barley Mow along with four CID officers. Another double-crewed BTP car also appeared. The CID team informed Inspector Bhatta that a Senior Investigator was on the way. That meant that Bhatta was to remain the officer-in-charge for a little longer. He deployed the CSI to take steps to cordon-off where they anticipated forensic evidence to be found. Further to that, they were to photograph and video as much as possible. The CID were tasked to create lists of people who were unaccounted for and to begin with the most recent electoral register.

The press began to arrive at the cordon. Bhatta had given specific instructions as to who should be allowed in. The press pack was not on the list at that time. Their enquiries were to be referred to the force Press Liaison Office, although they would, in all probability, not readily accept being told that. The local paper was there first followed by a collection of TV, radio and national newspaper journalists. Questions were fired at the police officers who were neither authorised nor inclined to answer any of them. When they began to outnumber the police officers, Bhatta went to the cordon to deliver a reminder and an appeal for some space in which to work. The appeal went unacknowledged.

"BBC News," declared one impatient reporter whose face was vaguely familiar from appearances on regional TV. "How many confirmed dead so far?" A colleague with a large camera on his shoulder hovered next to him. The cameraman scanned the landscape as the reporter focussed on Bhatta. Another hopeful stepped through the throng brandishing a pass. No attempt at dignified conduct was evident. It was competitive and relentless.

"I'm with The Mirror. Can you tell us what caused the crash?" called out a tall woman wearing a colourful scarf and a waxed-cotton jacket. The end of that sentence went unheard under the urgency of the next one.

"Come on, give a humble freelancer a slice, eh?" This came from a woman in a big coat who, when compared to the other, did not look old enough to be a reporter. She was soon elbowed out of the front row of the melee by those more aggressive in their manner.

Outside the cordon, a Salvation Army trailer had been deposited and was distributing hot drinks and high-sugar snacks. Some villagers had supplied garden furniture at which the refreshments could be consumed in relative comfort. The Salvation Army Captain was a caring soul named Clive O'Flindal and it fell to him to convey the suffering of the people of Eckscarfe, although, if asked, he would have had been compelled to admit that he had never before visited Eckscarfe, nor had he any connection to the place.

He was good at it. His experiences of bringing tea and sympathy to the traumatised had given him an innate ability to choose the right words and to deliver them in the right way. It was what the hacks were after and the nation was presented with Captain Clive O'Flindal's oratory on collective grief.

"The village of Eckscarfe is in shock today. Its peaceful community torn asunder by circumstances beyond the control or understanding of any of its people. Horror has come to Eckscarfe and the decent, honest and God-fearing people of this tiny corner of the world are dealing with it in their own way, with dignity, quiet reflection and a determination that life will go on. A lasting memorial is being considered and will serve as a permanent testament to those who may have lost their lives in this appalling and tragic event."

The idea of having a lasting memorial was O'Flindal's. He was sure that it would have been discussed at some point, he was merely anticipating that development. Several of the residents had watched his oratory on television and were initially irked that this non-resident had been allowed to speak for them. On closer consideration, most of the affected viewers accepted that the natural spokespersons for such a duty would have been the Parish Council, and the fact that most of them were missing presumed dead put the Salvation Army Captain's television broadcast into clearer perspective.

The editorial content of the early morning newspapers had already been determined. However, the later editions could still be redrafted to tell of the horrors and human tragedy of the Eckscarfe rail disaster. Soon, the entire country would know the name of the village. Suppositions, assumptions, unattributed observations and photographs of unnamed people placing floral tributes to a railing which could have been anywhere, filled the columns whilst the journos dug around for something more compelling. That included going door to door and asking the stunned residents to pour out their expressions of grief.

*

Detective Superintendent Janette Lane-Wright was the force cover officer for the Major Investigations Unit. She had travelled to Pendale to meet with the Chief Constable and establish her own technical staff in the process of activation of the computer access necessary for the Incident Room. By the time she was ready to attend the scene, daylight was breaking and Inspector Bhatta was getting near to doing the same.

Bhatta was getting a second wind when the sun rose. He tended to be a poor sleeper under normal circumstances, but the added factor of shift work created an endless condition of disorder. The bags beneath his eyes went from mild to heavy but were never absent. He was directing an early shift to their respective deployments at different parts of Eckscarfe when an ungainly yawn emanated from him. Acutely aware of the presence of the national and local press, Bhatta was swift to cover his mouth.

He had enjoyed a mutually productive and cooperative relationship with the local newspaper staff, but it was the national pack who he feared might seek to misrepresent him and his officers in order to show the police in a poor light. This was not founded on any of his own previous experiences. His attention was brought back to the 'here-and-now' by Janette Lane-Wright. She was also feeling the weight of fatigue but had gained more experience of managing it.

She was a better manager than she was a detective and, if in the right company, would have happily accepted that observation. She was methodical, corporate and meticulous. Little of what she did was on instinct and whilst that may have seemed to limit her effectiveness, her track-record of gaining detections and leaving no loose ends was more than enough to quieten her critics. She was of the firm belief that criminal convictions achieved by the police would only be assessed by historians. Her attention to detail was, to some, unnecessarily pedantic. She was a strong enough character to ignore such views. High office had been muted but Janette Lane-Wright had found her niche as a senior investigator and would not be easily tempted from that path.

The night team of detectives had compiled a summary of the incident so far. The first search of the rail carriages for signs of human life had been completed. There were no confirmed fatalities from the train alone, although five remained on the critical list. At least two had lost limbs. A continuous flow of ambulance traffic had made it difficult to count the injured, but the team had put the number between fifty and eighty. The driver of the train, Simon Butters, was alive but unconscious. No account could be gained from him at that time.

The revelation that the Village Hall had contained people at the time of the crash had caused the Fire and Rescue crews to re-evaluate their approach. After the explosion and subsequent fire, the plan was to saturate the partly demolished structure with high-pressure hoses. Anticipating that this measure could result in the drowning of any trapped survivors, the Fire Chief had opted to focus his hoses in a less expansive manner. Once the gas and electricity supplies were cut and the remaining pockets of flame extinguished, a physical search of the rubble could take place. Plans of the Village Hall were obtained from the archive at Fire HQ. They enabled the search teams, both fire and police, to get their bearings.

The snooker room, or where the snooker room had been, was to be the priority. Roof joists had fallen over that part of the building, but the engine had not gone that far. Rubble was taken out, one breeze-block at a time and thrown aside. Pauses to listen for any cries from within were frequent. Some of them were borne of hope, some of overactive imagination, but the determination to preserve life, any life which still prevailed, was immense.

The first significant find was the remnants of the snooker room. Among the furniture were human remains. They were that of a white man with grey hair, his clothing rendered colourless under the plaster dust. Darkened and dried blood had obscured his face. His features could not be described but his clothing matched that described to the CID by Mrs Kathleen McAulden as being worn by her husband Frederick. Peter Keld was on hand to preliminarily identify him. He agreed that it was Fred McAulden.

Hope-destroying as such a find undoubtedly was, it served to focus the search and, to some degree, justified the actions of the search teams. It also spurred them on to look for more in that location. Recovering the first body from the Village Hall caused the Fire Chief to reassess the scene. He had noticed that the shape of the rubble and timbers was not consistent with the area near it. There was a wide mound of rubble, which he could not identify. He authorised further careful examination and soon a second, lifeless form was uncovered. By the same method of preliminary identification, this was confirmed to be Leonard Hurlington.

The search continued into the warm, morning daylight. The sun shone brightly on the scene of unfolding desolation. The Village Hall body count had remained at two for over an hour and the pile of rubble seemed to be as large as it had been when they had first begun the search.

At five am, the search team found a gap in the blocks, fallen roof-timbers and dust, a chasm of darkness despite the bright daylight. Previously stowed torches were retrieved and trained on the gap. In what seemed to be a low-roofed burial chamber of the type found by archaeologists in Egypt, it was the space beneath the snooker table, which had withstood the impact of the fallen roof. The heavy, slate-bed table had remained intact throughout the building's collapse. The first sign of humanity was the sole of a shoe, quickly followed by a matching one. The fire officer reached in and touched one of them. It didn't generate a response. He scanned the tomb and he could make out a perfect, flat roof only two feet from the floor. He also saw the snooker balls sitting in the net pockets of the table. As the light passed across the lifeless frame, the firefighter put down his torch and reached to pull the body out. As he did so, the left foot lashed out at him and caught him on the edge of his fire helmet.

"Ahhh!" he exclaimed.

Other rescuers rushed at the exclamation from their colleague. He gabbled incoherently in his shocked state. When he had managed to compose himself, he clarified the reason for his temporary hysteria.

"He's alive! He's alive!"

The surge of energy this brought to the rescue team was evident. Rapid removal of adjoining debris resulted in the recovery of the semi-conscious form, who was quickly identified by Peter Keld as Jonathan Ullenorth. He was carefully lifted onto a wheeled stretcher and taken to the nearest point at which an ambulance could be manoeuvred.

"There should be another one in there," said Keld to the team.

The aperture exposed when Ullenorth had been extracted looked like a dusty mine tunnel. A firefighter with a helmet lamp climbed in and commando crawled along the length of the table.

"I see him," he called, surprised at how far he had crawled. It must have taken him beyond the far end of the snooker table. A roof-beam had fallen and come to rest on an angle against the end of the table. It had formed a protective canopy over the heavyweight Graham Posner.

"I have him, I can't move him, give me a hand here!" he sounded exasperated and out-of-breath. A colleague entered the gap and shuffled along on his stomach. Inch by inch, they dragged the inert body out of the rubble and into the open air. There was no sign of life. A paramedic administered first-aid with heart massage and oxygen from a mask. The rescuers fell silent.

Keld confirmed that it was Posner. That explained the difficulty for the lone firefighter who was trying to shift him. The paramedic remained calm as the procedures were applied. People began moving away. Some to get on with their respective tasks and some to distance themselves from the voyeurism of it all. The mood became solemn, defeatist, until,

"We've got him. He's breathing, heart's going."

A cheer rang out from those in earshot. It took six men and women to lift Posner onto a gurney. The paramedics were concerned that the trolley would not take his weight, so it was lowered to the bottom setting and pushed along just above the ground.

Keld stayed until the snooker room area had been made safe, albeit on a temporary basis. He looked for

Inspector Bhatta and found him at the rendezvous point by the pub.

"The Parish Councillors are accounted for Sir. Two dead and two alive, but they are in a bad way."

"Thank you, Peter. Are you alright?"

"Once I heard my family were not involved, that was a relief, but these people are my neighbours. This will take some time to come to terms with, you know?"

"Yes, it won't be quick," agreed Bhatta. "There are no deaths among the train passengers, at least not yet."

A separate police van was brought in order to store the items seized for potential forensic evidence. Plastic crates and bags of various sizes were filled with a broad assortment of items. Some were the personal belongings of those caught up in the crash. It was impossible, at that stage, to identify what belonged to who, so anything that might later be claimed was taken into police possession. Wallets, jewellery, spectacles, shoes, handbags and mobile phones were recovered, labelled and stored. Inside the wreckage of the train carriages, several laptop computers were found. As they were of high value, largely intact and likely to be returned where appropriate, the police property clerk stored them separately. One of the Fire crews found a laptop partly concealed beneath the life-saving snooker table. He approached Bhatta with it. Bhatta looked at the dust-covered device and momentarily marvelled at how it seemed to have remained undamaged through such carnage. He referred the finder to the property clerk standing at the opened rear doors of the van.

"I've found this. It looks like an expensive one," he said, "Your boss over there said I had to give it to you."

The clerk looked at where the firefighter had pointed and saw Bhatta overseeing the search scene. She accepted the laptop and waited until Bhatta appeared able to speak.

"Inspector, this laptop was found in the rubble. Do you want it in with the found items or is it relevant to the enquiry?"

Bhatta took a moment to take in the request. It seemed so unimportant when compared to the atrocious events of the previous night. He was about to say something regrettably intolerant, but he held it in.

"It might belong to one of the dead. It may have sentimental value so keep it separate, please."

"Okay, will do." The clerk went back to her van. Bhatta's attention was drawn swiftly back to the rescue scene.

"Shhh! I think I heard something," said the police search team Sergeant.

His team paused, they adopted statue mode to aid concentration. A sharp, desperate voice could be heard. There were no discernible syllables, but the tone was a plea for help.

"It's coming from this carriage. We have searched it already, right?" asked the team leader. His team nodded in turn. A methodical visual search from a safe position was standard practice. Someone was still alive and speaking from somewhere in the damaged carriage. "Search this one again, in your pairs. Come on."

The team reformed and began a new examination of Coach E. They strained to see under broken furniture and beyond dangling luggage racks. Unclaimed items were strewn around among the broken glass. The carriage had remained largely intact. Several people had been rescued from it and led to safety during the initial search. A collective sense of annoyance permeated the search zone. How could they have missed any survivors? The mood changed in an instant when the voice could be heard more clearly than before.

"Help me!" It was a woman's voice, but where could she be?

"Keep talking, we are here to get you out," called the Sergeant. "Describe where you are."

"I'm in the loo," she wailed with a breaking voice.

"The search team changed gear and dashed to the end of Coach E where the view from the broken windows did not allow for a visual search to be made. Two constables clambered through the void and into the carriage. Efforts were concentrated on the darkened area where the toilet door remained closed. They reached the door and tapped it.

"Hello, it's the police. Can you hear me?"

"Yes, get the door open and help me out of this box." Her desperation was giving way to indignation.

"What's your name, love?" asked the searcher.

"My name is Mrs Barbara Hunter and I don't appreciate being called 'love' by strangers."

The cop momentarily wondered if this individual really did wish to be rescued. Had he been in that situation, he would have been more pragmatic in his words. He moderated his address.

"Okay Barbara, we are trying to get the door open now. Are you injured?"

"I have been thrown about like a pea in a whistle, how could I not be injured?"

She was able to complain well enough. That was encouraging, albeit soaked in ingratitude.

"Any broken bones Barbara?"

"No, I don't think so, but I'm not a surgeon, am I?" she snapped.

Her rescuer chose to ignore her attitude. He radioed an update on the situation in Coach E, asking for pry-bars and any available paramedics to attend the carriage. Meanwhile, the Sergeant maintained the strained conversation with the entrapped Barbara, offering what comfort he could to his distracted and impatient target. The conversation undulated but continued until the required equipment and personnel arrived.

"Barbara, I'm going to try to get this door open now. Please lean against the wall away from the door."

"It's dark in here, I don't know which side is the door," she snapped, failing to convince her rescuers that it was true. The pry-bars were applied and considerable pressure was exerted in the restricted space on the damaged carriage. Several unsuccessful attempts brought further protests from Mrs Barbara

Hunter. It proved helpful to simply ignore her outbursts.

When the required purchase was achieved, a gap began to appear through which Barbara could see the light from the torch beams. Suddenly aware of the undignified nature of her appearance, and how that differed from her usual public image, Barbara tried to improve her look before her rescuers caught sight of her, but it was a futile gesture. Unpleasant-smelling water from the toilet bowl had been thrown over her and had then dried, her clothing was torn and her make-up had taken on an Alice Cooper vibe.

As the door came open, painfully slowly, the rescuers and the rescued were unaware that there had been an increase in the personnel outside the coach. Standing next to the waiting medics were the press pack, handheld voice recorders and cameras already in operation. The press sensed a human-interest story of an award-winning standard. Among all of the death and destruction, a life had been saved and it had been fully recorded for the world to take heart. The TV journalists were anxiously tapping their microphones in anticipation. The rescuing police team were too preoccupied with trying to get Barbara out to have noticed what the reporters were doing.

Unseen by the waiting assembly, the toilet door had been prized open sufficiently to extract Barbara and to get her into the doorway of the coach. Barbara had lost her shoes and had to be lifted over the broken shards and debris. As she was being passed to the police officers on the ground below, the flash photography exploded into life. Photographs, which would normally have appalled Barbara, were being taken at an alarming rate. Her skirt had rolled up to reveal her underwear and a stifled giggle could be heard from behind the strobe of lights. The questions came before Barbara's feet had reached the grass.

"How does it feel to be alive?"

"What's your name?"

"Do you have anything to say to the people who have rescued you?"

"Describe the crash in your own words."

"What do you think caused the crash?"

The chances of getting answers to those questions at that moment were somewhat remote but that did not stop them from being asked. The police and medics tried in vain to protect Barbara and her dignity from the reporters. The result was a melee, an ugly spectacle of conflicting interests amid a cacophony of voices, each drowning the other out. It was brought to a climax by one compelling voice - Barbara's.

"I have something to say!" she broadcasted over all of the other contributors. She had not spent so many years as a headteacher without learning how to gain control of an audience. All fell quiet, apart from the continuing flash photography.

"I have been through a living hell. No-one could anticipate that a train journey would result in this." Barbara spoke from the heart and in high indignation of the ordeal she had been made to suffer. It was television gold. At the first moment of silence, the hacks swept in to fill the void.

"What have you to say to the rail operators?"

"Do you have a message for the driver?"

"Do you intend to sue for damages?"

The Sergeant stepped up and appealed for some restraint.

"People, please. This lady has yet to be medically examined. Your questions will wait until she is ready."

Barbara was not going to allow anyone to speak for her.

"I am fully capable of speaking for myself!" she pontificated her views with unmistakable clarity.

She stood up from the paramedic's chair and addressed the wider world.

"Whoever is responsible for this outrage will be made to pay for their incompetence. If anyone has lost their lives or is seriously injured, they must have justice." It was as though she had invested her time whilst incarcerated in the train's toilet in preparing the speech she was now delivering with Churchillian gravitas. "I will ensure that no stone is left unturned in the pursuit of the truth."

The press had found their goose who was laying golden eggs in abundance, and with no prompting required. Barbara was to personify the suffering of the innocents, caught up in a massive, corporate cover-up, which was yet to be even suggested. By the time the paramedics were permitted, by Barbara, to take her to a waiting ambulance, she was already being presented to the eager media consumer as the voice of the wronged, the face of the sufferers and the champion of justice. The newspapers varied little in their titles for Mrs Barbara Hunter. The commonly agreed epithet, reinforced by the pictures of her dignified stance whilst looking terrible, became 'The Angel of Truth.'

Barbara was finally getting the public adulation she had always felt that she should have.

*

The arrival of the Chief Constable and the senior investigating officer was heralded by a summons for Inspector Bhatta to brief them on the night's events as he had understood them to be. After this, the Fire Chief and a paramedic were also consulted. These conversations took place in the cordoned area of the car park of the Barley Mow. Only when the light morning dew began to settle and moisten the air did they relocate to a gazebo already erected in a neighbouring garden.

Among the updates given by Bhatta was the activities of the press. The decision was taken to conduct a press conference in the hope that it would add structure to the flow of information whilst allowing the emergency services to conduct their roles without distractions and inhibitions. The only room deemed large enough to accommodate the conference was the function room at the rear of the Barley Mow. The licensee, Markus Grejzni, was asked and agreed without hesitation. He stipulated that he wished to open the pub at 11am but the function room remained at the disposal of the police.

The press pack moved their cameras, microphones and light-stands into the function room and began to plug them all into the limited power sources therein. The top table housed five people, the Chief Constable, the SIO, a senior manager from the railway operator, an executive officer from Pendale Town Hall and the Chief Fire Officer.

The hacks were phoning in their updates and tapping the screens of their computers when they were asked to sit. As they did so, Mrs Barbara Hunter made a dramatic entrance. Wrapped in a health-authority blanket, she had overcome her recent unconsciousness and was bearing her injuries sustained in the toilet cubicle, with admirable stoicism. She strode up to the top table and demanded to know who was in charge. The reporters nearby had spotted her and recalled that she was the ideal foil for their questioning of the top-table officials.

"I am a survivor of the train crash and I will not be silenced," she announced.

Det. Supt. Lane-Wright stepped forward to speak to Barbara as the others looked for an underling to blame for allowing this troublesome interloper to approach them. Lane-Wright had recalled the part of Bhatta's briefing in which he had mentioned the press intrusion during and after Barbara's extraction from the coach.

"Mrs Hunter?" she asked, which, luckily, was how Barbara preferred to be addressed.

"Yes. Who are you?"

"Superintendent Lane-Wright. I shall be overseeing the investigation into what happened. I am relieved to hear that you are alright."

"Alright? Alright? Do you think that being in a train crash makes me alright?"

"No, of course. You have been through a terrible ordeal, but as people have lost their lives, and as you are walking, talking and not needing hospital treatment, you are comparatively alright."

Her tone was carefully pitched and expertly delivered. It did little to assuage Barbara's ire.

"This press conference, why have none of the survivors been asked to participate? Would you deny us a voice? Has the cover-up begun already?"

The Superintendent took in a breath then assured Barbara.

"None of those things apply, I can assure you. We are to give an early summary of what has happened. Nobody is covering anything up and nobody is being denied their say."

"I choose to have my say right now," demanded the OFSTED Inspector on a level of indignation witnessed by few before.

Sensing an ugly scene, which would be to the advantage of nobody but the press, Janette Lane-Wright spoke briefly to the Chief and the other officials who agreed to allow Barbara to take a seat at the top-table. Another chair was found, and the conference could begin. Barbara dispensed with the blanket and instead showed her torn clothing beneath. Like a plant, she appeared to thrive in bright light.

The Chief Constable opened the proceedings. Stating the obvious but taking care to eliminate any misunderstandings, he explained that the previous evening, an electric train had left the track at Eckscarfe and had collided with a building in the village. At least two people had lost their lives, and many more were injured. Rescue efforts ran through the night and the co-operation of the emergency services and the implementation of contingency plans had proven to be effective in preventing further loss of life. He expressed the collective condolences of his force to those who had suffered as a result of the crash, in particular, those who had lost loved ones. He handed over to Det. Supt. Janette Lane-Wright, who he had appointed to be the Senior Investigating Officer, to speak about the investigation.

"Although it is too early to say what caused this tragedy, I will head a team of investigators to work with our partner agencies; the Fire and Rescue service, the Ambulance Service, the railway operators and investigators, the local authority, the Forensic Science Service and the Coroner in order to establish what has happened. It would be improper to speculate as to the cause. There is simply not enough information available at this time to make any conclusions or judgements."

She adjusted her briefing notes and the only sound was the click and whirr of cameras. She lifted her head to indicate that she was ready to continue.

"Formal identification of the victims is ongoing and we will, when the families have been informed, give you the names of those who have perished. I can tell you that the driver of the train is alive and in a serious condition. We hope to be able to talk to him at some stage, when his condition allows."

Another member of the top table assembly had waited long enough. The mention of the driver was the trigger for intervention.

"I would like to speak to that driver myself!" declared Mrs Barbara Hunter from the end of the table.

Lane-Wright instantly regretted allowing her onto the panel and her despair momentarily manifest itself in the briefest of rolls of her eyes. Her attempt to placate Barbara had backfired and the press, and therefore the world, were witnessing all of it.

Muttered conversations ensued and a reporter spoke over the hum to ask.

"You are a survivor of the crash, I believe. Mrs Hunter, is it?"

"I am Mrs Barbara Hunter and I was on that train. I am lucky to be alive."

Lane-Wright and the Chief Constable were unable to take any action for fear of it appearing to be denying a critic the opportunity to speak. They had no choice but to listen to her along with everyone else.

"All of these glib words mean nothing to me. I know what happened. I was there. The train was delayed at Pendale for over an hour and the driver was going too fast trying to make up for lost time. It's obvious that's what caused the train to derail. It doesn't take a genius to work that out."

The cameras flashed more wildly than before. Barbara Hunter, wrapped up once again, and quite unnecessarily, in her NHS blanket was holding court and it made for a more entertaining spectacle than the senior police officers on the top table. Barbara was just getting started.

"It was terrifying. The carriage was being thrown around like a beach ball. It went dark, there was screaming, children too. All because that driver was in a hurry. Those of us who regularly travel on this line, we all know there is a curve on the track at this point and the train has to slow down. This time it didn't and with devastating consequences." She paused long enough for a reporter to chip in.

"Mrs Hunter, Hugo Latimer, The Times. Thank you for your account. Please confirm that you are formally accusing the driver, one Simon Butters, as being solely responsible for this disaster?"

"Who else could have prevented the derailment?"

The cameras shifted into hyper-drive and should have carried an epilepsy warning. Whereas most of the panel tried to shield their eyes, Mrs Barbara Hunter soaked it up like the sunshine on a freed prisoner. She was playing up to the press and loving every minute.

"Barbara, over here please."

"Look this way love."

Barbara overlooked the overall state of her appearance and conducted herself as would a self-righteous movie star on a red-carpet premier.

"Lift the blanket up," demanded a photographer in a grey waterproof jacket. "Hold it up behind you, both hands."

Barbara obliged the wishes of the newsman by picking up the blanket and holding it open behind her back like angel wings. The press had their picture. The Angel of Truth had spoken.

CHAPTER FIVE

"Two high-risk missing persons in the North of the County, a bogus doctor enquiry with some cases dating back ten years, the Football Riot enquiry has fifty-eight pending arrests and we are short staffed as it is Sir," protested Lane-Wright over the phone in the Incident Room at Pendale Police Station. The Chief Constable would not be moved.

"I understand your concern Janette and believe me, if I could find you more trained detective staff I would do it in an instant."

"Sir, this inquiry at Eckscarfe involves at least two deaths and countless serious injuries. I need more staff to get through this mountain of outstanding actions. What about the BTP? Can't they send more people?"

The protocol for who did what had been followed from the outset. The BTP, although holding overall ownership of the inquiry, had insufficient resources to carry out the investigation. They were to offer some support but the overall responsibility for the investigation fell to the County Constabulary. This support had involved a team of BTP officers taking witness statements from the survivors who had been travelling on the train when it crashed. Once that had been completed, they had returned to their normal duties. Other liaison roles were also performed by the BTP, such as the facilitation of the work of the Rail Accident Investigation Bureau. They also fielded the rail operators' issues, sparing the investigation team from having to do that too.

Lane-Wright was acutely aware of the task ahead. Her intended deployment of experienced detectives had effectively been undermined by the Chief. She was a victim of risk management and it was her who would be taking all of the risks. If the investigation was in any way unsatisfactory, it would be her fault. As a final appeal, she requested some help from the uniformed staff.

"I suppose we could do that," said the Chief. "I'll see what resources can be reassigned."

"Thank you Sir. May I ask for Inspector Bhatta and some of his team please? They have been very helpful at the scene and with the house-to-house."

"Bhatta? Yes, I know who he is. That should be okay. Leave it with me."

She replaced the handset and let out a long breath. She looked up at the staffing detail displayed on a piece of plain paper on the wall to the side of her desk. She mentally drew lines through the names of the detectives who had been redeployed onto other protracted inquiries. She picked up the phone again and dialled the Control Room. She asked that Inspector Bhatta call her when he was able to do so. When he did get through, he was put in the picture.

"Imran, I've been on the phone to the Chief and the staffing situation across the force is dire. We are all going to have to stretch ourselves on this one. I will remain SIO but I am also doing that on two other large inquiries. What I need is someone running this incident at ground level and that is going to be you."

Bhatta was initially surprised to hear that. He, as a uniformed Inspector had an important role to play but he had believed that his actions on the night of the rail crash had made up the bulk of his contribution. He had, prior to his promotion to the rank of Inspector, spent six months as a temporary Detective Sergeant. It had been a fixed-term secondment, which he had thought was nothing more than a 'tick in a box' for his future career advancement. He had not expressed any wish to dedicate any substantial period in an investigative role. He had learned a lot and generally enjoyed the posting, but all of the people he had worked with had been in the CID from being constables. There was some reluctance to accept any addition to the team who was seen as having not earned their place as they had.

He was used to encountering other cultural obstacles, the most obvious being his race. He knew how to handle that. What he was less prepared for were the other cultural barriers existing within the force. Lane-Wright was putting him in that role. Although he had no say in that decision, he had some suggestions to offer.

"If you think I am right for the role, then I will give it my best Ma'am," he said with his customary politeness. "What about my team?"

"Yes, I want your view on that," she said as though distracted by something. "You can have two support staff who are trained in major inquiry systems imputing, an exhibits and disclosure officer who I will get back to you about and you will need to find some uniforms to fulfil the enquiries and actions. Anyone in mind, Imran?"

"Peter Keld is the village bobby so he knows Eckscarfe better than anyone. A familiar face will be reassuring for the locals. That will be of value. I would like to have Melanie Sharpe too. She has applied for CID and this will help her with her aspirations." He was about to suggest some more names but Lane-Wright cut him short.

"That should be alright. Leave that with me to arrange their release from their current duties."

"Is that all I have, Ma'am? It seems a small team for such a big investigation."

"I agree, Imran. Ideally, you would have experienced detective staff but they are all deployed elsewhere. This is all of the resources we can provide for you. I shall lobby for more, but it isn't likely at the moment."

"Thank you Ma'am."

He put down the receiver and let out a long breath.

Melanie Sharpe was summoned into the office of the patrol Sergeant at Pendale Police Station where she was told that she was to be seconded onto the enquiry team for the Eckscarfe investigation. In the five years she had patrolled Pendale, she had forged the ambition to be a detective and was keen to take advantage of any opportunities which may arise. Her arrest tally, which for some was an indication of work-rate, was comparable to any of her peers and as she did not have children, she was not limited in the working hours she could fulfil. When she left the

Sergeant's office, she went into the car park where some of her colleagues went in order to smoke. She tapped the buttons, one-handed, on her mobile phone and listened to the ringtone.

"Hi, you busy?" she said.

"No, it's fine. Go on," was the answer.

"Good news, I had to tell you first. I'm on the enquiry team for the train crash investigation."

"Babe, that it brilliant. You so deserve it. Well done you."

"Thanks. Apparently, the Inspector, Bhatta his name is, he actually asked for me. Can you believe that?"

"I can, yes. I don't need any convincing. You have earned a chance to do something like this, Mel. This Inspector . . . "

"Bhatta, he's Asian."

"Bhatta, yeah. What's he like? Is he a good guy or a knob?"

"I think he's okay. I haven't worked with him much. He's very serious. I suppose you can't go joking around on such a big job, so it's just as well."

"Well, he's a good judge of character having you on his team Babe."

"Thanks. I've got to go. I might be late home."

"Not surprised Babe. Well done. So proud."

"Love you."

"Love you too."

*

The major incident suite on the top floor of Pendale Police station had been completely refurbished only one year before. The result was a continuous, white strip at waist height containing electrical points and computer lead sockets, a great deal of full-length glass, an equal quantity of light, beech veneer and an array of computer screens which could shame an electrical superstore. When not engaged in the investigation of a major enquiry, the facility lay dormant. This had been decreed at the highest level. Under no circumstances was the facility to fall into standard use and therefore be unready to respond to any emergency, which would befit its intended purpose.

At the end of the main bank of computer screens was a narrow corridor of glass walls, behind which were individual offices and at the end was a video viewing room with no natural light.

Bhatta had set up his temporary position by making a hastily written sign and sticking it on the outside of the door. This was because he believed that many of the people working there may not have known who he was.

His work in the legal profession, although several years before, had required him to take his appearance seriously. Over six feet tall, physically fit, always clean-shaven, and with short, neatly trimmed hair, he customarily dressed smartly and in-keeping with his role as a leader. As a lawyer, he had acquired several dark suits and, as he was of the same slim build as he had been then, he was, as far as the range of his wardrobe stretched, ready to assume the role of temporary Detective Inspector.

He contacted the partner agencies to arrange for an information exchange meeting. On his hurriedly prepared list was the railway company. Before he got a chance to make that call, a personal business card was handed to him by one of the office staff. On it was the name Robert Almoss, Chief Rail engineer and RAIB Inspector. The address was in Derby.

"And he is downstairs now?" asked Bhatta.

"Yes, at the desk," he was told.

"I'll go and speak to him. Thanks."

Bhatta came into the public area and saw four people. Not wanting to make assumptions from appearances, which he had been subjected to all his life, he called out "Mr Almoss?"

A large-framed man with a shaven head stood up and approached him. He would have been quite intimidating but for a thoughtful and concerned expression on his face.

"Hello, I'm Inspector Imran Bhatta." He shook hands and nearly lost his in the big man's shovel-sized mitt.

"Bob Almoss. I'm the Rail Accident Investigator. Thanks for seeing me. I know you will have a lot on."

"I was going to call you anyway," said Bhatta, "Please, come up to the office."

He led him up two flights of stairs making general comments about the tragedy which had brought them together in the respective roles. Almoss explained the role of the RAIB knowing that it was a recently formed organisation and was yet to become a household name. As they reached the Incident Room, Superintendent Lane-Wright entered through the door at the other end.

"Ah, the boss is here. She will want to hear what you have come for." Bhatta assumed correctly. Introductions were made as they entered Bhatta's office and closed the door.

"What exactly has happened?" asked Lane-Wright, who was already working out options for her investigation. Almoss opened a zip-edged, document file and pulled out a notepad.

"I have thoroughly examined the scene, in particular, the length of track on the approaches to the point of derailment at Eckscarfe. There is extensive damage to the rails at the point of the derailment."

"That's not a surprise considering that a train has left the track there," offered Lane-Wright. "How could that have remained undamaged after that?" Bob Almoss paused, glanced at Bhatta and back at the Superintendent.

"It has taken several hours to examine the track properly but I am now sure about what has happened. I would have expected the rails to become detached from the sleepers in the course of such an event. There is a finite breaking-strain and it was not a surprise to find that the rails were extensively damaged. It was the nature of that damage which I found unusual. A derailment, at moderate or high speed, will normally cause the line to be damaged, often severed. Once I had photographed the damaged ends, it became clear that the metal had not been severed in that way. Imagine pulling apart a loaf of bread with your hands, the result is rough, uneven. Then think of that loaf being cut with a bread-knife and compare the edges."

"Mr Almoss, are you saying that the track was damaged by something other than the derailment?" asked Bhatta, whose mind was working rapidly to consider the possible ramifications.

"I am saying that some of the damage to the track was caused by prolonged contact with something stronger in density than the steel of the track."

"Such as?" asked Lane-Wright whose face was giving away nothing of her thoughts.

"Such as a power-tool or an angle grinder. This is not a conclusion I have reached lightly but somebody has deliberately cut through the rails."

"Deliberately!" exclaimed Lane-Wright.

"Yes. There's no doubt about it. The rails, both of them, had been severed by cutting gear. This could not have been caused by the train's wheels." He paused again but this time to allow what he had said to be absorbed. Once satisfied that his message was clear, he continued.

"Whoever cut the rails was not taking any chances. It was a thorough job. They redirected the severed edges of the lines to make sure that the train came off the track. Probably by applying direct force using a heavy instrument, but they did it on both rails. This was no accident."

The realisation that the disaster investigation had become a multiple murder inquiry washed over the police officers. New motivations and rationale began to form in their minds. Lane-Wright was the first to speak.

"Okay, we are dealing with a different situation now. Get the rails forensically examined and alert the Coroner's office. They will probably want Home Office pathologists to do the post-mortems. Mr Almoss, do you think that there was an intention to cause the train to leave the track at that point in order for it to threaten the village?"

"That is going beyond my range of investigation but, erm, yes, that is a possibility. The cuts were made at the point where the curve begins. It was inevitable that the train would leave the track and travel toward the buildings on the edge of Eckscarfe."

"Could it have been aimed at any other buildings?" asked Bhatta. Almoss paused to find the best words for a layperson to be able to understand.

"The reduced speed of the train at the point of derailment has helped to avoid a far greater catastrophe. We can be thankful of that. Once it had left the track, the trajectory of the train would, on such a flat surface, be quite predictable. The train wheels are not designed to go anywhere other than on steel rails, so the friction of the wheels on the field would reduce its velocity at a considerable rate of deceleration. This has also helped. If whoever did this wanted to inflict maximum damage to the wider village, they would have failed."

"So, if the intention was to destroy only the Village Hall . . . ?" began Lane-Wright. Almoss answered her unfinished question.

" . . . their choice of 'weapon' was proportionate. This does not take into account the injuries and suffering of those on the train, of course."

Nobody spoke for a few seconds until Lane-Wright summarised what everyone else was thinking.

"We have a deliberate act, resulting in the destruction of the people and property of this community. Why would anyone wish such harm in this place?"

CHAPTER SIX

"Can I have a word Sir?" said Peter Keld who looked dishevelled but Bhatta was not going to mention it.

"Yes Pete, how are you?" he asked knowing that Keld had been there from the outset.

"A bit pooped but there are folks worse off than I am," he said. "I wanted to ask you about something that happened before the crash."

The initial thought to enter Bhatta's fatigued mind was to dismiss whatever Keld was going to say. It was swiftly followed by a flash of inner-embarrassment at his own narrow-mindedness. By the time he answered, he seemed to have been awaiting this revelation.

"Go on Pete, what is it?"

"The line was closed for an hour and a half before the crash. The derailed train was the first one through when the line was reopened."

"Yes, we know that," said Bhatta displaying nothing more than impatience.

"The reason for the closure was an anonymous caller saying that someone had jumped off the bridge on Shipley Road. I went to the bridge and found what I thought was a suicide case, hanging from the bridge. It turns out that it was a dummy, a boiler suit stuffed with polythene bags. Some idiot was having a prank, so I thought anyway. I think there's more to that now. It was connected to what happened."

"Do you think that it was done to buy time?"

"That's exactly what I think, Sir."

"Then the bridge at Shipley Road must be treated as another crime scene. I'm going to bring this up with the Superintendent. Thanks Pete, you did the right thing by suggesting it." He headed to the door but Keld had something else to add.

"Erm Inspector Bhatta, there's something else. Perhaps I shouldn't have done this, with hindsight, but I took the dummy down and got rid of it. Sorry, I thought it was just a prank." Bhatta stopped in mid-stride and rubbed his forehead. He turned to Keld and asked.

"Where? Where did you throw it?"

"In one of the skips behind the quarry office. It was the only bin big enough to put it in."

"So the skips cannot have been emptied by the Council, can they?"

"No, the cordons don't let anyone into the village. There hasn't been a collection since Tuesday."

"Right. Get up to the quarry and find that thing. There is forensic potential on it and I don't want to lose that."

"Yes Sir."

Fatigued, close to tears and still trembling from the events of the night, Peter Keld drove beyond the cordon and out of the village to the quarry. The morning sun dappled his windscreen through the overhanging trees and came back in full, dazzling force in the open of the climbing lane. He drove in through the only gate and turned a sharp left to the square of refuse containers. He began opening the rubber lids of the skips. After initially trying to minimise the risk of forensic contamination by using his baton, he considered that he had handled the dummy and therefore his forensic connection to it was already made. It was the potential, forensic connection to other people that was important. In the third skip, he moved some recently added crushed cardboard and saw the eerily-arranged, human-shaped piece of potential evidence. He pressed the transmit button on his radio and asked that Inspector Bhatta contact him on private mode.

"Hello Pete."

"Sir, I've found that dummy. It's still here at the quarry."

"Is it as you left it, no interference?"

"Looks like it's not been touched. There is some clean cardboard on it but it shouldn't affect the forensic evidence."

"Can you get it out and bag it up, Pete?"

"I haven't got any bags that big, Sir."

"I'll get some up to you – no, I'll bring them myself. Ten minutes."

Fifteen minutes later, Bhatta arrived in his police patrol car. He took the largest plastic forensic bags he could find and went to look in the wheeled skip. Keld directed him to the relevant one. They carefully removed the sheets of card to reveal the artificial body beneath. With surgical gloves, they lifted the form as though it was a real person and slid it into a body bag. Keld remembered that he had thrown the rope into the skip before the dummy so he climbed up to look for it. He pulled the length of brown woven rope up and placed it in a smaller evidence bag. Keld and Bhatta stood up and looked closely at their newly-found clues.

The form was a representation of a man and it was wearing an all-in-one boiler suit of rough, blue cotton. There were plastic carrier bags taped to the ankles with grey carpet tape. The same tape held on the hands and the head, also fashioned from plastic bags. The boiler suit was old and worn but was clean and, allowing for the night in the skip, quite serviceable. There was a rectangular patch on the left breast, which was less faded in colour than the rest of the suit. A name badge, or a works logo, perhaps. At that moment, a worker from the quarry site approached and asked what was going on. As Keld knew the man, he stepped forward to field the question.

"We have recovered some potential evidence in this skip," he explained. All three men looked down at the body in the bag. The quarryman initially thought it to be human, as Keld had done the day before. Once he knew it to be a dummy, he regained his ability to breathe once again.

"Christ, I thought it was one of our lads."

"What made you think that?" asked Bhatta.

"Well, the suit," said the quarryman as though it should have been obvious.

Keld and Bhatta looked at the boiler-suit worn by the dummy and then at the one worn by the quarryman. Although his was virtually new, they were of the same design and colour. On the breast of the one worn by the worker was a cotton badge, sewn on to the cloth. His read Neville Allerton and had Wilson's Aggregates written in smaller letters beneath it. The name badge was the same size as the space on the dummy's suit.

"Is this suit from here then?" asked Bhatta.

Allerton crouched to peer through the clear plastic bag. "Looks like one of ours, an old one."

"How many of these are there? In the Eckscarfe area I mean."

"Loads. There are forty-odd blokes working here and each of us has a few. They don't want them back when somebody leaves or retires so it could be hundreds."

"Do they vary in sizes?" asked the Inspector.

"I think so, small medium and large, I suppose. What is this to do with the police? I mean, it's not anything valuable, is it?"

"We can't go into detail at present but it might be connected to something important." Allerton guessed at the 'something important.'

"It's to do with the train crash isn't it?"

"As I said, Mr Allerton, I can't go into detail and it would help if our conversation remained between us for the time being."

"Oh, alright, I get it." Allerton gestured the locking of his mouth and the discarding of an imaginary key.

Bhatta returned to the Incident Room and spoke to Lane-Wright. He explained the fake suicide and that the mannequin had been recovered and was available for examination. The logic being that, if the person who faked the hanging did so to allow time and space for them to cut the line without any trains coming, this could lead them to the killer. Once convinced, and slightly impressed that this line of enquiry had been generated by uniformed officers and not detectives, she approved the submission and the relevant entries and accompanying witness statements were completed. Keld arrived shortly after with his own statement and that of Neville Allerton who confirmed the match to the industrial clothing of Wilson's Aggregates. The evidence bags containing the dummy and the rope were placed in a police van for transportation to the major incident evidence store.

*

The next press conference went more smoothly than the first had. Care had been taken to avoid letting Barbara Hunter know it was taking place. The top table was staffed by Det. Supt. Janette Lane-Wright and Inspector Imran Bhatta. Unofficially, and Bhatta was acutely aware each time this had happened, it was considered to be good PR for an ethnic minority police officer to be included in the line-up. Bhatta reconciled this position to himself by accepting such deployments only if they were in-keeping with his duties and rank. He had swerved some requests, which he had seen as exploitation of his ethnicity. He had also become adept at prioritising the integration of minorities into the police service. It was a constant balancing act. For a British Asian to be seen in an important role in the police was, he believed, one way of bringing down cultural barriers. For the incident at Eckscarfe, he had no hesitation in agreeing to participate. As one of the first officers at the scene and the deputy S.I.O., he felt deeply and intrinsically involved in all aspects.

Lane-Wright chose her words with care. She had set out to impart the news that they were treating the incident as a crime, but she wanted to avoid causing widespread panic. The motive for the damage to the rail-track was yet to be ascertained and wild speculation was unhelpful. The community and the press needed to know that they were safe and that the police were doing everything possible to find out what had happened and who, if anyone, was to blame for it. Lane-Wright outlined the death and injury count with appropriate gravitas, pausing for effect at key moments. She went on to praise the efforts of the rescue and welfare agencies, which sounded like a tired, old soundbite. Only when the planned missive ended and the floor was open to questions did the energy levels soar. Camera flashes and reporters talking over each other resulted in nobody being heard or answered. Finally, a voice could be heard above the din. It was that of the BBC's chief home affairs reporter.

"Superintendent, is this an act of terrorism, and if so, what was it for?"

The camera noises replicated machine-gun fire. Only when they had abated did Lane-Wright begin to answer.

"This investigation is at an early stage. It is too early to be able to say with any certainty why it happened. That is only a part of our inquiry. I can confirm that there has been no claim to this atrocity by any political, religious or protest group. Until the evidence suggests anything different, we are not treating this as an act of terrorism."

The melee erupted again, albeit with less volume. A female journalist broke through.

"If it isn't terrorism, what is the motive?"

"As I said, it is too early to say and speculation is unhelpful in such an investigation. We are pursuing several lines of enquiry and I appeal to anyone who may have any information, or saw anything they believe might be connected, however small it may seem, to get in contact with my team at the Pendale Incident Room."

The questioning continued and the entertainment value of the answers diminished in value as the exercise unfolded. Bhatta made no verbal contribution to the proceedings. Instead, he contemplated how to make the next scheduled press conference contain some evidence that the police were making some progress.

*

Actions were generated through the centralised computer system. Most of them were instructions for police officers to visit and take witness statements from named persons. Many of them began with the instruction 'Trace, interview and eliminate,' which meant that sufficient questioning should be carried out in order to eliminate that person from suspicion of involvement. A standing joke among jaded investigators was to misinterpret the term 'eliminate' and use it in its more homicidal context. The use of dark humour can help to get some people through their day.

Those who were still in hospital and receiving treatment for their injuries had to be handled with additional sensitivity, but their accounts were required in any case. Specially trained uniformed officers were deployed to obtain accounts from witnesses who had been identified as requiring such expertise. Less delicate actions were given to any officer who could be spared. Due to the number of visits to be made, those tasks in the 'volume' category were given to Inspector Bhatta and his team of uniformed officers, including four seconded BTP officers. House-to-house speculative calls fell into this band.

One such low-priority deployment was to seek and identify anyone who was in the area of the Shipley Road railway bridge on the evening of the rail crash. The nearest house, in fact the only house which could be described as near, was an isolated cottage on the narrow lane which ran parallel to the railway line. The lane formed the shortest route between Shipley Road and the point of the derailment. It was a tied cottage, owned by the farm estate and the old man had lived in it for many years. The cottage was a picture of old-world charm apart from a modern lean-to at the side covering stacks of chopped firewood and a small Fiat car. The house was occupied by an old, retired, farm worker named Rodney Brickshaw, a widower with no nearby relatives. He had no telephone or any other modern amenities other than a radio set, which was playing classical music on a low volume. The inside of the cottage was unchanged since its last upgrade in the 1930s.

Peter Keld, accompanied by Melanie Sharpe, called on Rodney in the early afternoon. Rodney was unused to receiving visitors and was initially hostile. Thinking that this was due to their being police officers, Keld reminded Rodney that he was the Eckscarfe village policeman and that they had met before. Rodney's discomfort was nothing to do with them being cops. He treated all callers in this way. He tended to value his privacy above his manners.

"I know who you are," he declared in the opened doorway, "I don't know what you want to speak to me for so state your business."

The householder was not prepared to waste time on pleasantries. Although advanced in age, he kept an upright bearing and his clothes were clean and pressed with precision. He wore a brown, corduroy shirt and baggy, beige trousers. His silver hair was neat and well-groomed but his spectacles were held together at the hinge by clear tape.

"You will be aware of the derailment, Mr Brickshaw?"

"Aye."

"Did you hear of it on the radio? Newspapers perhaps?"

"I 'eard it 'appen, across fields. Made a right din, it did."

"So, you were at home at the time?"

"Aye, I don't walk so far these days. I only take car out to shops on a Saturday and Church on Sunday. I'm home all week, you know."

Keld and Sharpe realised that there was only fields between Rodney's cottage and the crash site. With nothing louder than a tinny radio, and nobody to talk to, it would have been unmistakable. Keld explained that he wanted a witness statement and after he had outlined what it was for, Rodney agreed and allowed them past the threshold and into his living room.

The walls were of yellowed lime-plaster and the oak beams allowed only those below average height to pass beneath without stooping. A log fire burned constantly in the grate and the smoke permeated the living room as much as it travelled up the chimney. Further smoke was provided by Rodney's walnut, tobacco pipe. The only connections to the modern world were a stack of newspapers, which had yet to become discoloured by smoke and the transistor radio, which belonged in the 1970s. The music emanating from the radio was from an earlier century. There were Constable prints in poorly-varnished plywood frames on the walls. A coat rack on the wall by the hinges of the door held three coats, all owned by the sole inhabitant.

"What did you think the noise was?" asked Sharpe.

Rodney Brickshaw had no need of pleasantries. What was obvious did not, in his view, need to be explained. Suffering fools was for others to do. He didn't answer and Mel Sharpe took this as her cue to repeat her question. Recognising the only way to shut her up, Rodney eventually answered but he looked at Keld and had did so.

"South train just come past by a few seconds. Then there's curve, o' course. If 'train's going to come off 'track, it'd be at 'curve. T'was always going to 'appen, you know. Trains like straight lines."

Keld heard in Rodney's words an echo of the unspoken words of many other people he had met. He had a feeling that Rodney's in-build directness brought with it a compelling honesty which did not rely on hindsight alone.

"Can you describe the sound of it?" he asked.

"Metal," said Rodney. "Like metal dragged across land. Squealing and thumping the earth. It 'ad to be 'train. Couldn't be 'owt else."

There was a powerful simplicity in the descriptive skills of this barely-educated man. Inarticulate as he was, he left no doubt as to what he had heard and felt and how clear it had been to him. Keld felt that Rodney would make a compelling witness if called upon - and if he saw the point in it.

"We are interested to trace anyone who was near to the bridge on Shipley Road last night," explained Keld. Rodney had not been asked a direct question so he said nothing.

"Did you leave your house at any time, Mr Brickshaw?"

"No."

"Did you see anyone yesterday evening?" asked Sharpe, who had quickly adapted her approach to match Rodney's requirements.

"No."

"Somebody did something at the Shipley Road bridge that caused the line to be suspended," said Keld. Did you see or hear anything from about 7pm?"

Rodney paused and thought about it. He summoned his memory into action and processed its contents into an order he could use. Sharpe was about to speak but Keld raised a hand to stop her. It would not help to interrupt Rodney who was evidently trying to remember. When he did formulate his answer, his voice took on a depth of meaning which demanded silent attention.

"There was a motorbike, a four-wheeler. It come up 'lane from 'village to Shipley Road."

"What time would that have been?" asked Keld.

"Seven o'clock."

"How are you so sure of the time," asked Sharpe whose questions were finally complimenting those of her more experienced colleague.

"Radio," explained Rodney who was not at all irritated as he had been earlier. "I 'ad BBC on, Radio 4. I'm not bothered about the music but I listen to the news, then I like 'Archers. I couldn't 'ear 'news for the noise of that bike past my door."

"Did you see the motorbike, Mr Brickshaw?" Sharpe was getting into her stride and Keld left her to it.

"Aye, I did. I saw it go past then, when 'Archers was on, I 'eard it come back and I looked out again. It was the same bike, I'm sure."

"Can you describe that bike and the rider?"

"He had an 'elmet on, a black one, so I couldn't see his face. The bike was one of those little-engined things."

"Like a moped?"

"No. It 'ad four wheels. Aye, one of them."

"A quadbike?" suggested Keld seeking clarification.

"Aye, one of them. Passenger didn't have an 'elmet."

"There was a passenger?"

"Aye, and on a little thing like that, It's a wonder it would go at all," said Rodney. "The engine was struggling, making a straining noise."

"Can you describe the passenger?"

"No. He had his head dipped away from my side, couldn't see his face. I thought they were youngsters, you know. They can't take it on the road so they rode it down 'ere. Didn't want you to catch em." Rodney looked at Keld as he spoke, cracking a slight smile for the first time during their visit.

"Did you notice anything else when they came back?"

"Aye, that passenger wasn't there on the way back, just 'rider with that black 'elmet."

"So the passenger must have got off somewhere near to the bridge on Shipley Road?" deduced Sharpe.

"Aye, must have I suppose," agreed Rodney. "Can't tell you anything more about them."

"Was there anyone else passing by during the evening, Mr Brickshaw?" asked Sharpe.

"Not that made any noise there wasn't. I 'ad m'windows open, you know. Nothin' disturbed my radio listenin' until I 'eard 'train come off 'track."

Rodney was thanked and complimented for his contribution to the investigation. He remained unmoved by it. They sat to write Rodney's statement. As Mel Sharpe did the writing, Peter Keld looked around the room and spotted an old army platoon photograph. Rodney Brickshaw noticed Keld's interest.

"That was me, in 'Army. Malaya."

"You saw some action then?"

"Aye, more than I wanted to."

Rodney's terse manner had acquired a sharper edge. It ended Keld's idle questions of curiosity.

Keld and Sharpe left with Rodney's signed witness statement. Sharpe headed for the police car, which had been blocking the path outside the front of Rodney's cottage. Keld hung back and gazed up the lane, his lips pursed in a pensive expression.

"What is it?" she asked. "Have we missed something?"

"No, no, it's alright. I was thinking about that quadbike."

"What about it?"

"It hasn't rained so there may be some tyre-tracks," he mused, thoughtfully.

"Do you think there is some forensic evidence on this lane then?" asked Sharpe.

"Yes. I don't know if the high-ups in the Incident Room will think so but I do. I'll run it by the Inspector before I raise the question."

He called Imran Bhatta on a one-to-one channel and made his pitch. Bhatta agreed and said that he would pass it on. He also said that the backlog of CSI deployments may mean that it could be some time before they got to look at it. He suggested that Keld look for the tracks and take photographs, just in case. Keld kept a camera in the glove box of his car. They took it and walked along the grass at the edges of the path I order to avoid trampling on the tracks.

It soon became clear that there was a line of imprinted tyre marks on the dusty strips of path. In some places it was a single line and in others there were two, at varying distances apart. Keld hovered over the clearest tracks and took numerous photographs of the ground. They continued along the path toward Eckscarfe but were impeded by the presence of a line of incident tape. The scene requiring preservation stretched much further than the debris of the train and buildings. The tyre tracks went beyond the tape and continued further than they could see.

"I would very much like to know where these tracks start and finish," said Keld. Sharpe was trying to follow his pattern of thought.

"Are you thinking that somebody used that quadbike to get to the track and cause the damage?"

The point of the derailment was about three hundred yards away from where they stood. Both of them looked in that direction.

"I was thinking that whoever was on that bike, and there were two people initially, they were either involved in some way or they saw something important - something or someone who did the damage to the track. Why did the passenger get off and where did they go?"

"I can't hazard a guess at that," she declared. "We had better get that statement in to the incident room," she suggested, "and we can ask about looking further up the lane."

*

The CSI staff, which included a mutual aid contingent from a neighbouring police force, concentrated their search for evidence at the scene of the derailment. A microscopic examination of the cuts to the metal rails was under way. It was painfully slow. What could be reported back to the Incident Room was that the cuts were not made by a standard circular saw. It would have required a very hard cutting blade to have cut through the rails at all. Given the time allowed for doing the cutting, only a high-tensile cutter would have managed it.

An action was raised for the investigation team to trace, interview and eliminate any owner of equipment capable of cutting metal, regardless of its specific capabilities. That could be established later. The house-to-house team were told to add that question to their standard forms. As could be expected, private households registered a 'no' to that enquiry. The most likely was they builder's yard, owned and operated by the village's only builder, Tommy Liddle.

Liddle was Eckscarfe born and bred. He took over the building maintenance business from his late father who had run it since the 1930s. He had a reputation for good quality workmanship and prompt completion. He frequently voiced his disdain for tradesmen who, in Tommy's view, failed to reach that mark.

In his sixties now, Tommy lived in the stone house at the front of his business premises with his wife and, when they deigned to visit, his adult son and daughter. Rumour had it that there had been a rift in the Liddle family and they were seldom in each other's company as a result.

His wife, Alison was a timid woman, often publicly berated by her husband for her inability to live up to his exacting standards. Another recipient of Tommy Liddle's temper was his latest apprentice, Gary Nicholls, an eighteen-year-old from a farm outside the village whose family could not afford to keep him on the farm payroll, so he worked for Liddle the builder instead. Choices were few in that community. He was bullied by Tommy Liddle constantly and on most days he went home to the family farm and set to work again to help out there too. Gary was in the habit of stopping off at the homes of his old schoolmates in the village after work. Getting back late could easily be attributed to the tyrannically intolerant Tommy Liddle.

When the house-to-house enquiry team called at Liddle's home and yard, they were unable to gain any answer, despite the presence of several vehicles suggested that Liddle was at home. Either he had gone out, or he was refusing to answer the door. They left and visited the remainder of their allocation, but they returned at the end of it to try Tommy Liddle again. This time they saw Liddle standing at the kitchen window. He was stone-faced, devoid of any expression. His heavy eyebrows cloaked his unshaven and dirty face. The officers were in uniform, leaving no doubt about who they were. Liddle stared at the hapless visitors, ignoring their requests for him to come to the door and speak to them. He reached out both arms and pulled the curtain across to conclude their unproductive visit.

Gary's mates included the policeman's son, Noel Keld, and Hugh Barron, the son of a Pendale-based pair of doctors. Lately, their evening activities had become a mystery to their families. By the standards of most towns and cities, the youth nuisance problems of Eckscarfe were negligible. It was more mischief than crime wave. Nicholls, Keld and Barron were simply bored teenagers with the imagination to be able to amuse themselves. That the mature residents found great objection to their antics was simply added entertainment. It was not so much about what they did, it was more about what they represented. For people who were proud of their achievements, their status and their environment, anyone who appeared to have no such appreciation warranted a campaign of attrition. It was the age-old gap between generations, nothing more. Had the trio chosen to partake of their bottled cider and cigarettes of questionable content in more discreet locations, nobody would have had anything to complain about.

The rebellious nature of the youths' activities was manifest in their manner of dress. Whilst considered normal in South Central Los Angeles, their 'street' attire was woefully out of place in Eckscarfe. Even the other teenagers though it too much. Their self-amusement antics had achieved widespread condemnation in the neighbourhood. Pushing over cows in the fields after dark induced convulsive laughter, but only for the perpetrators. Stripping bark off mature trees and causing them to die enraged some residents and paint-sprayed graffiti bearing anti-establishment messages invoked further indignation from those who sought to preserve the 'chocolate-box' image of the village. Larking around on the railway line had involved a stern warning from the British Transport Police. The officer was acquainted with Noel's father and had erred on the side of leniency. Nevertheless, Peter Keld was uncomfortably aware of the delinquency of Noel and his friends. He knew that it could cost him his posting and therefore his home. Arguments about this in the Keld household had raged into the night on several occasions. For Peter and Helen Keld, the passing of this 'phase' of their son's behaviour could not come soon enough.

Most of the house-to-house calls resulted in more questions than answers. Concerned residents wanting to know who was actually dead and who was injured and how badly in each case. Nobody recalled seeing anything or anyone acting suspiciously on the day of the crash. When asked in general about behaviour in the village that caused concern, the offerings were equally scant. Some did, however, when pressed express their discomfort at the conduct of certain delinquents and a couple of residents went as far as naming them. The teenaged trio of Nicholls, Keld Jnr. and Barron had caused a generation rift which was being aired by those who felt strongly enough about it. There was a reluctance to confront PC Peter Keld about the problem, but it was acceptable to talk to other police officers about it.

Bhatta had not come across the lads before. He gathered that Noel Keld had to be the son of the Eckscarfe police officer, a connection which called for a sensitive approach. When the need arose to knock on the door of the police house, Bhatta knew that Peter Keld had been deployed at other addresses. After all, he could hardly carry out house-to-house at his own home. Bhatta did that call himself. The door was answered by Mrs Helen Keld who moved with the aid of crutches on the days when her multiple sclerosis made unaided walking impossible.

"Oh hello," she said in mild surprise. "Pete's not in at the moment."

"I know. I'm Inspector Bhatta from Pendale. It's you I want to speak to."

"Sounds ominous. You'd better come in."

As Bhatta assured her that it was not anything to be worried about, she shuffled around on her supports and headed off along the hall to the lounge door. Bhatta stepped inside and, without being asked, closed the front door before following her. Once seated in the lounge, he explained that every house in Eckscarfe was to be visited as part of the inquiry into the rail crash. Without realising it, she pressed imaginary creases out of her jumper and trousers in response to the revelation that the visit was formal. Bhatta opened his folder and took out a fresh house-to-house form.

"There are some standard questions Mrs Keld," he opened.

"Fire away," she said.

"Who lives here?"

"Well, besides Pete and me there are our two kids. Leanna is thirteen and Noel is seventeen."

"Who was home on the evening of the rail crash?"

"I was, I don't get out very much without help. Pete was on a late, due off at midnight. That turned out to be all night and into the next day. Leanna was in doing her homework in her room. She's very bookish, doesn't need any encouragement, not like Noel. He has to be pushed to do anything. That's lads for you I suppose. Do you have any kids?"

"Yes, I have two."

Bhatta thought about his own brood and how they were both what Helen Keld would have described as bookish. At least he thought they were, he was not at home long enough or consistently enough to be sure of that. He remembered why he was there and carried on.

"Was Noel at home on that evening?"

"No, he was out," she said almost absent-mindedly.

"Where was he?" pressed Bhatta gently but firmly.

"At a friend's house."

"What is the friend's name?"

"Oh I don't know. He usually just hangs around - that sounds bad doesn't it? His mates are Hugh Barron and Gary Nicholls. They have known each other since they started at secondary school."

Bhatta wrote all of this down on the form. When he looked up he asked.

"Is Noel at home?"

"No, he goes to college in Pendale, by bus usually. He'll be back around four - well, he should be. It's anybody's guess what time he will appear at the moment."

Bhatta completed the remainder of the form and stood up. "I'll try to call back later and speak to Noel."

"Is that necessary, Inspector? I'm sure our Noel hasn't anything of use to you." Bhatta kept the atmosphere light and avoided confrontation or offence.

"I'm sure you are right but, only when we know where everybody was can we work out who was out of place. That's why these things take so long, you know?"

Helen Keld accepted that and began to struggle to her feet, one crutch at a time. Her visitor assured her that he would let himself out and that she was not to get up unnecessarily. Once in the road outside, he perused his entries on the form, noting that a return was required.

It was only the will to avoid compromise, which had made him decide to make that call the Keld's home. It was to be expected that familiarity among his officers could result in a half-hearted job. He contemplated handing over the remainder to his team but, as the atmosphere in the Incident Room continued to depress him, he chose to complete that section of the village himself.

CHAPTER SEVEN

Imran Bhatta did not get home for two days, except to briefly change his clothes when his family and houseguests were out. He had managed to call his wife once during that time. Eventually, he made it back after midnight.

Entering at the front door, he saw a light on in the kitchen. She had waited up for him and a warm feeling came over him. It was Sunila, who helped him to get things in perspective. She said that he did the same for her too. He needed that now. He hung up his suit-jacket and pushed open the kitchen door. Seated at the table, alone and reading a newspaper was Ali. He looked up then back at his paper.

"Anyone would think you were avoiding us Imran."

"Not by choice. You may have read in your paper that there is a lot to do right now."

"And that is all down to you, is it?"

"I have my part to play. People have been killed and someone has to find out why it all happened. The survivors and families deserve that."

"You neglect your family to help strangers, eh? Is that it?"

Imran took a breath and let it out slowly and silently. He had no intention of answering Ali's question. Instead, he put a question to Ali.

"You must have put in some long hours in your career, especially in your early career. You were saving lives too. My job is not so different."

"Your 'job' cannot be compared with mine," snapped Ali. "It cannot be compared with the career you rejected either. You could have been at home with your wife every night instead of doing what needs no education. You have wasted your opportunities and you want my daughter to pay the price for your vanity."

Imran Bhatta was about to erupt into the anger he had suppressed for several years. Ali had judged him unfairly since he had turned his back on the career in corporate law, which, in Ali's view, had been the main reason for the marriage. Without that, he was not worthy to marry his daughter. Without the status of a big, London law firm, Imran was merely some chancer from a terraced house in East Lancashire, which was where Ali wanted him to return, albeit without Sunila. Once composed and able to resist the temptation to go toe-to-toe with his domineering father-in-law, Imran turned to go up to bed. At the door he paused and said,

"Did you know, I am the highest ranking Asian in this police force? It can be difficult sometimes, so many white faces, waiting for me to slip and prove their prejudices right. It is made more difficult when the people of my own race turn on me as well."

He slipped out, leaving Ali to his newspaper.

*

Several of the witness accounts recorded in statement form by the police team had mentioned seeing a large model Mercedes in the village on the evening of the rail crash. A couple had remembered enough of the registration number for the team to run a check and identify the registered owner. It was a leasing company, and the owner records stopped short of naming the likely driver on that day. As the driver of the car had not committed any motoring offences, the team were unable to demand that the leasing company reveal who the car was usually driven by. Another check on a different computer system showed that the car had been through an unmanned speed check-point near Preston a month before. That had resulted in a legitimate demand for the driver to be named. The record showed that the car was in the possession of Guy Maxlow.

Guy Maxlow described himself as a businessman. If pressed for further information he either declined to elaborate or alluded to the aspect of his business which was property development. Rarely did he speak in polite company about the other money-making schemes he was involved in. He was equally reticent about divulging details of his early life in Longsight, Manchester. Anyone who needed to know about that probably already did.

For those who did not know of his past, and this included all of his neighbours in the leafy suburb of Pendlebury, Guy Maxlow represented a working-class boy made good. The trappings of his success were ostentatious, tasteless and in great number: a fleet of executive and sporty cars lined the edge of the gravel driveway of his nine-bedroomed home, concealed from the road by overhanging, immature trees running from the black and gold wrought-iron gates which would not have been out of place at Buckingham Palace.

Maxlow had more fingers in more pies than he had fingers. His early criminal activities began with shoplifting in his own locality. After realising that there was more money to be made in neighbouring districts, he gathered an interchangeable team of helpers and moved up to more profitable enterprises. Burglary, street robbery, drug dealing, extortion and blackmail all fell comfortably into his broad portfolio of wealth-generating initiatives. As his ambitions grew, so did his empire, which, on face value at least, became increasingly lawful. A security company, existing for twenty years in the Manchester area, was acquired by Maxlow at a knock-down price and rapidly grown into the biggest provider of security patrols in the city. The company provided uniformed staff patrolling shopping centres, dog handlers protecting building sites during the night, door staff at night-clubs, bodyguards for visiting dignitaries, pop and sports stars and ex-servicemen and women to do armed protection overseas. A lifetime of committing crime had metamorphosed into a network aimed at preventing crime. The irony was not lost on him.

In rolled the money, and in ever-larger waves. All competition was actively discouraged by old-fashioned methods. A visit from Maxlow or a delegation of his longer serving employees was usually enough to achieve the desired objective. Maxlow became the monopoly holder of the security business. It was not enough. New avenues of business were sought and explored. Whereas the aim was to be legitimate and above reproach legally, any competitor or official who stood in the way of Maxlow's ambitions could find themselves being familiarised with those unaddressed issues surrounding his past. Anyone who got in the way of Maxlow's plans became a target - and he rarely missed. Disappearances, although rare, became the last resort after other methods of persuasion had proved ineffective.

Ever hungry for new challenges, Maxlow moved into the field of property development with renewed vigour. His ability to bribe or intimidate planning authorities with relative ease enabled him to reach the multi-million-pound contract bracket whilst incurring minimal risk to his own assets. Large, inner-city, planning departments could be manipulated once the paths through that minefield had been identified. Residential property in urban areas were easy because all concerned wanted the buildings to be built. The further out of Manchester, Salford and Stockport he went, the more difficult it became to win the favour of the planners.

The money that could be made by building expensive homes in rural locations was too great to be overlooked. In areas of outstanding natural beauty and in or near national parks, it was more difficult, and sometimes impossible, to be able to build new homes. Maxlow considered the word 'impossible' to be a challenge. He saw no reason why his tried and tested methods of persuasion would not be as effective elsewhere.

With the exception of some barn conversions and the rebuilding of some wartime prefab houses into more substantial structures, the village of Eckscarfe had seen no new houses in fifty years. The Village Hall, rebuilt with the help of a National Lottery grant, was the only modern architecture to be seen. When houses did change ownership, which was a rare event, they went for disproportionately high prices. The unspoilt rural surroundings, the picturesque lake and the dramatic mountain backdrop made Eckscarfe a highly appealing place to live.

Although most of his business dealings had been in the Greater Manchester and Cheshire area, Maxlow had spotted an opportunity to make money further afield. Aiming at locations which commanded the highest prices for homes, he focussed his efforts in the areas which had previously been considered taboo, in development terms. Anything in or near a National Park became his objective. Eckscarfe was too good an opportunity to miss.

His application for planning permission had been ambitious. He had intended to increase the population of the village by fifty percent. His projects did not include any houses valued at less than three million pounds. Whilst local housing by-laws addressed the need for the next generation of Eckscarfe people to be able to afford to continue living there, Maxlow's plans gave no importance to that cause. This was the main reason for the compulsory community consultation process. In Eckscarfe, that meant that the Parish Council had their say as well as the county authorities. Maxlow's applications were rejected out of hand. That was nothing new. Once the relevant individuals had been identified, a series of sweeteners were offered to the key players in order to unblock the blockage. For the community, they included a public park with imported trees, ornate gardens and a fountain, a quaint piazza in the style of a mountain village in the Dolomites and an outdoor bowling green. Several members of the Eckscarfe Parish Council were approached and all rejected the offers.

*

Inspector Bhatta and PC Sharpe visited Kingfisher Cottage in the middle of a bright, fresh morning. Passing under the floral trellis and crossing the immaculately manicured garden, they took a moment to admire it all. The cottage was a picture postcard glimpse into English history. The year 1633 was displayed in wobbly form above the front door, which was beneath a canopy porch with one pair of wellington boots standing to attention under a narrow bench. Sharpe accidentally kicked the wellies over when she stepped under the canopy to activate the door-knocker. She hurriedly put them upright again before the door was opened by an elegant, yet sportily-attired lady in her early sixties. Her body was well-maintained and her complexion clear and healthy.

"Good morning. Ms Loretta Rokestone?" opened Sharpe, glancing down at her list of people to visit that day.

"Good morning. I've been expecting you – and it is Councillor Rokestone. I am on the Parish Council and the County Council. Come in please."

She stepped aside to allow the two police officers to enter. The aroma of lavender gave Kingfisher Cottage an aura of the past. Passing the magnolia staircase in the hallway, they followed Loretta Rokestone's flowing cashmere wrap into an enormous lounge. The furniture and décor were perfectly in-keeping. Paintings of horses and hay-carts adorned the walls and the lavishly upholstered chairs surrounded a polished oak coffee table. The only personal touch was a portrait photograph of a slim, young woman in graduation attire, holding onto an ornate scroll. Bhatta had considered that it might be her daughter or even granddaughter. It wasn't relevant, he decided. There was no television or other hints at modern times. This was the home of someone who was in charge, if only of herself. It made logical sense that she should wish to be in charge of her village. Once Bhatta and Sharpe had introduced themselves, Councillor Rokestone bade them be seated.

The initial questions were asked and her full name was written down. She said that she had never married but she refused to divulge her date-of-birth, on the grounds that she saw no reason for it. Bhatta reconsidered the graduation photograph theory he had thought of earlier. This woman was not to be trifled with. She was only prepared to speak of things on her own terms. Bhatta asked her about the day of the crash. She settled down to retell her part as though delivering a much-anticipated speech.

"The Eckscarfe Parish Council meets at seven pm on the first Thursday of each month. Since the Village Hall was rebuilt some two years ago, we assemble in the Committee Room to carry out the business of the running of the village and surrounding area. Now, you might think that nothing ever happens in Eckscarfe but I can assure you that is not the case. We seek to preserve and protect this place, its residents and its visitors. Someone must take collective responsibility and that falls to the Parish Council. We work very hard to maintain the employment of the village and the care of the elderly and the young. For example, the sheltered cottages at Moorly Close were negotiated by the Parish Council and the facilities at both the primary school and at Eckscarfe Hall School were enhanced by our work."

Both Bhatta and Sharpe were desperate for the visit to progress or at least begin to address some of the issues they had come to raise. Councillor Rokestone was not going to be rushed. She continued to relate the work and achievements of not just the Parish Council but also her role as County Councillor. Bhatta waited until she paused to breathe before interrupting.

"Councillor Rokestone, sorry to stop you there but please tell us who else is on the Parish Council."

"Of course," she said without taking offence. "Apart from myself there are, or rather were, five members, elected to serve for five-year terms. Graham Posner, Leonard Hurlington, Fred McAulden, Jonathan Ullenorth and erm, who have I missed? Oh yes, Pamela Hazeldene, not that she turns up with any regularity. Hilda White is the Clerk to the Parish Council."

Determined to keep the reins of the conversation, Bhatta left no room for the Councillor to stray toward her own egotistical agenda.

"What was discussed on the night of the crash?"

"The Council's business was recorded by Hilda, as was the custom. She does shorthand, you know. She will have the details but I recall that there were several issues to be dealt with. The Council at Pendale reducing the frequency of bin collections at Eckscarfe, that was covered. Some recent instances of criminal damage in the village caused some concern. It was debated whether to approach Police Constable Keld and ask what he was doing about it. There was some reluctance because, well, can I speak candidly Inspector?"

"Certainly," he said.

"It is not a secret that PC Keld's son and his friends are making something of a nuisance of themselves of late. That makes some of the Parish Council uncomfortable, not me. It was decided on a vote not to speak to our policeman about it in case offence was caused. Nonsense! He is a public servant, we can't allow this behaviour to - "

"Thank you for telling me that. What else was discussed?"

"There was a brief discussion about planning applications. Very few achieve approval. Our job, as the representatives of the community, is to maintain the unique beauty of this place and that means saying 'no' to those who seek to change it. Only recently, we refused to approve a ghastly plan, which would have destroyed this village as we know it. Dozens of enormous modern houses, not to mention the calibre of people who would be occupying them, it doesn't bear thinking about."

"So, the Parish Council can veto such applications?" asked Sharpe.

"Oh yes." The Councillor was revelling in the demonstration of her civic power. "They can appeal to the County but I am on that body too. The developer was non-too pleased with the decision, by all accounts. Some fellow from Manchester I believe. No thought for the village, just wanting to make millions and leave the place irreparably damaged. We cannot allow that."

"I see, can I just – " Bhatta had lost the lead in that power contest of words. Loretta Rokestone was not in a listening mood.

"The developer made certain 'gestures' of protest when he came to the planning hearing. An ogre of a man, probably used to getting his own way, but not here he won't."

"What is this man's name? The developer."

"Guy Maxlow."

*

Hilda White was well over seventy and she gave the impression that she had always been old. Appropriately named for her hair and complexion, the diminutive and painfully thin pensioner peered over pink-framed spectacles in a permanent expression of worry. She occupied a one-bedroomed flat in the Moorly Close complex described by the more ebullient Loretta Rokestone. Bhatta made a silent comparison between the two and formed the view that it was a personality mismatch. How that played out in the machinations of the Parish Council could probably be predicted.

Hilda opened the door wearing an oversized woollen cardigan, despite the warm weather. She also wore blue, cotton trousers and moccasin slippers. Once Bhatta and Sharpe had introduced themselves, Hilda welcomed them into the bijou residence she called home and soon dispensed with formalities. She offered them a seat and whilst Sharpe took the only unaccounted for chair, Bhatta stood in the window bay.

"Oh it is terrible, those poor people. Taken in their prime." Hilda gabbled her modest commiserations to those who had suffered. She produced a handkerchief from the cuff of her cardigan and used it to dab the corners of her eyes.

"You are the Clerk to the Parish Council, I believe?" said Bhatta, keen to make progress.

"I am, thirty-eight years I have been keeping the minutes and writing the letters."

"There can't be much about Eckscarfe that you don't know?" asked Sharpe.

"I suppose so, love."

"You would have known Fred and Len pretty well?" Sharpe was showing the patience that Bhatta knew that he sometimes lacked. He was content to let her ask the questions. Hilda imparted her story.

"Well, yes. I used to see them up at the school too."

"At the school?"

"Yes. Before I retired, I was the secretary at the special school. It was bigger then, hardly any children are there now. All of the men on the Parish Council helped out up there. They began a group called 'Friends of Eckscarfe Hall School' and they raised money for the facilities there."

"That must have been helpful, for the children, I mean," said Sharpe.

"I suppose it was but, oh dear." Hilda looked more perplexed than was usual.

"What is it Hilda?"

"It's all in the past now so it can't do any harm to say."

"We will treat anything you wish to tell us with discretion, I can assure you." Sharpe's tone was caring and friendly. Hilda swallowed and settled herself before speaking.

"There were, erm, problems at the school. There was some heavy-handed stuff going on." She recoiled as though she had said something regrettable. "There was always some trouble there, it was that sort of place. The children, some of them, could be a handful, but there were more complaints than there should have been. I shall leave it at that. It doesn't do to rake over such things."

Hilda turned her gaze away as though to close the matter. Bhatta interjected.

"Before we leave the subject, were any of the 'Friends of the School' group implicated?"

"Not that I know of, but the Head did put a stop to it. She never let on why but the 'Friends' folded three or four years ago. The men were no longer needed."

"I see," said Bhatta. "How did they respond to that?"

"They were so very disappointed. They had done so much for the school, you know. The four of them would plan things together. They stayed after the Parish Council meetings, as they did yesterday, of course. That began in the old Village Hall. They had a Snooker Room built in the new hall too and they moved the old table into it. Do you know, I don't think that anyone other than Fred, Jonathan, Len and Graham ever played on it. It was as though it was their own, private snooker club."

"Have you met the property developer, Guy Maxlow, Hilda?" asked Bhatta.

"Good heavens no. I wouldn't want to either. He sounds ghastly. If he approached me I would call for PC Keld straight away."

"Has anyone else given you any cause for concern?" asked Bhatta in broad speculation.

"Well," Hilda leaned forward conspiratorially and lowered her voice to a whisper. "When they were planning the new Village Hall, that brute Tommy Liddle was there a lot, trying to get the work, I suppose. You know, I have often thought that most of the Parish Council's decisions were made in the Snooker Room without Pam, Loretta or me being there. Tommy Liddle did get the job of building the new place. I suppose it would have been because he is local. It can't be because of his manners. I'll tell you that much."

They thanked Hilda for her hospitality and assistance and left.

*

A message was passed to Bhatta. It came from Neville Allerton, the quarry manager he had spoken to after recovering the dummy from Keld's car. Bhatta drove up to the Wilson's Aggregates site and entered the car park to find Allerton waiting outside the fence.

"Thanks for coming," said Allerton looking more serious than on their previous meeting.

"Well, thanks for calling," he answered. "Is there somewhere we can talk?"

"Sure, come up to the office."

Allerton led him through the main gate, across the dusty yard and into one of a jumble of concrete prefabricated buildings. On the way, Bhatta noticed that there were Danger and Health and Safety signs attached to every available wall and fence panel. Speed restriction signs displayed a limit of 10 miles per hour on the site. There were old and weathered versions of the giant trucks sitting in line at the top of the access road into the quarry. That path became rougher as it passed by the buildings and continued up a rise, the top of which could not be seen from there. It seemed to end at the skyline, which was obscured by bright sunlight. Inside the office, the distant noise of the quarry machinery was shut out. Allerton wasted no time in imparting his news.

"That overall suit you showed me, the one that came from here? I have been going over it in my mind and I think there is something you should know."

"Please, continue," asked Bhatta, secretly preparing himself for a disappointment and trying hard not to show it. Allerton shifted in his chair awkwardly.

"Firstly, we have carried out a detailed inventory to try to work out where that particular overall came from. We think we have identified who it might have belonged to. Ruling out the larger and smaller sizes and staff who have not been here long enough to have an overall as faded as that one, we asked the remainder who all accounted for their allocation. We have one employee who is currently off on sick leave. It could be his."

"That sounds less than conclusive Mr Allerton. Can we pin it down to this chap?"

"Almost. We can rule out newer people because of the wear and fading of it. Current members of staff have been able to produce all allocated overalls. That only leaves people who we know have some but aren't currently at work."

"What about past employees?"

"That's the reason I can't be totally sure about this fellow."

"I see. Who is he?"

"His name is Wayne Crewgard."

"Do you have his current address please?"

"Yes," said Allerton as he reached into his desk drawer and shuffled the papers within. He pulled out a buff folder with nothing written on it. Inside he read through a document. "He lives in one of the old council houses in Eckscarfe."

Bhatta knew the small estate of houses in the village. They had been built in a hurry in wartime to house agricultural workers then they were reinforced into a form of permanency. They represented the only affordable houses in Eckscarfe but they never went on sale, being passed down the generations despite being council-owned. Allerton confirmed this as he described Crewgard's term of employment at the quarry.

Crewgard was forty-eight, he had lived in that house in the village since he was born. He had worked at the quarry all of his adult life. His parents had died and, as a lifelong bachelor, he remained there alone. The reason for his sick leave was for some undefined mental illness. This had manifest itself in a series of bizarre incidents, at the quarry and elsewhere. Crewgard had erupted in displays of anger at several of his colleagues and, after several warnings, had been on the brink of suspension. The decision was taken that he had a health issue and his three decades of service had also been taken into account. He had been off work for two months and was under the doctor for his condition.

Before his absence from work, Crewgard had made certain threats toward his colleagues, airing imagined and unevidenced grievances each time. Neville Allerton himself had been threatened by him. He went on to outline further concerns.

"Before Crewgard went sick, there had been several instances of sabotage to the vehicles and machinery. Nobody had been injured but there had been some near misses. Since he went sick, these had stopped."

"Do you suspect that Wayne Crewgard could be carrying out more of these? I mean away from here?"

"Well, he might. We couldn't prove he was doing it here. There's another thing you should know about."

"Go on," urged Bhatta, seeing that Allerton was acutely nervous in revealing his information. "I can assure you of discretion if that is bothering you."

"Well, we have been carrying out annual safety checks this week. We do minor ones all year round but we have a detailed one every year. This time we have found some deficiencies in the stock at the explosives store. The written records are also inaccurate. There has been no sign of any break-in so whoever has taken this knew their way around. Wayne Crewgard was one of those who had access to the explosive store."

"Let me get this clear in my mind Mr Allerton. Crewgard has mental health issues, angry outbursts, he tampers with machinery - risking lives by doing so - and he might have stolen explosives?"

"It sounds grim when you list it all like that." Allerton laughed nervously. Bhatta did not join in.

"This guy also has old, blue overalls, doesn't he?" confirmed Bhatta. Allerton nodded. He had already thought about it.

"I want details of what is missing from the store, what it looks like, what it is capable of and how to make it safe. Is that clear?"

Bhatta had taken on a less polite and more direct tone. An unstable man with access to explosives constituted an emergency and niceties had to give way to necessities.

A call to the force's main Control Room began the required authorities for a search of the home of Wayne Crewgard. His medical records had been obtained and the information had been taken into account in assessing his needs during and prior to his imminent arrest. A Firearms team was assembled and a tactical adviser, together with a Superintendent, convened a briefing at Pendale Police Station. PC Peter Keld was also asked about what he knew about Wayne Crewgard. Keld told the briefing about his previous contact with Crewgard including his illicit fishing activities, his obsession with model railways and his occasional transgressions whilst in drink.

The incident at the Barley Mow pub in the late afternoon on the day of the crash was mentioned but, because Crewgard had left the pub before Keld had arrived, he was unable to say much about it. The landlord had told him that Wayne Crewgard had been drinking all afternoon and had put away seven or eight pints of beer. He began shouting angrily at the other customers, threatening violence and retribution for reasons, which were unclear. He had left when he was told to, under threat of being barred from the only 'watering hole' in the village, knowing that an alternative was not practicable.

The press had somehow gleaned that something was happening, although none among them knew what was behind it. It was unusual for a Firearms team to be deployed in this sleepy part of the country and the press pack had picked up on it. Surreptitious photographs were taken through the rear gate and over the wall of the back yard of the Police Station. It all led to nothing more than guesswork. The Incident Room was home to a great deal of guesswork too.

Janette Lane-Wright led the proceedings. When all contributions had been made, she summarised the situation.

"So, what have we got?" she began. "Wayne Crewgard, aged forty-eight." A projector screen clicked into life with the staff ID picture of their target. "Quarry-worker for over thirty years. He lives alone at No. 5, The View at Eckscarfe. Not known to drive, he walks the two miles to work or gets a lift. Recently sent home on sick leave following some angry and erratic outbursts at his work at Wilson's Aggregates. We can't be sure it was anything to do with him but there may be some explosives unaccounted for. He did have access to that store. Between four-forty and five pm on the fourth, Crewgard was thrown out of the pub for an angry rant. A drunk, angry, loner possessing explosives. Today's objective is to locate and detain him and make searches of his home and anywhere he has reasonable access to in order to find this explosive material, if indeed it does exist."

She paused to sip water from a paper cup.

"It is far from a straightforward job. If there are explosives, it is vital that he isn't spooked into detonating them before we get him into custody." The screen changed to an image of a non-descript semi-detached house of grey pebbledash. "His house is in a cul-de-sac in Eckscarfe and therefore difficult to watch but we have put a couple of initiatives in place to establish his position. A covert team went an hour ago, catalogue sales, I believe. There was no answer at No.5. As you can see, the curtains were drawn but, according to PC Keld, that is not unusual for Crewgard.

"There's nowhere we can place a camera and there isn't time anyway. We need a low-profile approach, invisible preferably. We have the use of a horsebox vehicle, which has been borrowed for this purpose. Such vehicles are not out of place in the village. The house-to-house enquiries will, in due course, visit every dwelling and business premises. Inspector Bhatta and his team have yet to reach The View. We will change the plan so that the house-to-house will cover that today. That gives us eyes at the scene without raising suspicion toward No. 5."

Bhatta nodded his understanding of what was required. At the close of the briefing, there was an unspoken but evident cloud of tension among the police officers and admin staff. Nothing had been presented to them quite like this before. High danger of people getting killed, too many gaps in the intelligence available and nobody had yet come to terms with the recent train crash. The Firearms team went back to their vehicles and appeared to the peeping reporters to be returning their weapons and equipment to their original places. Once the gate was open, the press took barely any interest, particularly as there seemed to be no urgency as the police cars headed North, which was in the opposite direction to the road up to Eckscarfe.

By the time the innocuous-looking, bottle-green horse transporter arrived and parked on the main road just out of sight of the junction leading onto The View, Bhatta and Sharpe were knocking on their seventh door, having started at the high numbers and worked up their list. Trying, and largely succeeding, to carry out the visit as all of their previous calls had been done, they managed to observe No. 5 by adopting the practice of remaining on the doorsteps and standing either side of the householder like Greek pillars. Conversation between Bhatta and Sharpe about Crewgard's house only took place between the calls. At one point, a woman mentioned 'that bloke at No. 5' in the context of any recent suspicious activity in the neighbourhood. Wayne Crewgard had arrived home drunk and shouting several times recently. In that place, this was considered to be a noteworthy event. Others were too polite to mention it or had not noticed.

As Bhatta and Sharpe entered the gateway to their eighth house, an old model, silver-grey Vauxhall Astra with a pale blue driver's door swung off the main road and snaked around onto The View. It was the first vehicle to move during their visit. They dismissed it from their thoughts until it ground to a halt with whining brakes outside No.5. The driver remained in the car as the passenger door came open and a man stepped out and went to open the boot.

Bhatta recognised him from his personnel file photograph in Allerton's office. He transmitted instantly and the urgency in his voice gave away his lack of composure.

"Target has arrived, at the house, getting out of a grey car now. Go, go!"

The tailgate of the horse transporter fell open and the Firearms team ran out fully kitted-up. The team leader responded to Bhatta's message with a request for more information.

"Is he carrying anything?" He too sounded uncomfortably panicky.

"No, but he's opening the boot of the car," imparted Bhatta, rooted to the spot.

"Team making urgently to the scene. Stop him opening the boot of the car," demanded the voice, out of breath and desperate with every word. The hurried trudging of his team and all of their weaponry made his words difficult to grasp. Sharpe picked up the instruction and stepped forward onto the road toward the Astra.

"Erm, excuse me," she announced. Bhatta unfroze from his motionless state and stepped after her. Half vexed at her audacity and lack of awareness of their safety and half at his own slow response.

The driver of the car remained behind the wheel and the closed window. Wayne Crewgard did not acknowledge her attempt to gain his attention. He pulled up the tailgate and lowered his head out of sight beneath it. Bhatta foresaw the detonation of the missing explosives. His blood ran cold through his veins. Sharpe appeared to have ice in hers. She stepped up her pace, not quite running and looking toward the only entrance to The View for the Firearms team, arriving to save the day. She heard running footsteps before they came into sight. She had to do something to stop him.

"Hello," she raised her voice. "I want to ask you about something." Crewgard emerged from the back of the opened boot holding a fishing rod, disassembled into several three-foot lengths, which he placed against the low front wall of his own garden. He still did not appear to have heard nor seen Sharpe. The driver, however, did notice her and he stared through the side window at her. She was not interested in him. Wayne Crewgard was her sole focus of attention.

The Firearms team came into sight, no longer running but crab-stepping, hurriedly and in a line along the pavement. Crewgard went back to the boot of the car, oblivious to the police officers approaching him. The driver shouted to Sharpe.

"What do you want?" he asked in genuine curiosity. He did not get his question answered. The Firearms crew spread out like a moving firing squad.

"Armed Police!" loud and unmistakable, but people can sometimes fail to hear or comprehend such clear instructions. Crewgard did not change his course of conduct. The driver of the car opened the door and stepped out. He was dressed in a scruffy camouflage jacket, old blue jeans and wellington boots. He saw the raised guns seemingly trained on him and froze.

"Armed Police! Get down on the ground, now!" This time the driver got the message but Crewgard delved into the boot of the car as he had done before. Crewgard stopped what he was doing when he saw that the driver of the Astra was lying, face down on the tarmac. He leaned around the elevated tailgate and peered at him.

"What are you doing, man?" said Crewgard, whilst being drowned out by the shouts of the

Firearms team who were edging into a semi-circle around him. When Crewgard finally caught sight of the reason for his companion being prone in the road, his legs went instantly weak and his knees dipped. An unheard expletive emanated from him, but he remained where he was.

"Step away from the car. Step away from the car!" came the shout as another cop called for Crewgard to get down on the ground. Neither had the desired effect. "Do as I say or you will be shot."

All of the police team were acutely aware of the possibility of an explosion, which would kill all of them if they were close enough at the critical moment of detonation. Neither knew how far away a safe distance was. In a moment without anyone speaking, the driver shouted from his horizontal position.

"He's deaf, he's fuckin' deaf."

This was repeated quietly to the entire team. It had to be hand signals. The team spread out as wide as they could go, stepping into the gardens across the street, annihilating a fledgling hydrangea bush. Bhatta and Sharpe were told to move clear and did so immediately. Sharpe's role in distracting Crewgard now complete, Bhatta conveyed the situation to the Control Room by radio. After being gesticulated at to move away from the opened car boot and lie down, Crewgard finally got the message and did as he was bid. He was searched and handcuffed, as was the driver. Both men were escorted away to other police vehicles and a feeling of relief was felt by all of the officers involved. There had been no dreadful explosion and nobody was injured. However, there was still the matter of the missing explosives.

CHAPTER EIGHT

A cordon was thrown around the car and the house. Despite a high level of resistance and confusion, all residents were taken away as a precautionary measure as the Army Ordnance Unit carried out a search for the explosives. When they were satisfied that there was nothing to be found, the military handed over to the police to complete the search for non-explosive evidence. Photographs were taken of the car and the house whilst Bhatta and Sharpe employed all of their persuasive powers to reassure the displaced residents who were in the back room at the Barley Mow. Some were incensed at the inconvenience, some were thrilled at the drama of it all and some saw it as an impromptu visit to the pub along with neighbours they had not had the chance to chat with for a while – and there was so much to talk about. Inevitably, the press, who were using the pub as their unofficial headquarters, got wind of events at The View and arrived in numbers at the scene.

Newspaper and TV journos went to work seeking witness accounts from Eckscarfe residents. In some cases, they were already acquainted with them from recent interviews. The freelancer Marci Wicker was vying with Keith Marlin from the Daily Start and Dan Delerouso from the News of the World for a quote from Inspector Bhatta.

"Can you tell us what happened at The View today, Inspector?" asked Marlin, pushing a recording microphone into his face outside the pub. Wicker added her question without waiting for Bhatta to answer.

"Was the raid connected with the rail crash?" she demanded.

"Were the two arrested a threat to the community?"

Bhatta was not going to answer any of their questions. He referred them to the Press Office at force HQ and left them to seek accounts from the villagers inside the pub. He collected Sharpe and Keld before heading back to the Incident Room.

The debriefing of the firearms operation took place with minimal staff present. The subsequent assembly had a wider range of participants. Lane-Wright again chaired the deliberations. She summarised the operation at The View and invited comment from the tactical adviser who had little to report.

The senior CSI, Ian Carraway, reported that although the search of Crewgard's house had not produced any explosives, it had revealed something of interest. In the lounge/dining room, concealed by closed curtains, was an elaborate series of model railway constructions. The largest of which was a representation of the West-coast mainline as it negotiated the curve at Eckscarfe. On the plain rolls of lining-wallpaper beneath the track was a detailed diagram of the village. The electric engine was lying across the Village Hall.

"So, it looks like he planned out the rail crash," observed the CSI.

The assembled police teams let out a collective 'Yes!' and 'Got him!' Lane-Wright was not as swift to draw conclusions.

"Steady now Ladies and Gentlemen. We have a long way to go here. The interview team will try to gain an account from Crewgard and his associate, Alastair Sackler who was arrested with him."

The interview with Alastair Sackler revealed that he and Crewgard used to work together at the quarry. They were in the practice of going fishing and had done regularly for two or three years. They sometimes took Gary Nicholls with them. As the lake was strictly controlled by an Angler's Association, they had to travel further afield to be able to fish without being disturbed.

Sackler had left Wilson's Aggregates after his hearing had been impaired in a blasting accident nearly twenty years before. Since then, he been casually employed as a village tidy-up man, picking up litter and trimming the flowerbeds in anticipation of the visits of the 'Britain in Bloom' judges. He had also swept the floor of the old Village Hall after messy events such as weddings and children's parties. The new Village Hall needed no such service from him. He lived on an industrial pension and spent his time fishing wherever he could.

He had known Crewgard for many years and he had noticed that Crewgard had also been losing his hearing. Their fishing trips had taken on new importance because of the quietness of the places they visited to fish. Sackler had no interest in explosives, his experiences in that field having affected his health and livelihood. He was more interested in the consumption of cannabis and his clothing, all too infrequently washed, carried a stale aroma of past reefers. His candour in the interview stopped short of him admitting any offences in that respect. He was not in the habit of entering Crewgard's house. He had no recorded criminal convictions. There was scant evidence of his involvement in the missing explosives.

The interview with Crewgard was conducted very differently to that of Sackler. It also revealed a great deal more information. As Crewgard had only recently begun to lose his ability to hear, he had not yet learned any form of lip-reading or sign language. Lately, Sackler had been helping him to learn that. All questions were written on paper but his answers were delivered audibly and appropriately recorded.

The interview rooms at Pendale Police Station had been cells when the building was first designed. Changes in legislation created the necessity for a reallocation of the available facilities. Soundproofing and emergency wall strips had been fitted, tables were fixed to the floor and a tape-recorder and wall-mounted microphone sat above it. The five chairs were free standing and as Inspector Imran Bhatta and Constable Mel Sharpe entered the room, the detainee Wayne Crewgard and his legal advisor Yvonne Parry were already occupying two of them.

Sharpe explained how the interview was going to be conducted and she switched on the tapes. A low buzzing sound came and went then Sharpe explained who everybody was and what Crewgard's rights were. Before Crewgard spoke, Yvonne Parry explained that a statement had been prepared which she intended to read out.

"Can't Wayne read it out Ms Parry?"

"I can read it out," snapped Crewgard, offended at the suggestion that he was in some way incapable of reading. Ms Parry handed the paper to him impassively. She wanted her client to say nothing and stick to it. She knew that the more he said, even if it was written down, the higher the likelihood that he would be comfortable speaking and would say things that he may later regret.

Crewgard coughed and settled in his seat. He raised the paper up and began.

"I, Wayne Crewgard, after consoling . . . "

"Consulting," corrected Yvonne Parry, wishing she had insisted on Plan A.

". . . consulting with my legal represent . . . ta . . . tive,"

All persons present were willing him to get on with it and had to fight the urge to finish the job for him.

"I have this to say. Ahem." He momentarily looked up as he shuffled in his seat. "I have not taken anything from my place of work without the permiss . . . permission of Wilson's Aggregates, in the thirty years I have worked for them."

The missive continued amid excruciating pity but largely repeated the same message. When Wayne placed the paper down on the fixed table, he anticipated that the interview would be over. It was only beginning. Sharpe took the lead. Reaching under the table she produced the blue cotton boiler suit folded neatly in a large forensic evidence bag. The Wilson's logo was visible on the outside and the label in the back of the collar was also on show. He added that his recent eruptions of temper had been the result of going deaf and his unwillingness to accept it. His excessive drinking had further aggravated the situation. He feared that he would lose his job if his condition were to be fully considered. A single man living alone, the thought of him not being able to work was a grim one. He denied any improper access to the explosive store at the quarry and blamed it all on inconsistent record-keeping. When that line of questioning was under way, he realised why the police had detained him in the manner they did.

"Is this boiler suit yours, Wayne?" Sharpe held up the bagged item.

He looked mildly bewildered for a few seconds then he glanced at the plastic covered garment.

"It might be, I dunno. There are lots of them about. It's an old 'un, all the colour has faded."

"Have a closer look," pressed Sharpe, adding only a tiny degree of pressure in the tone of her voice. Wayne leaned forward and perused the item.

"It could be, ah yeah. It's mine. There's my initials on the label there. Have you got it from my house, 'cause I haven't nicked it, you know? We're allowed to have them. We take them home to wash sometimes and they don't want the old ones back anyway. I do my garden in it or it's another layer when I fish the lake in the Winter. It's not a secret. I wear them in public and I dry them on the line in my garden for all to see."

"Wayne, you have not been working recently at the quarry, have you?"

"Erm," he looked at Ms Parry for her approval before continuing. She nodded once and he turned to look at Sharpe.

"No, not for a few weeks."

"Why is that, Wayne?" Her tone was that of an infant's schoolteacher addressing a nervous child but it belied a steely purpose.

"I'm on the sick, been having some problems."

"These problems, is that what made you lose your temper at work?"

Wayne nodded and looked away sheepishly.

"You are nodding Wayne. The recorder only picks up what people say out loud."

"Yeah, I suppose."

"You said some unpleasant things, didn't you?"

"Yeah."

"Threats of revenge on some of the others at Wilson's, eh Wayne?"

"I didn't mean nothin' by it. I wasn't going to hurt anyone." His earlier defiance had all but disappeared.

Ms Parry scribbled copious notes and barely looked up.

"Meanwhile," continued Sharpe, "you have had some free time, haven't you Wayne?

"Erm, yeah."

"What have you been doing with that?"

"Fishin', fixing some things."

"Have you been going to the Barley Mow, in Eckscarfe?" Wayne instantly turned pink in the cheeks.

"A bit, sometimes."

"When did you last go to the Barley Mow?" It seemed such an innocuous question but Wayne knew that it was highly charged.

"On that Thursday."

"What Thursday?"

"When the train crashed."

"So, on the day of the train crash, you had been in the pub."

"Yeah."

"What time did you leave the pub?"

"About teatime."

"There was some trouble there, wasn't there Wayne?" Wayne knew where this was going and did not relish the imminent revelations.

"I had a bit of a falling out with the landlord. I'd had a few, you know? He said I had to get out."

"Was it another display of anger Wayne, like at the quarry?"

Wayne felt that the walls were beginning to close in on him. He had nothing to call upon to resist that feeling. He did not answer. Sharpe glanced at her papers and continued.

"You have another hobby it seems, building models."

"Yeah, so what?"

"There is a particularly detailed model on a low table in your front room. Tell me about that?"

"It's . . . it's a model railway but it doesn't have any working engines. It's just for display, you know?"

"What is it a model of?"

"Round here. The village, the lake."

"It must have taken a long time to build."

"Yeah, a year or so."

"It also includes the railway line. And it shows the positions of the train and the buildings."

Yvonne Parry interjected,

"What are you getting at, officer?"

Sharpe maintained her gaze at Wayne and said,

"What I am concerned about is that your boiler suit was used by whoever caused the train to derail and kill and injure people. I am also concerned with your eruptions of anger and threats of violence, your state of drunkenness on the day of the crash, explosive substances are unaccounted-for at your place of work and you have a model of the scene in your house that has been under construction for a year. I would like to hear what you have to say about that Wayne."

"Now just a minute," demanded Ms Parry. "I must consult with my client in private before this can continue. You are taking advantage of a vulnerable man here. If your enquiries had been more thorough, you would have known that Mr Crewgard lost his mother to a stroke only two months ago and he is experiencing the trauma of bereavement."

Bhatta paused to allow the tension to abate before saying,

"Ms Parry, I have the greatest sympathy for anyone who had lost a loved one but remember the families in Eckscarfe who are experiencing that right now. The best way available to me to help them to come to terms with that is to find out what happened and who was responsible. I am sure you want to assist in that endeavour. Interview suspended for further legal consultation."

As Crewgard was being taken from the interview room, Sharpe walked behind him up to the custody desk. The Sergeant directed that he be returned to his cell. They reached the cell door but before he went inside, Crewgard looked furtively around then said to her,

"It's not all bad news, what happened to them in the Village Hall, you know."

"People have died!" appealed Sharpe, incredulous about Crewgard's apparent lack of humanity.

"Aye, I know that, but maybe some of them deserved it."

"Get in there," she snapped, flicking her head to the side toward the cell. Crewgard entered and the door was closed. Sharpe pondered on what Crewgard had said. Was it simply small-town small-mindedness? or was Crewgard trying to tell her something, something that he was unable to say without it being disguised in some way? She had enough to think about without trying to psychoanalyse the words of a man who had been behaving irrationally recently. Back in Bhatta's office, Sharpe summarised the interview.

"He denied nicking any dynamite, he denied anything to do with the rail crash. He claims that the model of the village in his house is a coincidence."

"We don't have any firm evidence for Crewgard, do we?" said Bhatta somewhat rhetorically. "He is hardly likely to have used a boiler suit with his initials in it to make the dummy, and that suit would have been on his washing line and there for anyone to take it. Okay, we have to release him. Has the search of his house finished?"

"Yes, there was nothing else found of any importance," she reported. "Oh, there was one thing."

"Go on," he said.

"Crewgard said something to me after the interview. He suggested that some of the people who died after the crash had deserved it."

"He really isn't looking to make any friends, is he? What do you think he said that for?"

"I don't know, but he waited until the interview tape was off before he said it."

CHAPTER NINE

The landlord and landlady of the village pub were Markus and Sophia Grejzni. Both Polish by birth, they had moved to the UK in their teens. After working in other people's hotels, they took ownership of the Barley Mow and had recently marked five years as custodians of the village's only functioning public house. There had been another one, but it had been converted into a dwelling some years before. On the morning of Bhatta and Sharpe's house-to-house visit, Markus was in the bar on his hands and knees stocking the chiller shelves and Sophia was yet to make an appearance.

Whereas Sharpe was perfectly at home in that setting, Bhatta was not in the habit of patronising licenced premises. If not for the police custom of celebrating a colleagues' promotion, retirement or career-enhancing transfer, he would see no need to do so. He attended such events for reasons of respect to the individual who had warranted the gathering, and he invariably spent a token hour at the beginning of the evening nursing a glass of cola before heading home. He preferred to spend his leisure time with his family and, although he had no religious or cultural objection to the consumption of alcohol, he chose to abstain, applying the rationale that he simply did not enjoy its effects.

Sharpe had taken the opportunity to visit the Ladies' room whilst Bhatta scanned the bar to learn of the unfamiliar. In a moment of wild optimism, he considered that the identity of the person who had cut the railway track on the fourth would be revealed to him, if he looked hard enough for it. Only when he was alone did he harbour such unrealistic thoughts.

He examined the décor and objects of interest on the walls and high shelves. Horse-brasses and old ploughshares told of the agricultural past and the framed, watercolour prints reinforced that message. All of the exposed oak had a richness of both substance and age, which he admired. Things that had been made properly tended to last the longest, he had often thought.

There was a buoyant atmosphere in the bar. Small huddles of people gabbled in animated dialogue, undecipherable to those more than a few feet away, which all contributed to the overall hum of the busy hub of that community. Bhatta spotted one of the reporters who had harangued him following the train crash. He could not recall the man's name, only his attitude. He was talking into his phone and appeared not to have noticed Bhatta, who was now attired in civilian clothes and therefore, perhaps, less recognisable. He was, as usual, the only non-white person present. He moved behind a pillar at the bar to minimise the risk of an exchange with the reporter. As he did so, he overheard a conversation taking place on the other side of the pillar. He could not see the participants but he pictured two women in middle-age.

"Of course, you know what's happened, really?"

"What do you mean?"

"I mean the train crash."

"What about it?"

"It was done on purpose."

"Yeah, they said so on the news."

"Ah, but they didn't say why, did they?"

"Go on."

"Well, it's obvious, isn't it? Terrorism."

"You think so?"

"Of course. What else?"

"They attack main rail lines as they do with airports. It doesn't matter where. Think about what happened at Lockerbie."

"Yes, but - "

"These Arabs will do their nastiness anywhere. That's all I'm saying."

"You think it's to do with Iraq?"

"Or some bloody place like it."

"I don't think that's true, you know. It will have been a prank gone wrong, kids larking about on the line."

"If that is true, and I'm not saying I agree, we can guess at who was involved, can't we?"

"I know what you mean. Those lads are wrong-uns. It was always going to end in somebody getting hurt."

"It doesn't help when one of them is the copper's kid. How can he sort out their shenanigans when his son is the biggest problem?"

The conversation left Bhatta's range of hearing and the Ladies went to sit at a table as Sharpe returned.

Bhatta felt that the gossip was ill-informed and lacked evidence. It had incensed him. Prejudice prevailed wherever people were present to practice it. It demonstrated the small-mindedness of people with nothing better to do than air their unsupported opinions. However, he could not rule out the suggestions being made, and that frustrated him. The train crash might have been ideologically motivated and that might have been linked to the ongoing military activity in the Middle East. Noel Keld and his friends may well have done something, which had proven highly destructive. It was yet to be established if that was true. His thoughts snapped back to the task in hand as Markus Grejzni spoke to him from his kneeling position behind the bar.

Sharpe produced the requisite house-to-house forms and began to write on them.

The part of the form covering who lived on the premises brought on a note of awkwardness in the landlord's voice.

"Ah, that is just me and Sophia now."

"Was someone else staying here recently?" asked Bhatta, anticipating the disclosure of a bereavement. Markus let out a sigh and stopped filling the chiller.

The refrigerated unit clicked and hummed at having its door left open for too long.

"We had a fellow working in the kitchen. He stayed in a room above the function suite. A quiet fellow, spoke poor English."

"Where was he from?"

"He was Polish. He just arrived a couple of weeks ago looking for a job and somewhere to stay. As it was, we weren't really looking for anyone but I thought it would allow Sophia and me to have a little time to ourselves, you know? We only paid him a few quid but he had his meals and accommodation, so we weren't doing anything wrong. I can't understand why he went. He didn't even say goodbye, just vanished."

Sharpe clicked the button on her pen. Bhatta asked Markus,

"What name did the Polish chap give?"

"Gregor, I can't remember what he said his surname was. He was only here a fortnight. Never said much. He worked in the kitchen but mostly in the washing-up area at the back. You would hardly know he was there, particularly when the bar was busy."

"Did he have days off, free time?"

"Oh yes, we aren't slave drivers, you know. When he wasn't working he either stayed in his room, which he kept very clean by the way, or he went out walking on the fell or around the lake. He wasn't any trouble to anyone."

"You say his English wasn't good?"

"Yes, he had a heavy accent too, he was a quiet type, didn't have much to say and when he did you could barely hear him, especially in a busy kitchen."

"Can you describe him?"

"He was a short bloke, in his twenties maybe, average build, well, a bit leaner than average really. Always wore a cap - and glasses, he wore glasses."

"And his clothing?"

"He wore a white overall in the kitchen, I didn't see much of him otherwise. I think he was wearing a black coat when he first came here."

"When did you last see Gregor?"

"Well, that is the odd bit," said Markus straightening up and stretching his back. "He hasn't been seen since the day of the rail crash."

"Why do you think he went?" asked Sharpe. It was a question Bhatta would have avoided asking after hearing such stereotypical views from around the bar. Not all foreigners are terrorists. She pressed on. "Do you think he had anything to do with the crash?"

"Wow!" exclaimed Markus, "I hadn't thought of that. I can't think of any reason he would. I just thought that maybe he wasn't totally legal, you know, being in the country? He probably saw the village was full of cops and couldn't risk hanging around, try his luck somewhere else."

No photographs of the itinerant Polish kitchen porter known as Gregor were available so a police artist's impression was suggested. The artist, whose previous offerings had generated derision amongst the more seasoned investigators for producing the same portrait for each case he worked on, spoke to Markus and Sophia Grejzni at the Barley Mow and decided that the task was futile. He cited that the subject's habit of wearing a cap and spectacles made a portrait useless as a form of recognition for evidential identification. All that could be gathered in the pursuit of circulating Gregor was a basic description: white male, 5' 4" to 5", slight build, in his twenties, speaks rarely and in broken English. Known to wear a black coat with no distinguishing features. The specs were plastic and wire-framed and the cap was black but old and faded to grey.

*

The uniformed cops on night patrol in Pendale were also depleted in number, effectively having half of the recommended staff. On such occasions, an unwritten rule tended to apply itself to the service provided. The custom was to adopt Fire Brigade tactics by only attended incidents graded as urgent and to put off any proactivity or prevention until the requisite staff were available.

Returning from a domestic violence deployment where the offending party had run from the matrimonial home prior to the arrival of the police, a double-crewed car passed through the pedestrianised shopping street in the middle of town. The driver, PC Gary Watts was looking for broken windows or anything else out of the ordinary in the dead of night. He opened his side window in order to listen for unseen activity. By the tiny interior light, his passenger, PC Helen Quinn was trying to write up a summary of their latest call in her notebook. At a crawling pace, their car was the only moving thing in the town centre. Nobody else was awake nor any premises occupied. The street lamps and shop displays were the only other sources of man-made illumination. As the car reached a cross-road, which by day formed the hub of the commercial district, Watts turned the wheel to his left and glanced to his right. He saw something move in a shop doorway. It quickly darted back into the glass recess.

"Did you see that?" he said whilst still trying to focus on the site of the movement.

"See what? answered Quinn without looking up from her writing.

"Someone or something, down there in one of the shops."

She looked up and made a token gesture of searching where Watts had mentioned. She had no real intention to find anything, she merely wished to appear interested and continue to do so until such time as it became polite to resume her scribbling.

"Nah, you've seen a cat, or a fox. They come into town more these days." she returned to making her notes.

Watts was not sure he had seen anything. Fatigue and a variation in lighting was a combination, which could, and often did, play tricks with human perceptions. He slipped the car into first gear and continued to crawl away from the junction. As he did so, he looked in his rear-view mirror and saw a head pop out from the same shop doorway, someone was checking that the police car had gone. Watts slammed on the brakes causing Quinn to tip forward in her seat and skew a line across the page in her notebook.

"Thanks a lot!" she protested. He thrust the stick into reverse and manoeuvred back to the junction, stopping the car at the concrete bollards.

"There's someone there, in that doorway and they don't want us to see them," he explained without looking at Quinn. She accepted that he would not rest until he had checked the doorway so she replaced the book into her pocket and got out as Watts did.

Approaching from across the paved street, they saw that it was a branch of a large opticians' chain. The glass recess went back six feet and as their view of it became fully open, a figure darted out and sprinted away.

"Hey, stop!" called Watts, knowing that it was never likely to have any effect.

Without any idea as to why this fellow had run away from the police, both officers pursued their mystery man down the sloping concrete flags of the street. Their body armour and equipment slowing them down, Quinn slowed to be able to transmit a message to her colleagues to afford them some help in stopping the runaway, although she knew that there were very few of her peers available to respond. Watts took it personally that anyone would think they could outrun him. He sprinted after the faceless fugitive, losing his hat as he went. Quinn remained in sight but some distance behind when the man turned sharp left into an alley, she lost sight of him and soon lost sight of Gary Watts.

Watts entered the narrow passage and left all illumination behind. He kept running but had no bearings or awareness of what was in front of him. He slowed to a walking pace and reached out a hand to avoid collisions with walls and bins. With his other hand, he took his pocket-sized torch from his belt. Once able to see again, there was no sign of his quarry. He explored the narrow strip between the rear of the shops, kicking open doors into back yards and scanning the possible hiding places. It crossed his mind to ask for a dog-handler's help but he knew the likelihood of that happening and abandoned the idea. The only help he could rely on was from Helen Quinn. He called by radio for her to join him which she quickly did. She arrived at the opposite end of the alley and assured Watts that nobody had emerged from that end.

The search was methodical yet tentative. They opened every bin and every door that they could open. He could not have simply disappeared. Neither of them wanted to be the one to admit to having failed. Reasons for giving up began to stack up in both of their thoughts. They had had no crime reported to them, nor had they any grounds for stopping and searching the man if they could find him. What would they be searching for? Speculative searches were of questionable legality anyway. At that moment, Watts opened his mouth to air some of his reasons, Quinn saw something to keep the quest alive.

"Gaz, the ladder. It's a fire escape."

They both shone torches up the metal ladder with its peeling, black paint and underlying rust. Watts put his torch in his mouth and began to ascend. Quinn was relieved that he had taken the initiative because she was afraid of heights. He had not mentioned that he too was uncomfortable with such elevated positions. He reached the flat roof over the first floor where the ladder ended and began to scan the roof for intruders.

From below he heard a clattering and a shout, a woman's voice, wordless, high-pitched, desperate yet determined. He scurried down the ladder and jumped the last few feet. Along the alley was a huddle of arms and legs in a frantic struggle. Quinn rolled the form over, putting herself on top. As Watts reached them, she took control of the prisoner and her colleague.

"I've got his hands, get your cuffs on him Gaz." She was out of breath and her blood was pumping through her at an alarming rate. "He was in a bin, the cheeky sod," she explained.

"We looked in the bins." rationalised Watts who was admonishing himself for missing him.

"He must have been under something, either way, it doesn't matter." She put some perspective into their discussion. "Let's get this bloke out where we can see him."

The manacled man was lifted to his feet. They steered back along the alley and into better light. Only when Watts had recovered his hat did they stop to look at man who had tried to evade them. He was a below-average in height, unshaven and dirty.

"Alright, explain yourself. What are you doing?" began Quinn.

The man's eyes darted at both of them then down to the ground. He said nothing. Several similar questions failed to get anything from him.

"Put him in the car while I go back to the shop doorway," said Watts.

There was no fight left in the failed escapee. All of his resolve to resist arrest had evaporated and he showed his acceptance in his sunken shoulders. Helen Quinn took him to the car and placed him in the back seat. She activated the child locks as a precaution but there was no will in him to make a getaway. Gary Watts returned with a scruffy old rucksack. He placed it on the bonnet of the car and loosened the cord to open the bag. A rummage inside produced some clothes overdue for laundering, some cheap toiletries and a pile of papers and photographs. The images were of a family and looked old and weathered. The documents were largely letters, written in a language unfamiliar to either Watts or Quinn. They put the bag in the boot of the car and got into the front seats. Quinn turned in her seat and looked at their prisoner. Watts did so by peering into the mirror. Both of them were acutely aware that they had no real grounds to arrest this man.

"Okay, let's start with your name?" opened Quinn.

The unwashed figure looked up at her but did not respond. She pressed on.

"Why did you try to run from us?"

Again, he said nothing.

"Look, if you can tell us who you are and what you are doing, we might not need to take you to the police station. You could go on your way. Now, please, what made you try to hide from the police?"

Watts had a thought, stemming from the foreign language in the documents. "Maybe he doesn't speak English," he suggested. He turned in his seat to look at him.

"Do you speak English?" he chanted slowly, nodding encouragement in the hope of eliciting an answer.

The little man's eyes darted between the faces of his interrogators. When he felt that he could speak he answered in broken English.

"I have a bit English."

"Good, now tell us who you are?"

"I have done no wrong. I am homeless, not a crime, eh?"

"No mate, it's not. So why run off like that?"

"I look for work, not find work in police station."

Quinn and Watts looked at each other in unspoken understanding of what to do next. Quinn stepped out of the car. Watts turned down the volume on his radio.

She called the Control Room and explained the situation. She was unable to offer the suspect's name but she did give a description of him. When the reply came back, she got back into the car and turned to look at him.

"Is your name Gregor?"

The man stared at her saying nothing.

"You fit the description of somebody who has gone missing from Eckscarfe. The rail crash investigators want to speak to you. You are coming with us."

CHAPTER TEN

The end of the initial house-to-house phase of the investigation was getting near. Bhatta tried, when other commitments allowed, to attend as many of the calls as he could. When he was unable to, he made a point of reading the completed forms before they were typed up onto the Incident Room I.T. system.

The fourteen to sixteen hour days were beginning to sap his energy. This had a detrimental effect on his ability to concentrate. Headaches ensued and made all conversation difficult. Only a complete break from the Incident Room would bring him back to a place where he could continue with the job he had to do.

The people at, or near, the top of the police food-chain had shown, in his opinion, insufficient confidence in him since his early elevation from the bottom rung of the career ladder. As one of the few ethnic-minority officers in the force, he felt the weight of expectation upon him from two sides. Many of the people from his own ethnic community still held prejudicial views about the low social status of the police. Historically, his family caste was of a higher stratum than that, although his upbringing was humble in U.K. terms. Similarly, the police force culture in a part of the UK where there were very few non-white people, contained an element of distrust of the unfamiliar. When he had rationalised his decision to become a police officer, he believed that he could, to some degree, bring down some of those invisible barriers. The steps may be small, he thought, but they were in the right direction.

His university experiences had been largely positive and he had felt that many of the old, cultural divisions were in the past where they belonged. He was further encouraged when he was promoted to Sergeant after only six years. A year on a planning project team and eight months as a custody officer followed. The spell as temporary Detective Sergeant in the CID then another promotion to uniformed Inspector made him feel that he was breaking down those barriers and blazing a trail for others. That initial optimism had crumbled as he had been repeatedly been held up as a poster boy for the force minorities recruitment programme.

He had become convinced that he was being used in order to display the force's Diversity credentials. It was a form of exploitation, although cloaked in a veil of fairness. His commanding officers had, when he raised his concerns, told him to 'see the bigger picture' whilst many of his family and friends in the British Asian community offered him a 'we told you so' philosophy on the subject. The result was that he felt that he belonged in neither camp. He felt isolated, misunderstood, misplaced.

His wife, a paediatric doctor, earned more than he did and their children enjoyed an idyllic existence in a delightfully affluent small-town community where their racial origins played no part in their lives. These factors had contributed to Imran Bhatta's sense of being trapped. In all but his ethnicity, his choices had been his own. He loved and respected his family and his best times were when he could be with them, away from the things that frustrated him. He also loved being a policeman. Helping those who were unable to help themselves gave him an inexplicable intrinsic satisfaction, which eclipsed the irritating politics of his police career.

The final strand of the house-to-house phase included a row of eight bungalows, which housed the elderly. The last one was occupied by Nadine and Victor Leshman. Nadine answered the door in the same startled manner as everyone else seemed to do in Eckscarfe. Once their reasons for visiting had been outlined, Nadine showed Bhatta and Sharpe into the house. The only unusual element of this visit was that Nadine was no older than fifty, and therefore appeared too young to be living there. Perhaps, thought Bhatta, her husband was old enough to qualify for residency. When he entered the lounge/dining room he found Victor Leshman in an armchair by the net curtained window. Countdown was on the television and a fug of cigarette smoke hung in the air and on the furnishings. Victor turned to face his visitors who both made a silent gasp at his appearance. Victor Leshman had hair only on the right side of his head. On the left was a red and white expanse of reconstructed skin, crumpled and shiny in parts. He had no left ear.

Remaining seated whilst Nadine fussed over their official houseguests, Victor turned down the volume on the television. Politely declining the obligatory offer of tea of coffee, Sharpe prepared the form and began writing. Nadine answered all of the questions but Bhatta wanted to involve Victor too.

"And what about you Mr Leshman?"

"Hmmm," he uttered, "What?"

"I was just asking Mrs Leshman about the day of the rail crash."

"Oh, I'm not interested in that," said Victor with surprising bitterness in his voice.

"I'm sure you are interested in helping us to get whoever did this, aren't you?" asked Sharpe, trying to appeal to Victor's sense of reason.

"I told you, I'm not bothered. It's got now't to do with me."

"People have been killed," appealed Bhatta.

"None that are related to me. People die, that's that. When your times up, your times up."

It was the first time the extensive house-to-house enquiry had produced that response. Victor's appearance made any challenge to what he was saying seem inappropriate. Bhatta knew that this was irrational but he felt it anyway. Victor turned to watch the quietened television. All subsequent questions were answered by Nadine.

Nadine confirmed that her and Victor had been at home watching television on the evening of the crash. It was a rarity that they spent their evenings any other way. Victor did not like going out since his accident four years previously. He disliked the staring and uncomfortable atmosphere, which prevailed in the presence of new people. She worked as a supervisor in the kitchen at the Special School and held some responsibility for the planning of the catering needs of the residents as well as the cooking and serving of meals. She came across to Bhatta as a put-upon soul, being a full-time nurse on top of her job. In his manner, Victor seemed to be depressed and was probably difficult to live with.

When the interview was over, Nadine escorted them outside, closing the door to avoid being overheard by her husband. As she did so, Sharpe caught sight of a graduation picture similar to the one on display in the home of Councillor Loretta Rokestone. The thought at first that it was of the same person but she soon decided that it was not. Mrs Leshman spoke in a whisper.

"Victor has not been himself since his accident. He gets rather grumpy, understandably. He used to be quite active and good-natured. Please don't take offence. He can't help what he is."

"What was the nature of his accident, Mrs Leshman?"

Nadine glanced at the closed door, checking that she would not be overheard. "He was burned at work. He can't work now."

"Did he get compensated for his injuries?" asked Sharpe, instantly sensing her question to be intrusive and impolite. Nadine showed no offence.

"You would think so, wouldn't you?" she said with evident cynicism. "They wouldn't pay out. They said it was Victor's fault. It's going to take years to settle this. They can afford a bus-load of lawyers, we can't. It isn't fair."

There wasn't any phrase of consolation which seemed appropriate under the circumstances. Only a brief expression of gratitude for her hospitality and cooperation was given before they set off to the next house.

Back at the Incident Room, they met with Peter Keld and compared notes on the highlights and lowlights of the house-to-house phase of the enquiry. When they mentioned their visit to the Leshman residence, Keld had some additional information to offer.

"Vic Leshman was quite a happy-go-lucky kind of bloke. He went cycling a lot, I remember, before he got his injuries."

"His wife mentioned that," said Bhatta. "A bit of a saint, don't you think?"

"Yeah, she bears the brunt of it, I suppose. Can't be easy for her."

"Do you know what happened to him?"

"He worked for the rail company on track maintenance. Travelled up and down the country doing it. Apparently, the acetylene welding gear malfunctioned and it went up in his face. You've seen the result - and that's after skin-grafts."

Bhatta's mind had locked on to the part about Victor Leshman's work on railway lines and he was not taking in the rest of what Peter Keld was saying. He interrupted and asked.

"So let me get this straight. Victor Leshman worked on the railway lines using, amongst other things, acetylene equipment and he has an ongoing grudge against his former employers who he sees as having legally bullied him out of a compensation pay-out."

His suggestion became clear for both Sharpe and Keld. Sharpe spoke next.

"But his wife has given him an alibi for the time of the rail crash."

"She has, but he should still be highlighted as a suspect. She might be covering for him because she is scared of him. She gets the brunt of his bad moods. She could be lying out of fear."

*

The foreign man detained in Pendale was spoken to by the Custody Sergeant who was satisfied that his grasp of English was sufficiently fluent to enable him to be spoken to without an interpreter. He claimed that he was Albanian, his name was Pietri and he was looking for work in the UK. Bhatta went to the cells and escorted Pietri to the interview room.

The duty solicitor, who had been present on another matter, had expressed his concern that the arresting officers has no grounds for the arrest, nor any evidence of an offence being committed. It was not against the law to run away from a police officer. He was informed that Pietri was suspected of being in the country illegally and had used another name. His true identity, as well as his movements, had yet to be determined. If he was in the country legally, he would be allowed to go free. The duty solicitor, a plummy-voice, old brief, well beyond retirement age, accepted this, once he was sure that he would be getting his fee from Legal Aid.

"I am Inspector Imran Bhatta and this is PC Mel Sharpe. We must ask you some questions about who you are and where you have been recently. Do you understand?"

Pietri looked at his legal representative who nodded his approval of his answering the question.

"Yes, I understand, Sir."

He was small and insignificant, round-shouldered and uninspiring. It seemed inconceivable that he was capable of getting across Europe by his own endeavours.

"You were arrested during the night in the town centre of Pendale. Tell me how you came to be here."

Pietri swallowed and settled in his seat.

"I come to UK to work. I an Albanian. I have family. Things are bad back home."

"When did you arrive here?"

"Feb'ry seventeen, Sir."

"February the seventeenth, this year?"

"Yes."

"What work have you been doing?" asked Bhatta, relieved that the language barrier was not adversely affecting the interview."

"I do any work. I dig potato in, erm, in Norfolk." He pronounced the normally silent 'L' in Norfolk. "Then I try to go work in forest, Scotland forest. I cut trees."

"Do you have a passport?"

"No, passport lost now."

"Have you used the name Gregor since you came to the UK?"

"No, I am not telling lies. Only my own name."

"Have you worked in any kitchen in a pub or restaurant?"

"No."

"Have you been to Eckscarfe?"

"What is that?"

"The village, near here. Eckscarfe?"

"No Sir."

"You worked in the kitchen at the Barley Mow pub for a man called Markus Grejzni, didn't you?"

"No, no, I did not work in pub."

"Are you really Albanian or are you Polish?"

Pietri looked confused. He looked again at his lawyer who offered no guidance.

"I am Albanian, I tell truth, Sir."

"I think that you have been working and living at Eckscarfe under the name Gregor . . ."

"No. Is not true Sir."

" . . . and you left on the evening of the fourth, when there was train crash. Did you have anything to do with that crash?"

Both Pietri and the solicitor were visibly shocked at this allegation.

"I must say, this is unexpected Inspector," said the solicitor, "If you are accusing my client of criminal involvement, I must have full disclosure of the facts and a further consultation with him in private."

"You can have all that, don't worry," Bhatta assured him. "Meanwhile, I want his fingerprints and a photograph of him before he leaves here. If he is who he says he is, he can go. If not, I will get the Immigration lot in. I can't tell you how long that may take." Pietri answered for himself.

"Yes Sir, I will do it."

*

The Incident Room's computer system had managed to match certain aspects of the evidence gathered so far. Several sightings of vehicles had been recorded. Many of them did not include registration numbers, which made it difficult to eliminate their occupants from the inquiry. Three people had recalled seeing a large, gun-metal grey Mercedes in the village. Two referred to it as a limousine. It passed through at least twice and was seen on the car park at the Barley Mow. Because the registration number was eye-catching in its brevity, the witnesses were able to include that detail in the description given to the police.

The car was traced to Maxlow Estates with a head office address in Manchester. Bhatta and Sharpe set off to visit the office to establish who was in the Mercedes on the day of the crash and the reason for their presence there. After some initial reluctance from the reception staff, a person in a supervisory capacity told the officer to come back with a warrant. The visiting police officers were not prepared to accept that snub. Bhatta pointed out that if he did not get answers to his questions, he would place a warning marker on the police national computer, which would result in every cop in the country stopping and checking the car and its occupants every time it set out on a public road.

This made the previously obstructive administrator make a phone call, the content of which changed her attitude. She answered the questions and gave the name of the driver as Andrew Fentley. Further persuasion resulted in a further call and ten minutes later Andrew Fentley entered the reception area and begrudgingly introduced himself.

He was a lean, bony figure in a beige suit that had been made for a wider man. His mousey hair had been teased up into a quiff and held in place with gel. His brown eyes constantly darted around and seemed to focus on not focussing on anything. Despite his 'can't be bothered' manner, Fentley did answer the questions in a fashion which was more concerned about getting it over with than actually trying to be helpful.

He accepted that he had been in Eckscarfe several times but couldn't be sure of the dates. He explained that his boss was trying to build houses there and insisted on looking around the area personally. He said that his job was mainly as Guy Maxlow's driver but he did other work for him too. When asked if he ever drove the car alone he said that he took it home at night but did not go anywhere without the boss unless he was sent. When asked if he was ever sent to Eckscarfe alone he hesitated before saying that he might have done but he could not remember.

"Is Mr Maxlow here now?" asked Bhatta.

"What does it matter," said Fentley, "he won't see you without an appointment."

"Okay," said Bhatta. "Make me an appointment to see him."

"When for?" asked Fentley.

"Now!" demanded Bhatta.

Fentley spoke in whispers to the officious receptionist. A further call was made and Fentley was briefed to confirm that Maxlow was in a meeting but would see the officers in twenty minutes.

"Good," said Bhatta. "Is the car here?"

"Erm, yeah," said Fentley with some uncertainty.

"So that gives us time to have a look at the Mercedes doesn't it?"

"Erm, what?" Fentley was in unfamiliar territory.

"I'm sure your boss won't mind. Shall we go and have a look at it?"

Fentley led them outside to a 'Staff Only' car park where the huge car sat like a king among his subjects. It oozed affluence and quality. When asked, Fentley opened the car and allowed Bhatta to inspect. There was nothing of any interest in the car but when the boot was opened, he saw several well-worn tools. There was a pair of bolt croppers, a long jemmy, hammers, screwdrivers, chisels and plastic tubs of nails and screws. Lying next to these were three power-tools: a chain saw, drill and an angle grinder. At that moment, a figure arrived and stood next to the car.

"What the fuck is going on?"

No introductions were necessary. Guy Maxlow had made his entrance. He was in his fifties, tanned and well-groomed but with a weathered and lined face, which spoke of a tough life. He was wearing a light-grey suit and a blue shirt with an open, white collar. Dangling from his neck and wrists were several ostentatious displays of gold.

"They are the police," announced Fentley in a nervously higher pitch in his voice.

"Shut up. I'll deal with you later." Maxlow's anger was directed at Bhatta and Sharpe. Bhatta was not going to be intimidated.

"Mr Maxlow, I presume?"

"Who do you think you are, coming here and snooping around? This is my car. You have no right to be anywhere near it."

Bhatta quickly formed the opinion that this was Maxlow's default position. He was probably this angry with everyone.

"I need to speak to you about your presence in Eckscarfe recently. I have some questions I need answers to."

Bhatta's calm manner was in stark contrast to the brusque and aggressive communication style of Guy Maxlow. Maxlow found it supremely annoying that he was unable to browbeat Bhatta into capitulating and doing his bidding.

"I'm not answering any of your stupid questions. You can piss off, both of you!"

"Not ready to leave yet Mr Maxlow. We have things to do here." He turned to Sharpe and said, "Get onto GMP. Ask for a tow truck to attend to examine this car." Sharpe took out her phone and began making that arrangement. Maxlow's anger hit new heights.

"That's my car, you can't do this. I've got connections around here, you fucking prick."

"Keep your abuse under control please Mr Maxlow. This car is being seized for forensic examination as part of a murder enquiry. You can have it back when it is no longer of evidential value."

Maxlow was close erupting. He turned to Fentley.

"Get on the phone to the lawyers, tell them what's happening. Go, now." Fentley headed off at speed back into the building. Bhatta calmly explained the grounds for his actions.

"This car was seen near to the scene of a rail crash at Eckscarfe, I'm sure you have heard about it in the news."

Maxlow glowered at him but did not speak. Bhatta continued.

"Somebody used cutting equipment to damage the rail track which caused the crash in which people died. You have some gear for that in the boot here. I want to know if this equipment was used to cut that track. If it wasn't, you can have it back, the car too. If it was, I will be arresting you and your driver and questioning you about it. I take it I have made myself clear?"

Maxlow's face was still red with rage. He had realised that there was nothing he could do about it.

"Do what you like. I have other cars." He turned and headed off to the building. Sharpe ended her call.

"The local CID will send a truck and a CSI to preserve it."

"Good, thanks Mel."

Fentley returned, flushed and flustered. He was about to speak to Bhatta and let out some of the venom he had absorbed from his boss but Bhatta cut him short.

"I'll be needing these," he said, snatching the car key from Fentley's hand. "And I need you to open the barrier to the car park when the tow truck gets here, alright?"

Fentley had nothing to offer by way of resistance.

CHAPTER ELEVEN

When the redoubtable Mrs Barbara Hunter was ready to impart more of her thoughts about the crash, there was no selectivity in her choices of journalistic platform. Everyone was invited. She was the voice of the victims, at least of the train passengers. Whilst no fatalities had occurred, the injuries sustained by her fellow travellers ranged from minor bruising to broken bones, an amputation and one induced coma to manage a bleed on the brain. The news items charted this tragic aspect in fine detail. When it emerged that the train driver, Simon Butters, had regained consciousness and was able to talk about what had happened, the press pack arrived at the hospital in Pendale before the police officers who intended to take his statement.

The press had conducted themselves without any evident cooperation between them. Any opportunity to gain an interview, a quote or a photograph was taken as a chance to steal a march on their competitors. The first few press conferences had been conducted by Janette Lane-Wright but her other commitments had resulted in that role being delegated to whoever was trained and available. Thankfully for Imran Bhatta, he was not called upon to carry out that role. At the hospital, Bhatta had to run the gauntlet of rapid-fire questioning before he could enter the building.

Sitting up in his hospital bed, Butters was frequently reduced to tears as he tried to recall the events, which had changed every aspect of his life. Through many forced interruptions, he remembered setting off from Glasgow and that there was nothing of any consequence through the Scottish part of the journey. The arrival and departure times were met without incident. Only when he received the message whilst stationary at Pendale Station did his working day differ from the norm. He had sat in his cab for over an hour awaiting the all clear to proceed. He had been told that there may have been a suicide attempt from the bridge before the Eckscarfe curve.

From talking to his family, Butters was aware that he had initially been blamed for the crash, that he had negotiated the curve at excessive speed and been unable to keep the train on the track as a result. He was adamant that he did adjust the speed to within safe limits for the track layout. When he was told that the track had been interfered with, he experienced a bewildering range of emotions. From relief of the official acknowledgement that he was not to blame for the crash to bereavement for the souls who he did not personally know who had perished in the path of the giant machine he had been in control of.

The press were out in numbers and the hospital security staff, along with some uniformed police officers, were preventing the news crews from entering the individual hospital room occupied by Simon Butters. Marci Wicker had tried to cajole several members of the hospital into allowing her an audience with Butters. Hugo Latimer of The Times had a superior budget to that of his freelance competitor, but even offers of financial incentives could not get him the interview they all sought.

Keith Marlin and Dan Delerouso were of the same school of aggressive journalism. Although one worked for a Daily and the other for a Sunday, they vied without restriction for the hot stories and their motives were rarely altruistic. It was the thrill of the chase for them, getting the information that others could not get and all was fair in love, war and journalism. In that endeavour, they had come to outdo each other, and this had been played-out many times with underhand pranks and misinformation aimed at throwing the other off the scent of the scoop. Wild goose chases stemming from the thinnest of leads and created solely to cause annoyance became the norm, whilst still chatting like old chums over a drink as though they were on the same team. The animosity between them was purely professional. Developing the required degree of dermatological density was part of the way of life.

Hugo Latimer distanced himself from most of this seemingly undignified conduct. His burning ambition was the acquisition of awards for the quality of his work. He regularly drifted off to sleep imagining himself on a huge stage in an auditorium of cathedral proportions, wearing a dinner suit and a silver bow-tie as he took possession of a glittering prize whilst receiving the rapturous applause of his spontaneously upstanding fellow journalists. There had, thus far, been no indication that he was capable of such feats. He believed that it was simply a matter of opportunity. All he had to do was get himself to the scene of any big story and work his lyrical magic. The spoils would inevitably flow.

Marci Wicker was so far down the pecking order of hacks that the others considered it charitable to acknowledge her presence. Most of the time they did not even do that. As a newcomer, she lacked the connections as well as the budget, but she was not lacking in her work-ethic and commitment to unearthing the real stories. Her unique selling point was that she was not as confrontational in her manner when speaking to potential witnesses and other sources. Unlike her competitors, she did not adjourn customarily to the pub to maintain the use of an expense account. She had no expense account.

Her other challenge was to get her work under the noses of newspaper and magazine editors and negotiate acceptable remuneration. It was hard to find an editor who was prepared to pay her for copy when they were already paying a salary and expenses to their permanent staff. She had tried her luck in New Zealand and after two years of the same problems, she had recently returned to the UK to restart her career in journalism. The Eckscarfe rail crash was the first big story she had set out to cover since her return.

The senior administrator for Pendale Hospital was standing on the grass outside the main entrance, reading from a prepared statement. Chief Operating Officer Alan Humbould summarised the progress of Mr Butters and took the opportunity to heap praise on his hospital staff for their professionalism during the Eckscarfe incident.

Anticipating that most of the hospital staff not directly caring for patients were fully occupied, the seasoned hacks set out to get to Butters. Delerouso telephoned the hospital and asked to be put through to the ward where Butters was being treated. After claiming to be a lawyer appointed by the train diver's union, Delorouso demanded that Butters' legal rights were being denied to him unless he was allowed unrestricted access. The ward clerk had been warned to expect such tricks. She took a message and added it to a list, which would be given to Mr Butters when he was well enough to consider it.

Marci Wicker had simply left a card bearing a phone number on it at the hospital reception. She then went back to Eckscarfe to look for new witnesses and heart-wrenching stories. Hugo Latimer turned on his old-school charm and tried to use it to get his interview with Butters. Looking for anyone connected to the hospital who had been educated at Cambridge, he got through on the phone to one of the hospital trustees who, he had learned was of the appropriate alumni as well as being the sister of a peer of his. Once pleasantries and old connections had been established, he made his pitch for access to Butters. He was politely told to follow the official channels and not to call her again.

Dismissing his rivals as lightweights, Keith Marlin acquired a set of hospital scrubs and an official-looking buff folder bearing the Hospital Trust logo. He proceeded unchallenged through the building, using the corridor and elevator signage to find the ward. Passing the central workstation which served as the hub of activity on that ward, he got as far as the door to Butters' room. The door opened and a woman with a ten-year-old child emerged. Looking through the open door and over her head, Marlin tried to get a glimpse of his target by moving his head from side-to-side as she moved in front of him. This action gave his ruse away. The woman was Mrs Emily Butters and, unlike his professional carers, had no better use of her time than to protect her husband from unwanted visitors. Marlin may have been dressed as a hospital doctor but he was not behaving like one. A real doctor would have entered the room without delay and introduced himself with similar timeliness.

"Who are you and what do you want?" snapped the fiercely protective spouse of the train driver.

"I, I'm Doctor Green. I have just come on duty and I want to see this patient," he gabbled, regaining confidence as he spoke.

"I.D!" she demanded.

"I beg your pardon. Who are you?"

"I'm his wife. Show me your Identification."

The custom of wearing a photo I.D. card on a lanyard around the neck was uniformly practiced in the hospital. It was noticeably missing from Marlin's outfit.

"Can we go inside and discuss this?" he said, stepping forward to touch the room door behind her. She remained as a barrier, holding her arm across the doorway whilst holding the hand of the wide-eyed child.

"No, tell me who you are. You are clearly not a doctor." The game was up but Marlin was not about to cave in.

"Okay, you are right. I'm with the Daily Start. I want to offer you and your family a substantial cash sum for an exclusive interview with – "

"Enough. I'm calling the security."

"Wait," he persisted, "I'm talking twenty grand here. He's going to be on the sick for some time. Think about it."

"You are scum, you realise that, don't you? My husband was in a rail crash. He was the guy at the front of it. He is in hospital because he was injured - badly injured. He is lucky to be alive. If he has anything to say to the newspapers, it won't be for some time yet. You, you," she struggled to find the words to express her anger, "are despicable!"

Her curled lip showed absolute contempt but her tone was moderate in order to avoid upsetting her daughter who was already traumatised at seeing her father in such a state.

"I'll bet you have a lot to say don't you Mrs Butters? I could make a payment for your story and another when your husband can speak to me." He wrestled a business card from his pocket and thrust it into the pocket of her jacket. She recoiled in revulsion then turned to face the work-station along the corridor.

"Security! Get security here now please!" she shouted. Marlin had already begun to make his retreat. Two nurses responded to the shouts and headed down the corridor toward them. Marlin barged by them and disappeared out of the ward. Emily Butters told them what had happened and showed them the business card. The staff recorded the incident as Emily and the little girl returned to the room where her husband had been listening to the commotion.

"What's going on?" he said breathlessly.

"Hacks, cheeky devils, eh?"

*

In its two-hundred-and-seventy years, the parish church of Saint Gerard had been a constant hub of the community of Eckscarfe. As well as christenings, marriages and funerals, the weekly church services had brought the people of the parish together to spiritually refresh and be seen in their Sunday clothes. Its old, stone walls, unchanged but for the inevitable signs of weathering and decay, stood as a monument to both Christianity and the resolve of the human race.

For the previous eighteen years, falling church attendance and stretched diocesan budgets had meant that the village no longer had its own parish priest. Instead, Eckscarfe had to share a vicar with two neighbouring parishes. The Reverend Francis Broughton spent his Sundays driving between the villages, dispensing prayers and hymns in a time-honoured fashion. The church organ at St Gerard's, referred to in the district as St Jed's, had lain idle and unserviceable for over ten years. Instead, the hymn music was provided by a music cassette and loud-speaker arrangement.

The only Sunday service took place at 10.30am and, on the first Sunday after the crash, the movement of people toward the church began over an hour before. Stoically grimacing families marched through the roads with evident purpose. Red-eyes and over-wiped noses told of the pain felt by everyone. Small children, unaccustomed to such grim formality, responded to the mood with significant efforts to behave. Dignified postures abounded in the cooling summer breeze.

The Ladies and Gentlemen of the press continued with their photographs and snatched conversations albeit with a slightly muted approach. The Reverend Broughton, resplendent in his white surplice and purple sash and holding a token bible, stood sentry at the ancient arched gateway to the churchyard where the victims of the crash were likely to be interred. People shuffled with stunted steps under the arch to emerge into the tree-dappled sunlight within. The benign Reverend exchanging pleasant and welcoming greetings to all, taking care to avoid appearing in any respect upbeat or happy. Uniformed police officers were deployed with press intrusion in mind but there was no need. The press kept a dignified distance in the road outside the gate.

The pews filled up within minutes and the folding chairs, borrowed from the school were claimed soon after. Standing room at the back was marshalled by the volunteers who also handed out hymn-books, which had run out. By ten-twenty, the church was full, and yet more people arrived and took their places outside. The Reverend Broughton took advantage of the fine weather and told the helpers to leave the main double doors open for those outside to be able to hear and participate. Once satisfied with the arrangements, he went up to the altar, which also housed several families, and nodded to the volunteer at the controls to cut the recorded organ music. Over the crummy PA system, he welcomed one-and-all and led the praying.

Mumbled, robotic responses were returned by the congregation. Only the seasoned orator in purple and white could be understood with any clarity. He called upon the Salvation Army Captain Clive O'Flindall to deliver a reading, the subtlety and relevance of which was appreciated by very few. It was a passage from the Old Testament and could have held contextual relevance but was lost on the majority. Once those able to do so had retaken their seats, the priest spread out his hands on the sides of the brass eagle adorning the pulpit and embarked on his sermon.

"In the name of the father," began the priest, stirring those on the packed, oak pews to join in in a half-hearted mumble for the rest of the mantra.

"Friends, we are gathered here today, in the house of God, as we have never had to do before. Disaster has come to this normally tranquil community and we, all of us, have been touched by it. Nobody is exempt from involvement. As well as those whose lives were lost, there are their families, their neighbours, colleagues and friends. It is right that we face this terrible experience and face it together. Here, in this old church, we may find a haven of peace amongst the chaos and seek God's help and support to come to terms with what has happened and begin the long journey to rebuilding this damaged place."

Bhatta felt a chill, raising his skin in goose-bumps. Was it because the temperature in the ancient, stone church was several degrees below that outside, or was it because his presence in a Christian church was so alien to him that is body was trying to react adversely? There wasn't too much difference than in his own faith, not that he had been a particularly keen attender in adulthood. The supplicant kneeling, the symbols on the walls and windows and the clothing of the priest was all similar. Perhaps the denomination was not the issue. Perhaps it was him. He could have been suffering such chills in any place of worship. The sonorously formal priest continued.

"It would be easy to say that this was simply the result of bad luck, an event which could have happened anywhere and to anyone. But, are we right to try to label such an occurrence in that way? For that is the path to self-doubt, recriminations, to attribute this disaster to the 'will of God.' Well, I must tell you that this is not the will of God. For our ever-merciful God is not vindictive, does not inflict His power to bring this torment and misery to His people. The Old Testament tells many stories of fire and flood to show those without faith the error of their ways. Our God is not destructive or vengeful, He is the path through this challenging time. It is through faith that we shall be able to see beyond the cloud of desolation, to the clear skies of understanding and acceptance."

Bhatta's body temperature became less distracting. Representing the Constabulary, he had attended in uniform, black tie, stiff collar and ceremonial tunic. His Inspector's cap was in his hand. He was standing at the side of the altar in a tiny chapel cordoned off by a low railing. The insignia on the wall next to him was of a military nature, commemorating those lost in war. Around him were twelve other people squeezed in to the nine square yards. He was behind two people who were shorter than him which afforded him the view of the congregation he was seeking.

He scanned the open area and to the pews. Extra chairs had been laid out between the pews and the altar. Two rows of servers in black cassocks under white surplices lined up on benches turned to face inwards. The priest, in God-like robes, held the throng in the palm of his hand.

People were visibly moved. Many had their heads bowed throughout, tissues and handkerchiefs were fully utilised. Bhatta saw some people he recognised. Marcus Grejzni was on the second pew accompanied by a blonde woman who, Bhatta guessed, was his wife Sophia. Marcus remained impassive whilst Sophia delicately dabbed the corners of her eyes. Peter Keld, together with his wheel-chaired wife and their young daughter, was there in his capacity as a resident and not as a police officer. He was therefore in a suit and not in uniform. The Ambulance crews were with the Fire and Rescue contingent. Bhatta considered, momentarily, that he should be with his partners in the other emergency services, but it was too late to do anything about that.

Councillor Loretta Rokestone stood as sentinel at the end of the front pew. Next to her were the chief mourners, Mrs McAulden and Mrs Hurlington with who appeared to Bhatta to be accompanied by their respective adult offspring. Two rows back was Nadine Leshman, wearing a hat with a black mesh across the front. Bhatta saw a smart, upright yet elderly man with clear tape holding his spectacles together. He was sitting next to Neville Allerton from the Quarry toward the rear of the church along with several other faces he recognised but was unable to attribute names. On the front row on the right sat the train crash survivor-in-chief, Barbara Hunter. Her arm in a muslin sling and her able hand holding an aluminium crutch. Her face was a study in defiance. Behind her sat Guy Maxlow, whose sneering expression suggested that he was more interested in how many apartments he could convert the church into than he was about paying his respects.

"It is also appropriate," continued the priest, "to pay tribute to those who, when it was needed the most, worked tirelessly to regain some order out of the chaos. The Salvation Army were there, providing refreshment and support as they so often do." He glanced at Captain Clive O'Flindal who was still clutching the good book from his earlier reading. "The emergency services, many of whom are here today, without whose strenuous efforts the suffering and injury wold have undoubtedly been far worse. We are indeed blessed to be served by such dedicated people."

Bhatta was the only one in that group at the front and a large number of the congregation turned to look at him.

"But the ones I have saved until last for special mention are the people of Eckscarfe who took in strangers, helped the injured, provided blankets and care when those directly affected needed it the most. That is the true meaning of being a Christian."

Bhatta stifled any show of discomfort. He had to be the only obvious non-Christian present. He felt as though he was being looked at once again, although he was probably the only one who had thought so.

As the service progressed to the closing hymn, the gathering rose to their feet and filled the high-vaulted ceiling with song.

'Abide with me, fast falls the eventide . . . "

Bhatta turned and shuffled through to the back of the chapel and to an emergency exit. He slipped out, taking care to close it again, and headed past the weathered gravestones to the front of the church where another hundred people were amassed, unable to find room inside. Huddled awkwardly was a group of teenagers. Dressed in customary casual wear, not in any gesture of disrespect but more out of a lack of awareness of convention. That they were there at all was the main issue. If they were local to Eckscarfe, they would inevitably have been affected by the train crash and its aftershocks. They had as much right to be there as anyone. They stood in dignified silence, not knowing what else to do. Bhatta noticed that there was only one girl in their group. She had a mane of flowing, blonde hair and seemed out of place in that set.

Beyond the grey, stone wall was the obligatory press contingent. Television cameras, all trained at the church gates by bored-looking technicians. Still cameras with preposterously long telescopic lenses, aimed at the church as though they were anticipating the second coming but being operated by people who did not care what they were there to snap.

Bhatta passed by without impediment. They were not there to see him. He approached a plain, grey, long-wheel-based Ford transit van parked on the narrow lane at the side of the church. After checking to see if he was being observed, he tapped on the rear door and was let in. Mel Sharpe and a guy called Howard from Technical Support were seated at consoles of screen monitors, all trained at the entrance to the church.

"How was it in the church Sir?" asked Sharpe who appeared uncomfortably warm in that confined space.

"I managed to dodge the lightning bolt they call down for infidels like me," he joked. "Other than that, it was tense and emotional. I have to salute priests for what they do at things like this. I mean, who, other than priests, could hold it all together and not choke?"

Mel Sharpe and Howard the technician nodded in agreement.

"Maybe we should get the press to read the sermon," she suggested. "They seem to be unmoved by it all. Just a job of work to them."

"So it would seem," he agreed, "and our role here is the same as theirs. We need footage of everyone who leaves the church. Then our intelligence analysts have to put names to as many of them as possible. The Chief took some convincing before he would grant me the authority to do this covertly. He was more bothered about bad publicity than he was about intrusions and privacy rights. I managed to convince him that it was a virtual certainty that the crash was caused by someone with a connection and a grudge against people in the village and that they were more than likely to attend the memorial service."

"Once we have named the congregation, what then?" asked Sharpe.

"We generate more actions to find out why they were here and what they might have against Eckscarfe."

Howard spotted movement on the monitor.

"Look. They are coming out."

They gathered around the screens and saw that the crowd outside was dispersing to allow room for those inside to leave. Several strayed onto the grass between the graves and others headed out of the gates where the press had assembled. Two concealed cameras were simultaneously recording the egress of the mourners. The clicking and flashing of still cameras could be heard from outside. Bhatta was satisfied that the objective was being achieved so he slipped out and re-joined the throng.

He passed by the press and saw familiar faces. Dan Delorouso was on his phone and speaking animatedly. Keith Marlin was holding recording equipment and was trying to get quotes from people seemingly at random. Marci Wicker was in intense conversation with an elderly lady who Bhatta did not recognise, and Hugo Latimer was trying to get a meaningful contribution from Councillor Loretta Rokestone. The TV crews had adopted a more discreet position across the road. Bhatta made a professional yet convivial greeting to both the Fire and Ambulance representatives before going to speak to the Grejznis.

"I was hoping that Gregor might be here," he said, hoping to provoke a revealing reaction. He did not get one.

"Oh, he'll be long gone, that one," Markus assured him. "Left in a hurry, didn't he? Do you know, he asked to borrow an old DVD player to use in his room. We said he could have it and we gave him some films to watch. Sophia thought it might help him with his English. We told him it was his to keep but he still left without it. Do you still think Gregor had something to do with the train crash Inspector?"

"All I can say about that it that he disappeared at the time of the crash and hasn't been seen since. I can't rule him out until I catch up with him. Until then, he remains a suspect."

At that moment, a change of tone came over the churchyard. Mrs Barbara Hunter had limped with her crutch to the church entrance. The press had already crowned her The Angel of Truth, although one had gone with The Queen of Eckscarfe, and they dashed forward, ignoring earlier etiquette, to get another invaluable soundbite. She had no hesitation in answering that call. Barbara held celebrity status for the first time in her life and she was determined to milk it for all the attention she could get.

Without waiting for Barbara to reach the gate, the questions came thick and fast.

"Barbara, how are you feeling today?"

"Who do you think cut the track, Mrs Hunter?"

"How angry are you that the police haven't caught who did it?"

"Are you going to sue for compensation, Mrs Hunter?"

As Barbara Hunter held court and delivered a speech, rich in indignation, which took in none of the questions being put to her, Bhatta spotted an opportunity to slip away without getting embroiled in the press-engineered confrontation, which was brewing around Barbara Hunter. If she wanted to complain about how the police were dealing with the investigation, good luck to her. There was nothing he could do about it. In any case. there were more pressing matters in his in-tray.

CHAPTER TWELVE

One such message was in the handwriting of Janette Lane-Wright. It was a 'request' that he call her about one of his team. Negativity ran through him along with the names of the officers and staff currently working on the enquiry. It was unlikely that she was going to give him more people to deploy.

"Ma'am? Imran Bhatta."

"Ah thanks for calling back Imran. Something has come up and we need to act on it."

"Okay."

"Peter Keld."

"Is there a problem with him Ma'am?"

"With him? No. With his son? Yes, there is a problem. Noel Keld has been arrested by the BTP for spray-painting a railway bridge in Pendale today. He was with a lad called Hugh Barron. They were given formal cautions for criminal damage. This has brought to light the issue of Peter Keld's position. There is, as you already know, some murmurs of a lack of confidence in him in the village. Some people suspect that young Keld and his mates were responsible for cutting the train track, although I know there is nothing to support that. We have kept this low-key until now but we cannot allow this to undermine the rail crash inquiry he is working on. It is too important. I'm reluctant to do this Imran, but he has to come off the team."

"I appreciate that Ma'am, but Peter Keld has been highly effective for us here. His knowledge and relationships in the village generate a lot of intelligence. I would prefer to keep him."

"Can't be done. Sorry, Imran. He has to be redeployed. Public confidence and all that. He will remain in the village police house and respond to the village if necessary, but he will be working in the town - for the time being, anyway."

Bhatta looked up and saw, beyond the glass wall of his office, Peter Keld standing with a member of the support staff and peering at a computer screen. Bhatta took a deep breath, stood up and went to the door.

"Pete, can I have a minute, please?"

*

The action generated to identify and locate any equipment capable of cutting through the rail lines remained unresolved. The Incident Room suggestions began with two obvious ones: Wilson's Aggregates were likely to use equipment designed to cut through stone so it flowed on logically that it could also cut through metal. Sharpe was able to address a part of the task by recording that an item of machinery found in the boot of Guy Maxlow's car was capable of cutting through steel and was already at the Forensic Laboratory awaiting examination. Looking further afield, she considered who else was to be considered.

The builder, Tommy Liddle, was the other likely owner of such things, and for similar reasons. It was also included in the action to ask at these places who else in the area would have cutting gear. It was also important to look for an accompanying implement capable of knocking the severed lines out of line from the rest of it. Liddle continued to evade the police by refusing to answer his door.

Meanwhile, Sharpe went over it in her head. There was no way for the perpetrator to arrive and leave in a car because the access track did not allow for that. It was too rough and narrow for any vehicle designed for use on a road. This brought up the earlier description of the quadbike provided by Rodney Brickshaw from the old cottage near the Shipley Road bridge. A quadbike could negotiate the harsh terrain of that pathway. There were several points that allowed access for a quadbike from the main road of the village to the path leading to the railway line. Any one of these could have been the route of egress of the offender. Tommy Liddle's builder's yard was next to it. She scribbled her thoughts into note form to avoid forgetting any of it.

Bhatta was thinking aloud as he put his take on this to Mel Sharpe in his office.

"According to Rodney, that quadbike carried two people which would have been asking a lot of the engine. The added weight of a metal cutter and a sledgehammer, or a similar item, would have slowed it down to walking pace. Rodney was sure that there were two on the bike as it passed the first time but only one on the way back." Sharpe offered another factor into the mix.

"If the passenger got off somewhere near Shipley Road, where did he go?"

"There were no sightings of anyone on the Shipley Road on that evening," pondered Bhatta as he stood up to look at the wall map of the area.

"Well someone had to be there to drop that dummy off the bridge," she said. "The rope was tied to the rail at the top."

"So where did he go after and, if they did get a lift on the quadbike, why did it go without him?"

"It must have been the one on the bike who went to cut the line. The other one could have been acting as a lookout for him. You can see the beginning of the curve from there." Sharpe was offering ideas in the hope that Bhatta would make sense of them.

"No, that doesn't work. If they stayed as a lookout, Peter Keld would have seen them when he checked the scene for the jumper," he added.

"Unless they were out of sight of the road, Sir."

"Do you mean off the road? Keld checked under the bridge too remember. The only thing he saw was the dummy swinging under the bridge." His voice slowed as a revelation came to him. "The dummy, someone took it there and left it there. That quadbike . . ." Sharpe understood his train of thought, even though he barely understood it himself.

"You mean that the passenger who Rodney Brickshaw saw on the bike was really the dummy?"

"Why not? How else could they have got it there without being seen by anyone on the road?"

"So, the rider of the bike takes the cutting gear, the hammer, the dummy and the rope to Shipley Road by the narrow track past Rodney's house. He leaves the bike out of view, waits until there is nobody driving by on the road, then he ties the end of the rope to the bridge rail and he slings the dummy over."

Bhatta continued for her.

"Then he gets on the bike again and rides back along the track to cut the lines."

"Yes, but wait a minute." Sharpe's mind was racing again, "Somebody called 999 and reported that they had seen somebody jump off the bridge. If they made the call, it must have been on a mobile. I'll check the original message and see what it can tell us about it."

"Yes, log that, will you," said Bhatta trying to balance his role as a supervisor as well as an investigator. "There's another thing. Where did that bike go after the cutting? It didn't go back past Rodney's cottage. He doesn't miss a thing." He turned to the map again, following a series of lines. "It had to return to the village."

*

The police radio operator's voice carried an unmistakably serious tone.

"Patrols to attend Pendale General Hospital. There is a patient on the roof threatening to jump off."

A scramble of responses was taken as confirmation that everyone was heading to the hospital. The first patrols to arrive were greeted by frantic staff, both nursing and administrative. A space had been cleared in front of the main building. Five floors above the ground was a figure in a pale green hospital gown. He was leaning on a pair of crutches and facing the void beneath.

"What's going on?" demanded Helen Quinn as Gary Watts set about establishing a cordon around the area. She was addressing a woman in a business suit and a high-viz vest over it.

"A patient has gone up onto the roof," said the woman. That much was clear already and Quinn had to bite her lip to avoid saying so.

"Who is it? What's his problem?" she probed, raising her voice to be heard over the siren of an approaching fire engine.

"We don't know. We're doing a head count on the wards now," said the woman in the suit.

"Has anyone been up there to speak to him?"

"No. We didn't want to scare him into jumping off."

"Alright," said Quinn. She relayed the initial information to the Control Room and headed inside to ascend to the roof. Watts remained on the ground to keep people out of the cordoned zone.

On the top of the four floors, she was steered to the metal stair-rail leading onto the roof. At the top of the ladder was a hospital porter, a junior doctor and a man in a suit bearing a name badge, which said he was a director of something. They all spoke at once and had to be silenced by Quinn who picked the doctor to speak first.

"He's told us not to approach him," he began, "we have tried to talk to him, but he won't."

Quinn's first thought was that she should try to speak to the man, but she hesitated. Was it expected of her to do so? What if the doctor was right and she became the final factor in his demise? She couldn't simply do nothing. A trained negotiator would be preferable but how long would it take for get one to the scene? She decided to try a different approach. She stepped out onto the roof and slowly walked toward him.

There was gravel underfoot and raised skylights were laid out in formal rows like flowerbeds in a park. An eight-inch high, raised lip ran around the edge. The temperature was lower than it had been at ground level, at least it felt colder to Quinn. The wind-speed differed too. It was strong enough to affect Quinn's balance. The man in the patient's smock seemed unearthly to her. He spotted her and turned his head whilst remaining on his crutches. He was barefoot and eerily out-of-place. The wind on the rooftop swept across with unsettling force.

"Get away from me!" he screeched as he turned back to face the edge of the building. Helen Quinn stopped and said,

"I just want to talk to you."

"No, no you don't," he snapped, "You want to grab me and stop me from jumping, I know you do."

"No," she answered, "Look, I'm going to stay here." She sat down on the felt and gravel, cross-legged and unthreatening.

"You might as well go. There's nothing you can do," he said in a more rational tone. There was a deep resignation in his voice. He was a man who had given up on life.

"I'll stay here for a bit," said Quinn, hoping to defuse the evident tension by sounding light-hearted whilst her own heart was trying to beat its way out of her chest.

Neither spoke for a minute. Voices could be heard from the ground below. Quinn's radio passed messages, which were being fielded by Gary Watts, who knew that she was unable to report the developments herself. She broke the silence.

"You could tell me your name."

He glanced at her through puffy and tearful eyes then at the gravel beneath is feet.

"Simon."

"Simon. My name is Helen. Can you tell me why we are both here please?"

"I can't take any more of this. I can't handle it anymore. All the grief and the guilt."

"What have you got to be guilty about Simon. Whatever it is it can't be as bad as it looks right now."

"I was driving, and they are all dead, how is that not my fault?" His voice rose in volume as he spoke. His shoulders shook in rage. Quinn joined the dots and worked out who he was.

"It wasn't your fault Simon. Somebody cut the track. That's what caused the crash. You tried to save everyone. You're a hero. It's in all the papers."

"Papers! Those bastards have been pestering my wife and my kid. They don't deserve any of this." He was tearful and appeared unable to take in what she was saying to him.

"You jumping won't help, Simon. They need you alive. You are getting better every day, stronger. Who would have thought that you could get up here today eh?"

He did not respond. Cautiously, she got back to her feet. Her confidence was no higher than when she had arrived. Had she said too much? She knew that she was not a trained expert in such practices, but Simon was still there, alive.

"We will protect you and your family from unwanted press attention. You don't have to talk to anyone you don't want to. Will you come with me, please?"

Simon Butters screwed up his eyes and shook all over as he sobbed. He let go of his crutches and slipped down to sit, slumped in dejection on the gravelled roof. Quinn dashed forward and, kneeling by him, she held his head on her lap. He opened the floodgates and wailed aloud. Quinn leaned forward and hugged him, partly to show care but mostly in her own relief. She too had tears in her eyes.

The intensity of the situation washed over her. She barely noticed that the party of hospital staff who had been watching from the top of the stairs had come forward. Two more people had joined them. They began to carry Simon Butters back to the stairwell. Quinn was reluctant to let go of him. When it became obstructive, she did release her hold. She made an excuse that she had to examine the scene and would come down presently. As they carried Butters down the stairs, she remained alone in the breeze, shivering and emotionally exhausted.

*

Jonathan Ullenorth's rate of recovery was alarming, physically, at any rate. His family were calling it a miracle. His fortuitous proximity to the Village Hall snooker table at the precise moment of impact had undoubtedly saved his life, having protected him from the falling masonry and roof-timbers. The concussion he had suffered carried no lasting effects and the bruises and inhalation of brick-dust were all-but cleared-up. Jonathan was able to walk unaided and allowed to return home. He did so in a blaze of press attention, although he said nothing. Instead, his wife and daughter spoke to the assembled press-pack as he looked at the ground.

Once in his four-bedroomed, detached house with a sweeping lawn down to the lake path, and behind closed curtains, Jonathan felt the full magnitude of what had happened to him. His brush with death, his gratitude to those who had rescued him, the support of his family and his neighbours all combined to give him a tearful appreciation of his continued life. The dawning reality of surviving where others had not, brought with it surges of overwhelming guilt and the loss of his friends added the cloying swamp of bereavement to the challenges facing him.

A brief visit from an occupational therapist was followed by a longer one from the family G.P. Certain medication was prescribed and walks in the garden became the norm. Night terrors punctuated the otherwise tranquil darkness of the Ullenorth household. During the day, a near-constant barrage of visitors to the house required the family to adopt a rota of receptionist duties. Well-wishers were easy to deal with, however, the ladies and gentlemen of the press invariably proved more difficult to get rid of.

Offers of recompense were forthcoming and rejected, sometimes accompanied by sharp words. It did not deter the journalists. When Bhatta and Sharpe arrived by arrangement at the Ullenorth residence, they were mistaken for reporters and given a frosty response. The production of the relevant identification and an authoritative introductory speech by the Inspector resolved the situation. A statement was taken from Jonathan Ullenorth, which revealed nothing new. He recounted the events of the evening of the train crash, going from leaving his home and walking to the Village Hall as he had done on the first Thursday of the month for several years. He had participated in the routine meeting of the Parish Council along with his now-departed colleagues before adjourning to the snooker room to play and drink whisky. At that point, his emotions got the better of him and a recess was called-for. Cups of tea all round, then the statement was eventually completed.

Throughout the police interview, Ullenorth was unable to maintain eye-contact with either of the visiting police officers. Both were used to the pitfalls of trying to gain an account from a traumatised witness. Once the well-meaning but occasionally obstructive family members had offered their own form of support, the process had been allowed to progress to a satisfactory conclusion. Bhatta assured the Ullenorth family of his commitment to maintaining their safety and privacy. He asked that they inform him of any press intrusion. As he did so, the phone rang. Mary Ullenorth answered it.

"Hello?" she paused. Her face gave away her inner contempt. "No, my husband does not wish to give an interview. Please stop calling!"

She replaced the receiver with significantly more force than when she had lifted it. Bhatta stood up and ushered her into the hall to speak to her away from Jonathan.

"Perhaps we could get the telephone company to put a temporary screening service in for you? It can be done in a day or so."

"We shouldn't have to do things like that. Why don't they just leave us alone? It's bad enough what we have been through. I have to grab the phone before Jonathan gets to it. It can only upset him. He's a nervous wreck as it is."

Her protective instinct was in full flight. Bhatta felt that she would need it in the face of the persistence shown by the reporters. He doubted that Jonathan was capable of sustaining such resistance. Understandably, he looked drained and exhausted. He also seemed to Bhatta to be consumed with anguish. Bereavement, he reminded himself, was a cruel torturer.

As Sharpe and Bhatta walked away from the Ullenorth home, she turned up the volume on her radio, having silenced it inside the house. She heard a police patrol giving a report to the Control Room. Bhatta noticed that she was concentrating on the radio. When she lowered the set from her ear, he asked,

"What's happened?"

"There has been an 'incident' in the village. The press lot have been trying to get Crewgard to talk to them about his arrest."

"He has a short fuse," he recalled. "Did it get heated?"

"Yes. He was getting into Sackler's car and the reporter was standing too close when the car moved." She stifled a smile. "He ran over the bloke's foot. The reporter called the police to report it as an assault."

"That doesn't sound like an assault to me," said Bhatta.

"No," she added. "The bobby who dealt with it though so too. Insufficient evident of deliberate intent, victim put himself in the path of a moving vehicle, no further action."

"The press have their own ways of dealing with things like that," he said. "They tend to write about it, and it won't show the police in a good light."

*

Sunila prepared dinner in full anticipation that Imran would miss it. She had gone to more trouble than usual due to the presence of her parents. She felt it appropriate to stretch her cooking abilities to show respect for Lania who had taught her how to do it. Although due respect was maintained, there was, she felt, little point in aiming to please her father. As she began to fill the plates, Imran came through the door. It was the first time he had been home before the children had gone to bed since the day of the rail crash. They left the table and affectively attacked him as he tried in vain to slip off his shoes on the doormat. He hugged them in turn then clapped at them to playfully scare them into returning to the table. Lania and Ali sat patiently as this overdue family reunion unfolded. Sunila recalled how that joyful informality had not been prevalent in her childhood.

Imran sat down and greeted his in-laws. Once settled, he encouraged the children to tell of their daytime activities. Sunila served the meal, her husband first then her father, her mother, the children then herself. The on-going tension between Imran and Ali, although still present, played no part in the conversation. It was not to last.

The meal concluded and the children went to get ready for bed. Lania helped Sunila to clear the table and Imran went into the lounge with a pot of coffee. Ali arrived with his newspaper and sat down in the lounge in silence, to begin with. They sat for a few minutes. Ali spoke first.

"I have been following the press reports on the case you are investigating Imran." He seemed to be genuinely interested, although he kept his air of cynicism throughout. "Are you any nearer to finding out what has happened?"

"We are getting there, it takes time."

"I am particularly interested in the extent of the injuries suffered by the people on the train. I have never operated on anyone who was injured in such a disaster. Is it true that there were some amputations?"

Bhatta was initially uncomfortable talking about the investigation out of the safe environment of the Incident Room, but, as the story was in the public domain and any non-confrontational conversation with his father-in-law would diffuse the tension between them, he was happy to sate Ali's professional curiosity.

"Yes, there was a limb amputation. Another passenger had a bleed on the brain, but he is stable now."

"It is marvellous how the design of the train carriages has spared lives."

"I agree," answered Bhatta. "The fatalities were all in the path of the derailed train."

The conversation took an unexpected turn. Ali's tone was conciliatory and somewhat more respectful than it had been the day before.

"I thought about what you said, about the white people waiting to judge you. I have experienced that. There are many, many Asian people in medicine in London now. It was not always so. You are doing that here and whilst I think that there are more reasons for living in the city, I don't overlook the good in what you are trying to do."

Imran was surprised and suspicious. Was Ali being truthful? Had he listened to Lania and Sunila in his absence? He had to take it at face value.

"Thank you Ali. I understand your concerns about Sunila and you want what is best for her, so do I. Her opinions should be respected too. Sunila likes living here. It is good for the children and the hospital is the same as any hospital anywhere. I will not tell her how to live. Our decisions are made together."

"Ah, this modern thinking, it is the road to trouble." He folded his newspaper and went up to bed.

*

Mel had called ahead to Claire to say she was heading home. They agreed to meet in the pub and have a meal. Claire was already at the table when Mel arrived. The pub had certificates of achievement for its food adorning the walls beneath the optic rack and pleasant people serving it. That it was only two minutes' walk from their apartment made it an obvious choice.

It had been Claire who had suggested dining out. The main reasons were that she seemed to have been alone at home for days and that she could not be bothered to cook. Mel arrived in her work suit, which, being the only smart suit she owned, was looking ready for the dry-cleaners. She kissed Claire on the cheek and sat down to eat.

A large glass of house red and a pint of lager were already on the table. Mel's mind was still racing with the need to proceed and analyse the storm of information she had absorbed. As Claire told her about a fourteen-year-old pupil who had hit a classmate with a badminton racket during a lesson, Mel found that the pressure she was feeling had begun to abate. It was normal for them to exchange anecdotes of their daily experiences, but Mel's absences had put that custom on hold. She had missed it. She had missed Claire and, listening to her school-based stories, Mel managed to put her work into a box for the evening.

Within twenty minutes, she was laughing. It was the first time in days. Claire did not ask Mel to relate any aspect of her day. She was there to listen if Mel needed her to, but she recognised that Mel had more demands on her than was usual at that time. She knew Mel well enough to know what her needs were. Claire's needs were also being addressed. Hearing Mel laugh was exactly what she needed.

CHAPTER THIRTEEN

Eckscarfe's recent upheaval had been unprecedented. The village's history included invasions of Vikings, Roman's and various other ancient tribes, but it had survived all of that to go on, probably for another thousand years. Amidst that turmoil, the sweeping fell-slopes and lush greenery of the trees and fields remained a haven of tranquillity. The old houses remained standing, the sun continued to shine and the clouds swept by on high winds.

At the edge of the village, the lake lapped over grey pebbles in a gentle rhythm. Three old, rowing boats lay idle on the stones with grasses growing around them showing that it had been some time since they had seen meaningful use. A short jetty intruded into the water and two, more-modern, boats dipped up and down on the tame ripples. At the point nearest the village, there were signs declaring that fishing was prohibited, unless the participants had the express permission of the Eckscarfe Angling Association.

Gary Nicholls did not have any permission to go fishing on the lake. This did not put him off. Tolerating the volatile Tommy Liddle in his working environment was undeniably challenging and could drive any soul to distraction and, because he did not have the money to go drinking, he resorted to the peace and quiet of the lake to take his chances with the brown trout and pike therein. Wearing an old, camouflaged cotton hat, matching jacket and chest-high waders, Gary knew better than to take up a position in view of the buildings of Eckscarfe. Instead, he entered the wooded area and followed the narrow but well-trodden rough path, which took him into the shade of the overhanging branches. Denied sunlight, the ground was permanently wet and the soil formed into clinging mud. The path widened at certain points as did the mud. Gary was well-equipped for this. His fishing waders afforded uninhibited progress and he strode confidently through the low weeds and grasses, at peace from the turmoil clouding over his home village.

The third inlet from which he could gain proper access to the water came into view and he swung his basket down from his shoulder. Fitting together the sections of his fishing rod, Gary found himself humming a tune. He could not say what the tune was until a few of the lyrics crept out and into the air. He was at a loss to know why it was Abba's Dancing Queen, which had permeated his consciousness, but there it was.

"You're in the mood for dance," he attached the reel to the rod and threaded the line through the loops. "And when you get the chance." He flipped open the plastic bait-box and attached something unsightly to the hook. "You are the Dancing Queen," he stepped into the water up to knee height and waved the rod in the air ready to cast it across the lapping waters. "Young and sweet only seventeen." One practiced sweep and flick and the baited hook flew out and plopped into the lake twenty-five yards out. "Dancing Queen, feel the heat from the . . ."

Gary froze. His song halted into silence in mid-lyric. Had his hook contained a world record of a fish, he would not have felt it. His breathing was suspended and a cold shudder ran through him. Unable to comprehend or respond he simply stood still, gripping his fishing rod with both hands.

A bird flew across the lake and into the trees behind Gary. It served to snap him out of the trance he had been cast into. With that came the overdue rush of air into his lungs and a reawakening of his situation. The form floating in the water between him and his hook looked like a wet, grey rock rarely exposed by a low water level, but Gary knew there was no such rock there. When the thing moved in the lapping waters, he saw the zipped pocket of a jacket.

He knew that there was nothing he could do to help the poor soul who was wearing it. He stepped forward then hesitated. What to do with his fishing rod? Irrational, he knew it was, but anyone would think irrationally in such circumstances. He clambered back onto the shore and put the rod on the basket without reeling in the line. He was about to venture out toward the body again when another irrational thought occurred to him. He was not supposed to be there. By raising the alarm and summoning the police, he was likely to drop himself into trouble he did not need.

Gary knew that he had no obligation toward the deceased. It didn't matter to him, or her, who found the body, or when. He could simply forget the whole thing, get on with his life, come back and fish another day. He sat on the basket and rolled himself a cigarette. With trembling fingers, he rolled the untidiest excuse for a fag he had ever made. Eventually, he managed to light it and drew heavily on the misshapen roll-up. The smoke served to bring a degree of calm to him. Putting away his petrol lighter, he took out his mobile phone and chewed over the possibilities and consequences of calling the authorities. He had no signal anyway. What was the right thing to do? He decided, on the basis that the drowned soul could have been a member of his family or a friend, or even himself, that he had to call it in.

That meant leaving to get to a place where he could make a call. The body wasn't going anywhere – or maybe it was. He knew that bodies in water could sink after a while. It would be a devil of a job to find it if that happened. He considered going for help from his fellow anglers. Wayne Crewgard and Alastair Sackler often accompanied him in illicit fishing sessions. Alastair didn't own a phone because he couldn't hear it ring and Wayne, although he could hear much better than Alastair, had been so angry of late, Gary quickly dismissed that idea as impractical. He threw away his fag end and strode into the lake.

The water was up to his navel when he reached the dead form. He grabbed the grey jacket and, purposefully avoiding looking at the face, he dragged it across the surface of the water to the tiny inlet from where he had set out. Once in the shallow water, the task became more strenuous. Gary heaved the uncelebrated human shape out of the water and onto the grassy mud of the inlet. He felt by then that it was that of a man, or a very heavy woman. He let go and straightened up to correct his aching back and breathe more freely. After a minute, curiosity got the better of him. He pulled at the jacket and rolled the casualty onto his back.

"Bloody hell!" he exclaimed, putting his hand over his gaping mouth. "Shit! Shit! Oh Shit!" he pulled his camouflaged hat off his head in reverence. "It's Mr Ullenorth!"

*

The Forensic team had to be kitted out as Gary Nicholls had been, only with the added burden of new waxed-paper over-suits, hats, gloves and facemasks. An approach path was established through the woods, which minimised the potential interference to the scene. This was rather hopeful due to the plain fact that whilst the body had been brought ashore there, there was no suggestion that the inlet was where Ullenorth had entered the water. Their painstaking examination would not be hurried by anyone. Cordon tape was placed in a wide arc around the scene and all approaches to it. Sealing off a lake was unrealistic but if they could have done it, they would. The body was photographed at the scene before anyone else touched it. Once the crime scene manager and the senior detective were content that it was acceptable to move it, the body was lifted onto a rigid metal stretcher. It was carried over the rough path between the trees by a team of six police support unit officers. Exhausting labours done, the strained efforts of the team delivered the covered body to the waiting black estate owned by a Pendale undertaker.

Across the field and bending the cordon tape, the press pack had assembled. Bhatta saw them and heard their cameras as the stretcher party arrived. He was confident that nobody in his team had told the press who it was under the elasticated cover and Gary Nicholls had not had the chance to, but a part of him knew that they must have found out from their own persistent observations.

Ullenorth's story was too juicy for them to resist. Surviving the devastating effects of the train crash only to drown in the lake a few days later. Eckscarfe really was the gift that kept on giving. Bhatta spotted the faces who had been making a nuisance of themselves in pursuit of the 'story within a story' that inevitably followed a high-profile tragedy such as this.

The CSI manager, Ian Carraway, strode across the field on the approved line of access. He was a rotund but healthy middle-aged man who had worked for the police in a civilian role for over twenty years after serving in the Army for ten years. Organised and thorough, he had progressed in experience and capabilities to the grade of Crime Scene Manager, effectively heading a small team of fingerprints officers and other gatherers of physical evidence.

Although there was no evidence that suggested that Ullenorth's demise was anything other than suicide, or at least misadventure, the decision had been taken to treat it as suspicious. Carraway was content to allow others to make such decisions. He stuck to what he was good at and was respected for his work. In his dealings with the elevated ranks of the police service, Carraway maintained the formality of address he had learning in the military.

"Inspector Bhatta." He greeted him in a tone which befit two professionals in the same organisation who had met only twice before.

"Hello Ian. Is it too early to ask . . ." but Carraway held up the palm of his hand to stop him from continuing to ask his question.

"All I can say is that he is definitely dead. You have it from the chap who found the body who it is.

Anything else will have to be confirmed at the path lab. Do we have a Home Office pathologist for this?"

"I think that the Pendale hospital staff will carry out the P.M." said Bhatta, who was not in position to decide on such things. "Shouldn't it be done by a Home Office pathologist under these circumstances?" asked Bhatta, albeit to the wrong ear.

"You sound disappointed, Inspector?" said Carraway.

"I would have preferred this to be treated with a higher priority," he admitted, stopping short of openly criticising the decision made by those above him. "The proximity of the train crash would suggest so. We can't separate the two events."

"Ah, well that's for the 'powers that be,' I suppose," pondered Carraway. "Do we know who saw him last?"

"It was his wife, last night. I saw them both only yesterday evening." Bhatta recalled Jonathan Ullenorth's difficulty in taking in what was said to him. "He was a troubled soul. That was clear to see."

Carraway started to remove his outer protective garments, popping them into a fresh forensic bag to preserve anything that may have clung to them. He paused and looked at Bhatta, differently this time, with more intensity and purpose.

"It might not make any difference," he began. Bhatta jerked upright in anticipation. Carraway was not given to speaking informally, but he continued, "There may be a factor which could be of use to you, to raise the stakes, so to speak."

"Go on Ian, what's on your mind?

"Well," he wriggled out of the forensic over-suit as he spoke, "The deceased was dressed somewhat unusually, for a chap who knew he was heading out to drown."

"In what way was it unusual, Ian?"

"Under the grey jacket, he was wearing a bullet-proof vest. I won't speculate as to why, not my place and all that, but if you want evidence that this was suspicious enough to warrant a top-drawer P.M. this might tip the scales in your favour."

"Yes. Thank you, Ian. I have to make a call before the body gets to Pendale."

*

Bhatta and Sharpe returned to the mobile Incident Room at Eckscarfe. They were about to return to Pendale when Sharpe spotted some activity outside.

"What is it Mel?"

"Some kids, teenagers. I know they have to hang around somewhere, but does it have to be here?"

"You are not yet old enough to be so grumpy about the young," he warned her in mock parenting. He peered out and saw them. He was about to resume what he had been doing when a spark of memory came back to him. He remembered the blonde girl from the group outside the church at the memorial service. She was among the gathering outside. He looked again. There appeared to be some quietly intense discussions taking place. They were trying to nominate an envoy to enter the Incident Room. Bhatta saved them the trouble by stepping out to speak to the group.

"Hello, I am Inspector Imran Bhatta. Is there something I could help you with?"

There were four in the group. Bhatta remembered the other young mourners from the churchyard. They seemed unable to express themselves although it was clear that they had arrived there with a purpose.

"Why don't you all come inside? I am interested to hear your concerns."

He moved aside and allowed them to step up into the portable building. There was a room just large enough for them to sit on a metal bench. Bhatta sat across the table and smiled. "What's on your mind? Who is going to kick us off?"

They looked at each other before one was silently appointed as spokesperson. He was a thin youth with greasy hair and a difficult complexion. His eyes showed an alertness and intelligence which the others lacked.

"Erm, I'm Adrian, Adrian Hallimond. This is Charmian, Freddie and Neil. There is something we think we ought to tell you but, it's complicated."

"Okay, I have to take complicated things and make them less complicated. If you tell me what it is, I might be able to help." Bhatta assured them.

Adrian looked at his friends then back at the Asian policeman in the suit.

"We are in a band. The Proles," he began.

"Good!" answered Bhatta light-heartedly.

"We practice, or we used to practice in the Village Hall."

"I see. You have nowhere to play your music now. Is that what you came to talk to me about?"

"No, it's not that. Something happened before the train crash. It might have something to do with it," said Adrian in evident discomfort but showing the will to carry it through.

Bhatta had formed the view that their visit could be categorised as a section of the community seeking reassurance at a challenging time. Perhaps to express their disappointment at having no facilities for young people in the village. He had to change his mind-set to be able to take in new information about the murder enquiry he was conducting.

"Tell me what happened Adrian. Take your time."

Bhatta intended to gain individual written accounts if necessary but for the moment he listened to a tale being told by all of them.

Bass player Adrian Hallimond, drummer Freddie Parr, guitarist, Neil Debicki and vocalist Charmian Vallasarias made up the band. They told Bhatta about their former friend, Perry:

Perry Vanaugh had found himself as the front man of The Proles. Centre-stage was where he believed himself to belong and all of the perceived and expected adulation was well-deserved. The Proles were to be merely a vehicle to facilitate his ambition. Once the band had served its purpose, they would be consigned to music history as the band that supported Perry Vanaugh during his early successes in show business. He was a major star in the ascendance. He was, however, the only person in existence who held this view.

Perry was unable to read music, nor play any musical instrument, although he did shake a tambourine on occasions. The others did possess some musical ability and, when called upon, could hold together a tune and entertain an audience. They were average and they largely knew it. When the decision was made to replace Perry with Charmian, it brought to them a renewed sense of fun.

Charmian Vallasarias had stage-presence and she could sing. Unlike Perry, she knew the lyrics of the songs. The band knew that having a good-looking girl singer could be a winning formula. As an additional benefit, Charmian was a team player, she did not believe that the world revolved around her or otherwise owed her any favours. The atmosphere in rehearsal was positive, it had laughs where there used to be arguments.

Perry's opinion of the revised format was no secret. On the Thursday before the crash, Perry had arrived at the Village Hall, stating his interest in how their performance was coming along. The band had made a series of uncomfortable gestures of greeting in the hope that Perry would recognise that there was nothing there for him, and he would leave them to it. Perry had other ideas. He had tolerated only a few bars of their first song when he let rip with what he really thought of them. It began with a slow handclap.

"You think that is going to give you your big break, do you?" sneered Perry as he lit a cigarette.

"You can't smoke in here Perry," declared Freddie, fully expecting an escalation in the already tense atmosphere.

"I'll smoke where I fuckin please!" announced Perry with increasing volume as he stood up and approached the stage. Mimicking in a high-pitched and infantile voice he chanted back "You can't smoke in here Perry." What a bunch of pussies. You think this is what it's about? Do you?"

The band remained still and kept quiet. Apart from Charmian, they had become used to his temper tantrums. He tended to erupt then storm out with a comically dramatic strut, usually kicking something over on his way out. He had become so predictable that they were looking for objects he could kick. Perry's rant began to gather momentum.

"You know this is shit. You must know that. You're supposed to wake people up, give them a shock, not sprinkle sugar on them." Charmian, unused to the pattern, tried to reason.

"You probably mean well Perry, but we . . . "

"Nobody wants to hear what you have to say, sweetheart, and I don't mean well. You can't see how pathetic this has become. Tell you what, I've got a new name for you, 'Barbie and the Boring Bastards,' yeah, that works."

Freddie had heard enough. He rose from behind his drum kit and threw down his sticks. Despite some tame murmurings of discouragement from his bandmates, he jumped down from the stage and headed with evidently physical purpose toward The Proles' former frontman. Perry stood his ground, firm in the belief that this was mere posturing and confident that nobody was as proficient in posturing as he was. He was about to be proven wrong.

Freddie hurled a wide but accurate haymaker and connected with Perry's cheek. It made the drummer's fingers sting, but that paled into insignificance when compared with the fractured cheekbone sustained by Perry Vanaugh. He did not just drop to the floor, he was knocked sideways and skidded along on the polished wood.

Initially, the feeling among the band was one of horror. They had been brought up in a nice village community, it was hardly gritty and urban. Displays of violence were the stuff of the movies. This soon gave way to feelings of renewed admiration for Freddie. He had taken action which reflected the collective will of the band, but perhaps he had additional motivation for doing what he had done. Perry was the first to offer his take on it. Holding the side of his face, he rose to his feet and laughed, it was sardonic and malicious.

"Oh now it becomes clear," he revelled in the attention. "We know why she's in the band now, don't we?" The band looked around at each other, but mainly at Charmian. Nobody knew of any romance, requited or otherwise, between Charmian and Freddie. Perry saw his chance to undermine the group dynamic.

"You bastards will get what you deserve. You can't drop me for this fucking bimbo without facing the consequences."

Freddie played into his hands by stepping forward to plant another punch on him. Charmian yelled for him to stop, and he did.

"Ha!" Perry snapped, "You're pathetic, all of you. You'll regret this."

"Threats? Is that what you have been reduced to? Is it Perry? Is that the range of your abilities?" said Neil.

Perry stopped walking and turned to look at them.

"You have no idea what I am capable of."

Bhatta had found himself hunched forward as The Proles' story had been told. The others had contributed some small details but the bulk of it had been imparted by Adrian. Bhatta sat back in his chair and let out a long breath.

"Okay, thank you for telling me that. You were right to come here and I understand your reluctance to implicate Perry unnecessarily. It is because of the threat he made that you think he might have had something to do with it, right?"

They all nodded mournfully.

"You were supposed to be rehearsing on the night of the train crash?"

"Yes," said Charmian, "but the session was cut short because of some Council meeting or something. A man came in and sent us away."

Although nobody said so, it was clear that The Proles had had a lucky escape from the collapse of the Village Hall. Bhatta kept the youngsters' focused on the matter in hand.

"But Perry Vanaugh didn't know that your rehearsal had been cut short?"

"After what had happened the last time, we had nothing to say to Perry anyway. Nobody told him."

"Is Perry the hot-headed type then?" asked Bhatta.

"Yeah, he loses it sometimes," said Adrian as the others nodded.

"Okay. I want to see you all individually tomorrow to make statements. How old are you?"

"Sixteen."

"Sixteen."

"Seventeen."

"Seventeen."

"You two will need to be accompanied by a parent," he said to Adrian and Charmian.

"What are you going to do, about Perry I mean?" asked Freddie.

"I'm going to ask him what he was up to on the night of the train crash and check his story thoroughly. Remember," he sat forward again, "you have done the right thing today. Don't beat yourselves up about it. If Perry is not involved in the train crash, I will find that out, and if he was, I will find that out too."

CHAPTER FOURTEEN

Bhatta was sifting through the mountain of witness statements. He assured himself that the task would be made worse if not for the office staff he had deployed to separate the wheat from the chaff. Most of the pile had been placed in the 'unused' tray. The remainder contained accounts from individuals which could have some evidential value. A decision about each one had to be made, and it fell to him to make it.

It was brain-numbing work. Many of them covered the same elements of the story with only subtle differences between them. After every two or three of these submissions, he had to get up and walk around the room to clear his head. The spectre of him having missed some vital wisp of evidence loomed over him and provided another strain of motivation, as if he needed that. It was during one of these breaks that there was a knock on the office door.

"Come in!" he called, swiftly checking that his tie was straight and his appearance was consistent with his role. The door opened and Melanie Sharpe entered. Bhatta knew that she was about to disclose something sensitive when she closed the door before speaking.

"I am sure I've seen Guy Maxlow in the village."

"When was this?" asked Bhatta, recalling the heated exchange they had experienced with Maxlow in Manchester.

"Today."

"Tell me what you saw."

Sharpe perched on a chair against the side wall and relayed her story.

"I was in Eckscarfe, tidying up some outstanding actions when I saw a big, flash car I hadn't seen before. It wasn't the same one, but it did remind me of the Mercedes that we seized from Maxlow. This one was a BMW 7 series. I watched it go past me then it turned off the main road. I was on foot so I lost sight of it for a minute or so, but I saw it again and I am sure it was Maxlow getting out of it. He went into a house and was there about five minutes. I saw him come out and get into the back of the car. It drove away, I don't know where to."

"Oh did he now? I suppose it was being driven by his man, Fentley," pondered Bhatta, whose mind was racing with the possibilities, one of them that Fentley might have a lot to say if he no longer worked for Maxlow. "Did you get the car number?"

"Yeah, it came back to a leasing company, head office in London."

"Contact them and find out who they are leasing it to," he ordered.

"Will do," she acknowledged. "I was surprised about the premises he visited. Can't have been a social call."

"Go on Mel, whose house?"

"He went to the home of Councillor Loretta Rokestone. What do you think they were talking about in their five minutes?"

"Sometimes, the most direct route is the most appropriate," said Bhatta with a philosophical air. "Get your coat, we are also going to see the good Councillor and our conversation might take more than five minutes."

They reached Kingfisher Cottage at dusk. No artificial lighting was in operation but there was sufficient ambient illumination to get them safely to the door. A single light was on somewhere in the house. It took some time for the door ringer to be answered. When the door did open, it was only by three inches until the chain prevented any further movement. Bhatta recalled how there was no such security measure in place on the occasion of their previous visit. That was not the only notable difference. Loretta Rokestone's eyes were locked open in an unmistakable expression of distress. Gone was the confidence of the pillar of the community who missed no opportunity to tell everyone about it. Instead, there was a trembling and fragile middle-aged woman with smudged make-up and untidy hair.

"Councillor Rokestone, good evening," said Bhatta, fully expecting her to recognise them and open the door. She did not move. It was as though she was unable to process what she was looking at or what was being said. Bhatta ended the awkward silence.

"Councillor, you remember us? Inspector Bhatta and PC Sharpe. We would like to ask you some further questions please."

Still nothing. Bhatta and Sharpe exchanged a glance then looked back at the vulnerable little face peering over the security chain.

"Ms Rokestone, are you alright? You seem, well, not quite yourself." He hoped a change in tone would bring about a change in response. It did at least provoke some dialogue.

"I'm . . . it's . . . erm."

"Councillor Rokestone. I am concerned about you. Please allow us to afford you some help."

"No!" she snapped, "I don't need anything."

"Well," interrupted Sharpe, "you can reassure us of that by opening the door and putting our minds at rest about it. As soon as we have done that we can leave you in peace. How about it?"

Mel Sharpe's change of approach worked. The door closed and the chain was removed. When the door fully opened, the previously ebullient Parish and County Councillor appeared shorter and older than she had done before. She held the lapels of her cashmere cardigan tight across her throat in a futile gesture of self-protection. Sharpe led them through to the lounge where the only light was from an angle-poised desk lamp, rendering the rest of the room in a gloom. Sharpe switched on the main ceiling light and instantly lifted the ambient malaise.

"Has something upset you Councillor?" asked Bhatta in a tone more conciliatory than before. Loretta Rokestone had gathered her wits sufficiently to realise that her appearance was a mess and that she was emotionally delicate.

"I am sorry. I have just received some rather upsetting news. I would rather not speak of it, if you don't mind. It has knocked me for six. I'm sure I will be myself again when the shock wears off."

Bhatta was not going to be put off what he came for. The Councillor had recovered her faculties to a degree, which was sufficient for her to be capable of answering his questions.

"How was this news delivered to you?"

"I, don't know what you mean." She remained defensive but with an evident lack of resolve.

Sharpe considered stepping in again but decided not to. She had got away with it once, but another intervention would be pushing her luck. She remained silent whilst the Inspector occupied the driver's seat.

"Was it a visitor to your house, perhaps?" he enquired, knowingly.

"I don't see that it is any of your business who . . ."

"You have had a caller earlier today, haven't you Councillor?"

Loretta Rokestone froze once again.

"You know what it is that we are investigating, don't you?" asked Bhatta calmly and quietly.

"Yes, of course."

"And you understand that the questions we must ask are important and you aren't in a position to decide on that."

"I understand that, Inspector."

"So please tell me why Guy Maxlow came to see you today."

Sharpe was relieved that she had left it to Bhatta to pose the question. Cllr Rokestone took in a deep breath and closed her eyes. When she opened them again her voice had regained some of her customary strength.

"Have you been watching my home? I suppose you saw everyone who came here, did you?"

"No. We have been watching for certain activities in Eckscarfe, persons of interest, you understand. We are aware that Mr Maxlow came to this house. What for?"

Cllr Rokestone sank into an armchair and let out a heavy sigh.

"He came to tell me that he intends to submit another planning application for his proposed executive home development." She virtually spat the words in evident contempt. "He seems to think that his prospects for getting planning consent are now better than they were."

"Because most of those on the Council who objected to his plans are no longer in a position to do so. Is that what has upset you?"

She took out a handkerchief and dabbed at her eyes and nose. "Would that not upset you Inspector?"

"It probably would," he agreed. "Why did he want to speak to you alone? Why not communicate through official channels?"

"That is not the sort of man he is. He wants me to support his application and he doesn't want to wait until the formal hearing."

"Did he offer any inducements to you?"

"No nothing like that. I hardly need the money."

"Did he threaten you in any way?"

"I have answered enough questions for now." She resumed her timid manner again, rapidly dabbing her face with the hankie.

Sharpe and Bhatta silently agreed that it was time to go. They reached the front door, thanked their hostess for her help and headed to the car. The front door of Kingfisher Cottage closed and the hall light went out. Once in the car, Sharpe let out what she was thinking.

"Everyone who came here. She said something about us seeing everyone who came here."

"What are you getting at?" asked Bhatta in a manner aimed at facilitation of the airing of her thoughts.

"When I saw Maxlow leave in the BMW, I hung around for a bit to see if anything else was happening."

"And did it?"

"Well something did. I saw Nadine Leshman come to the house. She went around the back though.

She was still here when I left to come and tell you about Maxlow."

"Leshman, Leshman." Bhatta flicked through the virtual card-index in his head and found the one he was looking for. "That's Victor Leshman's wife isn't it?"

"That's right. I didn't know that there was any link between them. I mean, they are not exactly on the same social strata," she said, uncomfortable about playing to old, class stereotypes. Bhatta did the same but without the discomfort.

"Maybe she's the cleaner."

"Nadine didn't say anything about it when we did the house-to-house. Besides, Nadine works at the school, I recall," offered Sharpe.

"No, she didn't say anything to us," he mused. "What if she is friends with Loretta Rokestone? Unlikely, I know but, if you were to receive a distressing visit, on your own, from somebody who has tried to intimidate you, you would probably call a friend, wouldn't you? And that friend would come over and offer some crumb of comfort."

"She didn't look like she had received any comfort," observed Sharpe. "She looked like she had seen a ghost. That doesn't add up. She gets a visit from Maxlow about two hours ago. If they only discussed what she said they discussed, she has had ages to calm down from that. Maybe the friend, Nadine, didn't have any words of comfort to add. She could have made things worse."

"How?" said Bhatta.

"I don't know, but whatever it was, Cllr Rokestone didn't think it appropriate to tell us about her visit."

"There's another way of finding out," he said with a note of mischief.

"We are going to ask Nadine, aren't we?" Sharpe was beginning to predict his thought patterns.

"Yes we are. A bit late now but tomorrow, hopefully. There is something in my head that says that we are headed down a blind alley with this, but the devil is in the detail and this is one issue that is yet to reach any conclusion. I hope that Loretta told Nadine something that she didn't tell us. I know we are in the realm of hearsay but it is worth pursuing. This Maxlow bloke has a clear motive for arranging the train crash. Anything he has said to anyone has potential for evidence."

*

"Let's recap what we have?" said Janette Lane-Wright in the rail crash incident room. She summarised the sighting of the quadbike, the placing of the dummy under the bridge and the cutting of the track. A diagram was used to create a timeline of these events. It showed the proximity to the village and the access points which could have been used by the offender. When she appeared to have reached her conclusion, Bhatta and Sharpe exchanged a glance. He stood up and systematically dissected the suspects and outstanding lines of enquiry.

"Guy Maxlow, property developer. Clear motive because the Parish Council had rejected his plans for building new houses, big ones. Maxlow's car was seen in Eckscarfe in the evening of the crash. It could have been his driver, Andrew Fentley." Bhatta flipped a page in his notes. "Wayne Crewgard. Made a model of the crash in his house. Recently displayed erratic and angry behaviour, excessive drinking. The missing explosives at the quarry has fallen flat due to questionable record-keeping. A bit of a loner but not previously known to the police."

He rifled through his notes before looking up again.

"Perry Vanaugh. This young man made a threat to get his own back on his former bandmates in The Proles. He knew that the band were due to have a rehearsal in the Village Hall. A bit hot-headed, by all accounts. He was expelled from a boarding school down south two years ago, set fire to one of the buildings, apparently. Who has spoken to him since the house-to-house?"

Nobody responded.

"Right. We need to keep an eye on him. If he was involved there's every chance that he won't be able to keep it to himself. Speak to the people he would speak to and pin down his movements before and during the crash."

Sharpe scribbled on a notepad then she pushed another sheet of paper across the desk toward him. He glanced at it then continued with his summary.

"Victor Leshman."

A voice from the back of the room expressed some surprise.

"Wasn't he alibied out of it, Sir?"

Bhatta explained his reasons for not eliminating Leshman from the enquiry.

"Leshman worked on railway maintenance until he was burned in an accident at work. The investigation concluded that he was at fault and, as a result, won't pay out any compensation. The story was covered in the local press quite extensively at the time. The house-to-house team spoke to his wife, Nadine, who provided him with an alibi for the evening on the crash. She may be vulnerable to intimidation and has provided the alibi under duress. Victor Leshman has the clearest motive for seeking revenge on the railway company. We must also consider the possibility that Nadine could be involved."

A mass groan of disbelief wafted around the room. Lane-Wright interjected,

"I don't see why that is so hard to accept. Just because the perpetrator has cut though metal rails does not mean that it has to have been carried out by a man. Let's not be closed-minded to any possibility, please. Nadine Leshman has a motive every bit as strong as Victor's. The railway company's refusal to pay out has affected her too." The suitably admonished assembly fell silent once again. She nodded to Bhatta to press on.

"The group of teenaged delinquents in the village have come under suspicion, at least by their neighbours. All we know is that they have been carrying out a small-scale campaign of civil disobedience and the oldies are fed up of it. According to some luminaries of Eckscarfe they are master criminals, hell bent on overthrowing the functions of state. In reality, they are just bored teenagers getting their kicks by rebelling a little. The question is, did their mischief go horribly wrong and cause the crash?"

This generated some quiet muttering and exchange of views but no formal contribution to the briefing was made. Bhatta had more to add.

"What makes these boys difficult to overlook is that they were detained by the BTP spraying graffiti on railway property only yesterday. They seem to have something against the railway. I want the earlier accounts of their movements looking at again, please."

"Other potential lines of enquiry," he said by way of changing the subject. "The Parish Councillors who were killed and injured had, in the past, been involved in a voluntary capacity with the Eckscarfe Hall Special School. There were a lot of worrying issues surrounding the school. The Governors, and others, were blamed for its failings. The parents of the kids there were pretty vocal about their disappointments and there were some allegations to the effect that there was an acceptance, or a culture if you like, of aggressive discipline. They were investigated by the education authorities, but nobody was formally charged with any abuses. Either way, there remains the possibility of some animosity toward the people who had been running the school. McAulden, Hurlington, Posner and Ullenorth were all involved as volunteers."

"What sort of abuse was investigated?" Lane-Wright reminded everyone that she did have her finger on the pulse.

"Assaults, mainly. Corporal punishments, extra tasks, more exercise. Not good for those not cut out for that sort of thing," Bhatta answered.

"Any suggestion of sexual abuse?" asked the exhibits officer, "That can be a strong motive for revenge."

"Not that we know of," said Bhatta, "but we can trawl our own records of such allegations as well as the school archives. Speaking to past pupils is another possibility. They all had diagnosed conditions that would make it difficult to gain evidential accounts from them. It's all rather speculative, we have more specific lines of enquiry to concentrate on at the moment, but we will get around to it."

"What about the kitchen porter from the Barley Mow? Any news on him?" asked the S.I.O. Bhatta sighed,

"The action raised to trace, interview and eliminate him is still live and unresolved. We did have a bloke in custody at Pendale who we thought was the missing kitchen hand. He ran from the police during the night before last but they caught him and brought him in. He denied being Gregor. We took Sophia Grejzni to Pendale to identify him but she eventually confirmed that it was the wrong guy. I don't know what took her so long to decide, but she was sure in the end. The Immigration people are dealing with that fellow now. As for Gregor, if that is his real name, he arrived there two weeks before the crash and speculatively asked for work. According to the landlord, Marcus Grejzni, Gregor's language skills were poor but he could understand English. He put him to work in the kitchen and gave him some basic accommodation over the function room at the back. He hardly spoke to anyone, choosing to spend his free time, not that he had much, out walking by the lake and on the fells or watching DVDs in his room to improve his English.

"Then we have the builder, Tommy Liddle. We haven't managed to pin him down for an account of his movements on the fourth. He must know we are keen to speak to him but he is an awkward type, by all accounts. He has access to metal-cutting equipment but a motive has yet to emerge."

When the briefing was over and new actions had been allocated, Peter Keld came to the Incident Room to speak to Bhatta.

"Inspector, can I have a minute?"

"Sure Peter, come in."

As they walked to the office, Bhatta was anticipating some confrontation from Keld. Ever since the train crash, his life had been turned upside down. His son was a suspect, his reputation in his community was damaged and his future as the village copper was in doubt. This meant that his long-term occupancy of the police house, which was conditional to his deployment was also hanging in the balance. Bhatta steeled himself for conflict but it did not come. Keld was more professional than Bhatta had privately given him credit for. The reason for his visit was entirely operational.

"It took me a while but I recognised someone after the train crash. I've only just remembered where I knew him from."

"Who are you talking about?"

"Clive O'Flindall."

Bhatta took a few seconds to register that name, it was familiar but how? Keld sensed that delay and intervened.

"He is the Salvation Army bloke, dishing out the tea and sympathy in the aftermath."

"Yes, I've got him now," said Bhatta, still at a loss as to the relevance of Keld's concerns.

"Well," said Keld by way of preparing himself, "I've met him before, years ago, when I was a new recruit in Newcastle. He had a different name then. He was called Albert Kingston Halifax. I didn't nick him for anything but I remember escorting him to court and guarding him there. I hadn't seen him in twenty years, until now."

"Changing your name isn't a crime, Peter." Bhatta pointed out the obvious in the hope of moving the conversation on.

"No, it's not that. It's more about why he was here, considering what he used to get up to."

"Go on."

"He was a petty thief back then. A bit of a pathetic type, no mates, no status, you know?"

"I get the picture."

"Well, he came across a fire. It started in the basement of a block of old folks' flats. It had spread up to the ground floor and was getting really bad when Halifax, or O'Flindall, raised the alarm. He called out the Fire Brigade and ran in to get the old residents out. He carried several of them to safety before the fire guys got there. He inhaled smoke and was injured but he got them out."

"He's a hero then?" said Bhatta.

"Yes, well, he was. It got in the local papers, 'Hero saves pensioners from fire.' For the first time in his life, he wasn't a complete loser, he was somebody. It would have been a good news story but for what happened next."

"Go on Peter."

"He did it again three months later. The fire hadn't got going but it appeared that he had started it himself. There was insufficient evidence to charge him with anything at the time. Anyway, when I recognised him and could finally put a name to him, I did some ringing round to neighbouring forces. It turns out that he did similar things in other places. He claimed to have seen someone jump into the river at high water in York. He had jumped in to save them but couldn't get hold of them. He had got himself out before the police arrived. Another story happened in Leeds a few years after. This one involved him rescuing a mental patient from the roof of a shopping centre. The poor soul was a mute and the police only had Halifax's word for what happened. The last one happened in Carlisle. He rang 999 saying that someone was lying on the railway track in the middle of the night. The line was closed whilst they searched it all but it came to nothing. Now, either this is the unluckiest bloke in the country or he creates his own opportunities to be a hero."

"Some sort of fantasist, is he?" observed Bhatta, who was now getting the reason for Keld's visit.

"That's the consensus of those who have met him. Always insufficient evidence to charge him with anything but coincidence can only stretch so far."

"I don't like that Carlisle incident. If he has moved on to stopping trains, that could put him in the frame here."

"There's another thing Sir," said Keld, "I looked through the incident log for the night of the crash. There is no record of anyone informing the Salvation Army about the incident at Eckscarfe. I've asked around the people who were there on the night and they didn't call them either. It seems that Halifax/O'Flindall set up his Salvation Army tea wagon without any invitation. How did he get to know about the disaster?"

CHAPTER FIFTEEN

The parents of sixteen-year-old Perry Vanaugh were used to accompanying him into disciplinary meetings. All previous educational establishments attended by Perry had, at least once, carried out such interventions and one or both of his parents had reluctantly participated. It had reached the point where they argued as to whose turn it was.

They were both professional people and high earners in their respective fields. His mother was an accountant and his father a bank manager, although neither of them could manage or account for their son's woeful inability to keep out of trouble. Moving to Eckscarfe whilst Perry had been away at boarding school, they had hoped that a change of location would bring about a change of behaviour. Nice village, nice people, nicer Perry. That had been the plan.

Initially, there was some relief that Perry had steered clear of the more obviously delinquent assembly of Noel Keld, Gary Nicholls and Hugh Barron. His choice of friends was pleasing and their formation of The Proles had provided them with something constructive and wholesome to do. This did not fully divert from his sudden outbursts of temper. Perry had the shortest of all fuses and whilst his energy and enthusiasm for the progress of the group was undeniable, he rarely acknowledged that any decisions could be made by anyone but him. When the band took the decision to impose the ultimate sanction, he had been forced to play the victim. That was not right. He was never the victim. Others were his victims, that was how it was supposed to be – at least in Perry's world anyway.

"Perry," began Mel Sharpe once the formalities of introduction were complete, "you have been asked here today because of some things you said, some threats you made before the train crash. Can you recall what I am talking about?"

Perry shuffled in his seat. He may have been as tall as most adults but his manner was that of a small, petulant child, albeit a child with a swollen and bruised cheekbone. He initially refused to speak at all. His mother made some gestures but her meagre efforts had no effect.

"You have not been arrested, not yet anyway, Perry. You have, by your conduct, brought suspicion on yourself. Now, what I want to know is what you did on the day of the train crash. Is there anything you want to tell me about that, Perry?" There was no response.

"Alright Perry, let me put it like this. You made threats to your former bandmates in The Proles. You were angry that you had been replaced as lead singer and you went to the rehearsal in the Village Hall to express your disappointment. Am I right so far, Perry?"

At least this new line of questioning had made him look at his interrogator, but still he did not say anything. Sharpe pressed on.

"There was an angry exchanged of views which resulted in a fight."

"I was assaulted!" Perry broke his silence to put his case as the innocent party.

"Alright, you were assaulted. Who by?"

"Freddie Parr, the arsehole."

"And that was how you came by the injury to your face?"

"Yeah."

"Do you remember what you said as you left?"

"No."

"You said that you would get them back for what they had done to you, or words to that effect. Did you say that?"

"I might have said something that sounded like that but I didn't mean anything by it. There's only one of me and three of them, and that girl."

"Where were you at the time of the rail crash?"

"I can't remember."

"Yes, you can. Where were you when you heard about it?"

"My Dad told me. I was at home."

"So, now that you can recall that day, tell me about the rest of it."

"I didn't go to college, I'm suspended. I was here in Eckscarfe all day."

"Doing what?"

"Playing 'Call of War' mostly."

"Did you go out?"

"I went out for a bit."

"What did you do?"

"Why all these stupid questions? I've done nothing wrong."

"Just explain what you did please."

"I went out once."

"Where?"

"To the Village Hall. I wanted to wait for Freddie and get him back for this." He pointed to his swollen and discoloured cheek.

"When did you go there?"

"About seven o'clock, I suppose."

"What happened when you got there?"

"Nothing. I expected to hear them rehearsing but I heard nothing. I waited for a bit, then I gave up and went home."

"Did you go to Shipley Road?"

"No."

"Or the railway line?"

"No. Why would I?"

"You cause a lot of disruption when you have a mind to, don't you Perry?"

"Oh, you mean that thing at boarding school. That wasn't my idea. I was there, that was all. I didn't set fire to anything."

"But you were expelled for that."

"Yeah, but I wasn't the one who did it. I wouldn't do stuff like that."

"But you did threaten your former bandmates in The Proles, didn't you?"

"I'd just had my face broken! You would have been angry too."

"What did you mean when you made that threat?"

"Nothing. I meant nothing. I didn't go through with it so it meant nothing."

The interview was concluded and Perry was released without charge. He remained a suspect as the reasons for suspecting him were yet to be discounted and his account of his movements could not be verified. Bhatta felt growing discomfort at the number of suspects who could not be ruled out. If, as most investigations tended to be, it was a process of elimination, then why was he continually unable to eliminate anyone?

*

In the bar of the Barley Mow at Eckscarfe, Keith Marlin was having the Ploughman's whilst Dan

Delerouso had opted for the BLT. Each was accompanied by a pint of German lager.

"It's obvious that the cops are chasing their own tails and getting nowhere," declared Marlin. That Superintendent, Lane-Wright – "

"Lane-Wrong!" interrupted Delerouso, showing his command of language and spontaneous humour.

"Ha! Yeah, Lane-Wrong, good one." Marlin was keen to keep his train of thought. "She's hardly ever in the Incident Room and her lackey, Bhatta, doesn't know what he is doing."

"I like that bird, Melanie Sharpe. I could go for that," announced Delerouso as though he was bestowing a royal seal of approval.

"Anything in a skirt, eh Dan?"

"You can talk," objected Delerouso. "You've had some dodgy romps over the years." Marlin had to concede to that. He did so with considerable pride in how irresistible he was to all women.

"Any port in a storm, you know me. You gotta find your fun, even in a sheep-fest like this place. The only flesh I've seen was spilling out of hiking boots."

Delerouso paused with his sandwich only an inch from his open mouth. A smile grew on him as a realisation dawned. He knew Marlin well and had learned to spot the signs. He pointed an accusing finger at Marlin and said.

"You're screwing someone here aren't you?"

Marlin smirked then he tore off a hunk of wholemeal bread dipped in chutney and stuffed it into his mouth. When it was partly chewed, he said,

"Not yet, but I have my eye on our young freelancer, the conscientious Miss Wicker. There's something appealing about her."

"She's a bit naïve, don't you think?" suggested Delerouso.

"Yeah," laughed Marlin, "that's what's appealing to me. She's ambitious but green. I'll offer her an introduction to the big league and she'll be grateful, very grateful."

"You haven't got any influence like that, not in our industry."

"Probably not, but she doesn't know that." He crunched down on a pickled onion.

Delerouso's expression straightened into formality as he looked over Marlin's shoulder at the front door of the pub. Marlin turned his head and saw the object of his lustful intentions entering the bar. Behind her was the Times' man Hugo Latimer. Delerouso leapt at an opportunity to tease.

"It looks like that posh twat from Knightsbridge has stepped in before you Keith. You snooze, you lose, huh?" Marlin was not going to be put-off easily.

"She wants a real man, not some powder-puff plum-sucker like that. Besides, my expense account makes his look like a charity case. Same again?"

Delerouso nodded and Marlin darted to the bar, arriving just before Marci Wicker could order anything.

"Let me get that," demanded Marlin, "Gotta give our freelancer a slice of the expenses pie. What will you have?"

"I'll get my own thank you." She sent out a clear message, which Marlin instantly ignored. He turned to the barman and, without waiting for him to finish serving someone else, ordered a glass of medium white wine for the lady.

"You don't listen, do you?" she protested, "I don't want a drink."

"Oh yes you do," he said without looking at her. She was about to reiterate her declaration of independence, but she changed her mind when the landlord, Markus Grejzni, emerged from the door to the cellar steps and headed behind the bar. She turned away and without looking at Keith Marlin said,

"Bring it over here then."

Marlin allowed himself a smug grin, which he shared with the hapless Latimer. It was not by any means certain, but Marlin felt that Latimer also had designs on the rookie, and he had tried to push him out of the running. Latimer, whose refreshment preference was not included in Marlin's bar order, waited until the barman was available before ordering a small glass of Shiraz. As he waited, he leaned over to Marlin and offered him some advice.

"Go easy on the pickled onions, old chap. What?"

Marlin's expression was enough to show that Latimer had dislodged his self-confidence, at least for a moment. He sloped away to join Marci Wicker in a window bay near to where Delerouso was finishing his lunch. He curled his lip in contempt at Marlin's failure to buy him the drink he had promised.

Straining to stand due to a recently sustained foot injury, he limped to the bar to get his own drink.

Marci Wicker sat with her back to the bar and seemed to be looking out of the window and onto the main road. Ignoring his previous companion, Marlin slipped onto the bench seat and tried to turn on the charm.

"Glad you saw things my way, sweetheart. Cheers!"

She barely acknowledged his presence and swerved custom by leaving her drink untouched on the brass-topped table. She let out a heavy breath and without looking at him she said,

"The cops aren't saying much about this train crash. I reckon they are nowhere near a breakthrough. Have you heard anything?"

"I might have," he teased her by playing on her desire to get up the journo ladder, the one he believed himself to have ascended to a status worthy of her admiration, "I could give you some info about it - if you're nice to me." He slurped his pint without taking his eyes off her. She sipped her drink and swallowed harder than was necessary. She was no cover-model, but she wasn't ugly either. She had brown eyes made wider by obviously false eyelashes and short brunette hair with a fringe past her eyebrows. She had more energy than patience.

"Nice to you?" she enquired, demanding an explanation.

"Yeah," he grinned, "a bit of mutual back scratching never hurts. That's how this business works, you know?"

"And you are going to be my guide through the minefield of the world of journalism, are you?"

"You got it, babe." He wiped his mouth on his cuff. "Look, there's no point in me having this expense account if I can't 'share the love' as they say. I've got a room here." He darted his eyes upward indicating that the Barley Mow was his present domicile. "Have you got some digs or does your freelancer budget not stretch to that?" She chose to ignore that question and pose one of her own instead.

"What do you reckon about the crash? Who's behind it?" Whilst he was looking for some fun, she was looking for a breakthrough in the rail crash story.

Marlin was bored of that. He had better things to concentrate on, particularly her. The remote, rural community provided too narrow a range of leisure pursuits for his liking. However, he had suggested a mutual benefit between for them, so it was only going to happen if she felt that he was playing the game.

"Alright, here it is. As I see it, the CID are short of ideas, here. There's an opportunity for someone to make a name for themselves by cracking it before the cops do."

He meant her. He had, in his opinion, already made a name for himself.

"I have always thought, 'if in doubt, go with the money.' There's always 'readies' behind it, you just have to follow it and see who it leads to."

"So you think that somebody did this for money?"

"I have found that it is usually the case, yeah."

"How, in this scenario?" She leaned forward in a conspiratorial manner. He did the same.

"Who gains from the train crash? Let's start with the developer, Maxlow. He was turned down for planning permission for a site that would have netted him millions. He might have better luck with a new Council."

"Alright. Is that your theory?"

"It's one of them. There's the local builder, Tommy Liddle. Who gets to rebuild the damaged buildings? Liddle made a good earner when he built the Village Hall a couple of years ago. He has been on the bones of his arse since."

"What does that mean, bones of his arse?"

"Skint! No money, danger of going out of business. Christ, where are you from?"

"New Zealand, recently."

"Oh, okay, that explains it. Look, if Liddle gets the job of rebuilding the place, he would be back solvent again. Clear motive and he's right here with the equipment he would need to be able to cut through metal."

"Would he have meant to kill those people inside and risk the ones on the train?"

"He probably didn't think of that."

"That's a bit thin, don't you think?"

"Maybe."

"What's this Maxlow character like?" she asked, making mental notes of all of the key points.

Marlin was tiring of the conversation. He wanted an unearned and uncomplicated romp in the convenient room above their heads and such talk was delaying the inevitable.

"I don't know. A businessman, I suppose. He gets what he wants, one way or another."

"Well," she said in conversational conclusion. "Thanks for the drink," which she had hardly touched, "I must go. Lots to do."

"Erm, what about . . . you know?" his eyes darted toward the ceiling, suggesting that his bedroom suggestion had been already agreed. She paused and sat back down.

"I'll tell you what, Stud. You prove that these deaths were all a part of a money-making scheme by unscrupulous business people and corrupt locals, and I will reconsider your tempting offer. What's a girl to do?"

She blew a flippant kiss and swept out of the front door of the pub leaving Marlin, Delerouso and Latimer all staring at each other. Marlin was crestfallen but tried to brave it out. He felt as though he had spent the last twenty minutes vigorously back-scratching and had gained nothing more than an itch.

"Well, gentlemen," said the smooth-voice of Hugo Latimer. "That appears to be the way to a lady's heart these days. No place for chivalry, I suppose."

"Shut up Latimer," snapped Marlin. "If one of us does beat the cops to the punchline in this joke of a place, it will be worth more than a roll in the hay with her."

"I sense a challenge," beamed Delerouso. "This job just got interesting."

"That does make it interesting, I must admit," mused Latimer. "Of course, there is nothing in it for either of us if Miss Wicker gets there first."

*

Without a current address for Captain Clive O'Flindall of the Salvation Army, calls were made, by Incident Room staff, to the national head office. The result was that a message had reached O'Flindall who responded by calling Pendale Incident Room. It was arranged for him to attend to be spoken to by the team.

O'Flindall arrived in full military and religious garb. He was of average height, slightly overweight, jowly, and had a weathered complexion. There was a look of righteousness in his expression and his manner of talking was that of a Georgian parson. He spoke to Bhatta and Sharpe as though he were softening them up for full conversion to his ideas of faith. Both Bhatta and Sharpe privately, and respectively, anticipated racial and gender prejudice. There was no clear reason for this as he was yet to say anything. He was just the sort of pompous, narrow-minded person who would.

"Mr O'Flindall, thank you for - "

"Ahem, it's Captain O'Flindall actually," interrupted the Salvation Army man.

Bhatta had to make a decision as to how this was going to be. There was a golden rule in police culture that you must control the interview and not allow the interviewee to take the reins. The balance could usually be found later in court, where the lawyers had the upper hand. Bhatta chose to allow O'Flindall to be acknowledged as he wished to be. That was as far as Bhatta was prepared to stretch.

"Captain Clive O'Flindall," he said. O'Flindall nodded his approval. Bhatta continued.

"You were at Eckscarfe during the night after the train crash. Please tell me what your involvement was."

"Certainly. Anything to assist the Constabulary, you know. I was talking to the Chief Constable only last month about public support for his officers. I shall have something else to speak about next time I see him at a function."

Both Bhatta and Sharpe hoped that their thoughts were not being given away in their facial expressions.

"And on the night of the fourth?" Bhatta steered him back to the point.

"Ah yes, a terrible, tragic business. It is at times like those that the best and the worst in people comes to the surface. I staffed the refreshment cabin and offered what meagre spiritual support I could to those who had suffered." He put his hands together as though in prayer as he spoke. "People see us as a beacon of compassion in a storm of distress. It may come in the form of tea and sandwiches, but it is the human contact that counts the most."

The sermon would have gone on but for Bhatta's intervention.

"How did you get to hear about the train crash?"

"Ah, the Lord moves in mysterious ways," he smiled knowingly. Bhatta was losing patience. He hardened his tone of voice by a few degrees.

"How did you get to hear about the train crash?"

"Well, I received a call and I answered it."

"Who called you?"

"Is that important, really?" That I came and served the needy was the main thing."

"Where do you live?"

"Why, I live near York."

"Were you at home when you received that call?"

"No, I was away from home, doing God's work."

"Where were you?"

"I was quite near to this part of the world, actually."

"Doing what?"

"I told you, God's work." Bhatta consulted his notes for a few seconds then looked up at O'Flindall.

"You used to have a different name, didn't you?" O'Flindall stared blankly at him but did not speak. "Your name was Halifax, Albert Halifax. Wasn't it?" Again there was no answer. "You lived in the Newcastle area a few years ago and you came to the notice of the police there. You were suspected of staging events from which you could emerge as the hero of the hour. One of these incidents was at Carlisle. It involved interference with the movement of a train. Now, I am keen to know how a man who has done that in the past, happens to be near here at the time of the train crash, which was preceded by a similar impediment to the railway. Add that to the plain fact that you won't say why you were near here or how you learned about the train crash and that leads to where we sit right now."

"Are you suggesting that I had something to do with this tragedy?" said O'Flindall through erratic breaths and with weakening indignance.

"Answer my questions and reassure me that you are not," said Bhatta at the same pitch as before. "You were called Halifax, correct?"

"That was a lifetime ago. I am a different person now. A man is allowed to change."

"Yes, you are, but I am investigating murders here. People who don't tell me the truth when asked make me suspicious. Now, tell me about that night."

"I was returning from an event in Glasgow," began a more realistic O'Flindall, "I was in Carlisle when I heard it?"

"Heard what?"

"The police radio channel."

"You were listening to a police channel?"

"Yes, I have a monitor which enables me to do that. I know, strictly speaking I shouldn't, but that is how I can get to the places I am needed quickly. Tell me Inspector, were you there that night?"

"Yes. I was."

"And when would you have got around to calling for the Salvation Army to attend and minister to the suffering?"

Bhatta paused for a moment. O'Flindall's actions were wrong but if he was telling the truth, his motives were noble. What was clear in Bhatta's mind was that there was insufficient evidence to keep O'Flindall any longer. He had, when pressed, answered his questions. However, there was a nagging doubt in Bhatta's mind that anyone who was capable of doing the sort of things that O'Flindall had done in the past, then changing his name afterwards, was capable of anything.

*

"So let me get this straight," began Bhatta as he walked from the car park of the Barley Mow with Mel Sharpe, "The builder, Tommy Liddle refused to answer the door to the house-to-house team when they called on him?"

"That's right. He's got a reputation for getting rather heated with very little reason," explained Sharpe.

"Why does anyone hire him for work if he treats people like that?"

"He is a competent tradesman and he's the only one for miles. Other than that, I don't know. Maybe we can catch him in a good mood."

"I hope so. Besides the quarry and Maxlow, he's the only other fellow that we know of with access to metal-cutting gear. Which reminds me, we need an update from the forensic submissions. Remind me when we get back."

"Will do," she assured him.

They reached the gap in the terraced cottages, which served as the access road to Liddle's yard. The end house was a double-fronted, stone cottage with the year 1725 displayed on a limestone lintel over the doorway along with the initials of the original builder or occupant. There was a distinct absence of any life on display at the front of the house. The dark green painted oak door held the cobwebs and dust of disuse tightly against the frame and the windowpanes were well overdue for cleaning. There seemed no point in knocking.

They went down the rough path, which opened out onto an urban wilderness, a junk-scape, which was hard to take in. A series of lean-to structures barely protected the array of wood, stone, plastic sacks, bricks and machinery beneath. The nose of an old wagon peered out of a dark void and a flat-back transit van rested against the rear wall of the house. Dirty tarpaulin sheets partly covered the debris, which resembled a cubist's view of the mind of a madman - or a genius. They paused to take in the mayhem, unaware that they were being watched. The back door of the house came open silently. That silence was smashed by a loud and vicious voice.

"What business do you have here?"

Both Bhatta and Sharpe jumped involuntarily. They turned to see the builder standing on his doorstep with a large hammer in his hand. He held it as one may have held a weapon. He wore old, blue jeans with tears at the knees and with a layer of light-grey dust, a lumberjack shirt of mainly red tartan and faded yellow Cat boots. His expansive belly and several days of grey stubble told a story of self-neglect, but his frame told of a powerful musculature to back up the angry voice.

"If you've nothing to say, be on your way," added the indignant homesteader. Bhatta quickly regained his composure and remembered why they were there.

"You are Mr Tommy Liddle, is that right?"

"Aye, you'd expect no-one else here in my yard."

"I am Inspector Bhatta and this is PC – "

"If that means police, I've now't to say to you. I don't like police. Go on, get out!" He had found another point on his volume control.

Sharpe anticipated that the mood was becoming more confrontational. She also knew that Bhatta was not going to accept Liddle's demand. She slipped a hand into her coat pocket to find her radio, the lifeline for help if needed. Bhatta showed no such apprehension. He was fully calmed and ready to converse.

"I don't recall asking you about your likes and dislikes Mr Liddle." He walked up to Liddle and ascended the steps to reach his level. "But seeing as you have introduced the subject, I will share one of mine. I like it when people greet visitors with some civility. I'm sure you can do that when the need arises. Pretend that I am thinking of hiring you for some building work. That should put you in a better frame of mind."

Liddle released and wrapped his fingers in turn around the handle of the hammer. Bhatta maintained his unruffled manner. Liddle's scowl hardened and the venom in his eyes neared boiling point.

"Your turn to speak, Mr Liddle," said Bhatta staring into Liddle's eyes without blinking. "No? Nothing? Ah well. I shall explain the reason for our visit. You will want to put that hammer down, I expect. Imagine not being able to find your tools in this place."

Liddle stared, the hammer remained gripped in his hand. His bluff had been called and he had no option but to fold. He placed the hammer against the doorframe without breaking eye contact.

"Now Mr Liddle. My officers came to see you after the rail crash, but you chose not to speak to them."

"I've now't to say to you either," growled Liddle in a manner slightly less aggressive than before. "I can't stand your lot."

"My lot? My lot, Mr Liddle?" Bhatta suspected that Liddle's unpleasantness was aggravated by his opinions of race. Liddle had not gone far enough for Bhatta to be certain of that. He had to allow Liddle the benefit of the doubt.

"Yes, your lot, the bloody police! I've no time for you."

"That is because you don't know what I have to ask you. I'm sure I don't have to convince you of the importance of my visit. I am trying to find out who killed several of your neighbours. Murder, Mr Liddle, it doesn't get more serious than that, so I suggest that you get over your 'now't to say' attitude and tell me what I want to know. If you are unable to do that, I shall consider your conduct obstructive and I shall seek a search warrant for your premises. That may take several days, during which, you would have no access to your vehicles, yard or anything in it. Do we understand each other now, Mr Liddle?"

Liddle let out some air and acknowledged that he was beaten.

"No bloody choice, have I?" he snapped, swiftly picking up the hammer and striding down the steps to the yard.

Bhatta followed a few yards behind. He nodded at Sharpe who instantly understood that he wanted her to take notes. She took out her pocketbook and began writing. Liddle persisted in his awkwardness by moving things around in the yard. Bhatta noticed that he was moving the same things back and forth. He managed to get his personal details and those of the other residents of the house. He covered the fact that he employed Nicholls as a labourer.

"Tell me your movements on the day of the rail crash," asked Bhatta.

"Can't remember," snapped Liddle.

"No Mr Liddle, that's not true is it? Nobody in this village is unable to say where they were or what they were doing that day."

"I . . . can't . . . remember," insisted Liddle.

"Being a builder, you will have access to high-powered cutting equipment, that's right isn't it?" asked Bhatta, who gave no indication that he was losing patience with the belligerent builder, although inside he was nearing his limit.

"I might have," said Liddle, teasingly.

"Where is it please, Mr Liddle?"

"It's not here," he sneered, looking at Bhatta for the first time since the interview began in earnest.

Bhatta had heard enough. He reached behind his belt and swiftly snapped a rigid handcuff on Liddle. The second one clicked into place before Liddle could take in what had happened.

"What? Get these off me, I've done now't."

"You are under arrest on suspicion of causing criminal damage to the rail track." He had decided not to arrest him for murder as it may cloud the case at a later time. Criminal Damage was easier to deal with. What he really wanted was the authority to search that yard and Liddle's arrest would achieve that. He continued with his explanation whilst Liddle continued with his protest. Neither man paid any attention to the other.

"The grounds for your arrest are that you possess metal cutting gear which you are trying to keep from the police, your close proximity to the scene of the crash and your refusal to account for your movements of that day. It is necessary to arrest you in order for you to have a solicitor present and for me to be able to properly investigate without interference from you." He cautioned Liddle who, by then, was bellowing like a bereaved cow. His protests, however, were verbal only and when Sharpe had gone to bring the police car to the yard, he got in without any resistance.

The subsequent search of the builders' yard was laborious and time-consuming. Liddle had his own system of storage and security. Layers of dust, plaster and rubble lay over items of questionable value and use. What they were and what relevance they may have had to the investigation was open to broad interpretation. Anything which appeared to be capable of cutting through metal had to be the priority. However, the officers carrying out the search lacked the expertise to be able to determine the range of usage for the machinery found. Decisions had to be made on the spot. Any item which was too big or too cumbersome to be seized was to be photographed in situ for further examination.

Down the side of the main out-building was a narrow path, which also housed tarpaulin-covered items against the outer fence. At the end of that path was a broken gate and beyond that was the rough path which led along the edge of a field and to the railway line in the distance. The tarpaulin covers were so dirty, Mel Sharpe was uncharacteristically reticent to move them. She was wearing her only suit and could ill-afford to render it too dirty to wear. She recalled that Claire owned a suit and, because she spent all of her working day in a tracksuit, she would be happy to lend it to her.

She dragged the cover off, raising a cloud of dust, which made her cough and cover her face. Leaning against the side of the building was a blue plastic sheet, which was comparatively clean. The sheet was lifted to reveal a quadbike. Although it was old, it was clean and appeared functional. It was a Yamaha, with a faded yellow fuel tank. The key had been left in the ignition and it smelled of petrol. Bhatta was called over to inspect it.

"This is coming in," he declared to the team. "Preserve it for Forensics before it goes to the storage unit. It fits the description of the one seen by Rodney Brickshaw just before the train crash. Is there a helmet with it?"

"Haven't found one, not yet anyway," answered the finder.

"Well, keep looking. The witness said that the rider wore a black helmet."

"Do you think that this was used by whoever cut the track, Sir?"

"I'm not certain but it looks like it. It was hidden for some reason. It smells of fuel, so it is probably still capable of being ridden."

"That would implicate Liddle then?"

"It might. Anyone could have put it here but it is Liddle's yard. Wait a minute. What's the name of that lad who works for Liddle, his apprentice?"

Sharpe remembered the name. "It's Gary Nicholls."

Bhatta's memory made another link.

"Is that the lad who found Jonathan Ullenorth's body in the lake?"

"That's him," she confirmed. "How could that tie in with this?" She pointed to the Yamaha.

"I'm just juggling ideas here, but Nicholls 'finds' Ullenorth in the water and the motorbike used to get to and from the point where the train-line was cut is found at Nicholls' place of employment. There's a possible link for you."

"Should we bring Nicholls in for questioning?" she enquired.

Bhatta ran through the pros and cons in his head before deciding.

"Not yet. We have Liddle to speak to first and we haven't examined the bike yet. It would put us in a much stronger position if we had some forensic link to either Liddle or Nicholls and tyre tracks near the railway line or Shipley Road bridge. We can speak to Nicholls later."

"Are you going back to Pendale, Sir?"

"No. I am going to speak to the widow of Jonathan Ullenorth. I want her to answer the questions I can't now ask her husband."

CHAPTER SIXTEEN

Bhatta walked through Eckscarfe, passing the usual activities and features of English village life as he passed by. The sight of a Police Inspector, albeit in plain clothes, had once been worthy of interest, but the events of the past few days had made it commonplace. Life seemed, on the surface at any rate, to be returning to some version of normality. He caught snippets of conversations as he passed people. One such exchange was between an elderly man and younger woman seated on a bench at the bus stop.

"You mark my words," said the man to his disinterested companion. "These things come in threes."

Bhatta hoped that he wasn't talking about the incidents which had resulted in the deaths of the Councillors, but he knew that the people of Eckscarfe were talking about little else. Was the old sage predicting another fatality? Bhatta shook off that thought as he passed the village store where a huddle of women had gathered on the pavement outside by the fresh fruit display.

"They are saying that he did himself in through grief at losing his friends," offered one oracle of village events.

"Ooh, that poor soul. Where will it all end?" added a shorter woman clutching the handle of a small, tartan shopping trolley.

Bhatta carried on without pausing to hear more. He stopped to look at the floral tributes adorning the plinth of the village cross. An array of early summer colour, which should have brought joy but only expressed pain and loss.

Light traffic weaved along the main street. Were the drivers local people going about their business, or had they come to see the scene of tragedy, like ghoulish voyeurs feasting on the suffering of others? Bhatta had spent enough time there to be able to feel something of their collective angst, sense its indignation at this affront to its peaceful identity. To Bhatta, Eckscarfe represented an unresolved puzzle, a tragedy incapable of healing itself, the scene of desperation and limbo. 'Scratch the surface and what do you have?'

Across the main road the door of the butchers' shop was open, and a gathering of shoppers could be seen inside. They were all facing each other and were talking animatedly. Nobody was looking at the produce on offer. He silently asked himself. 'When will those people have something else to talk about?' He paused to cross the road, waiting for the slow-moving cars to give him an opportunity. 'Who among these people inflicted this pain on the community? Where did the hatred come from?'

He arrived at the house to find the curtains all closed. It looked as though the residents were away.

Only the almost-new four-wheel drive utility vehicle standing proudly outside the double garage suggested that anyone was at home. Knowing the custom in some communities of showing respect for bereavement by closing curtains, Bhatta remained hopeful that his visit was not in vain. He rang the doorbell and, due to occupational habit, stepped back to see if any of the curtains moved. The lounge curtain moved slightly.

An ashen Mary Ullenorth opened the front door. She peered around it through sunken eyes. Her expression was bereft of energy. Bhatta was about to offer his condolences for her loss, but she spoke first.

"I can't see anyone at the moment, I'm sorry." She was about to close the door, but Bhatta stepped forward to appeal for an exemption to her admissions policy.

"Mrs Ullenorth. I am sorry to impose upon you at this most difficult time and I will be as brief as I can be, but I do need to speak to you. I know you will want to know exactly what happened to Jonathan and it is my duty to find out. For that, I need your help. We don't want unanswered questions, I'm sure you agree."

As he spoke, he felt wretched. He was effectively putting pressure on this woman in a time of acute family trauma. The contempt he held for the ruthless nature of the work of the news people he had encountered recently came back to him and it was his own pushy approach, which had evoked that.

Mary Ullenorth dipped her gaze to the floor, resting her forehead on the doorframe. She squeezed her eyes shut, creasing her face for a moment before letting out a long sigh.

"Fine," she uttered in a whisper.

She opened the door to allow him to enter. He stepped inside and wiped his feet, more through habit than necessity. She was dressed in an oversized Arran cardigan and saggy, pink track-pants with the gusset hanging down. She was wearing suede slippers and was clutching a balled-up handkerchief.

She led him through the hall to a reception room he had not been in on his previous visit. He entered a vast yet tastefully furnished room with a baby grand piano at one end. Showroom-standard furniture stood on polished oak flooring between finely woven rugs. A French window let in what should have been ample ambient light, but this failed to lift the overall gloom of the house. She gestured for him to sit and he did so on a leather settee of bottle green. Photographs in frames told of the holiday travels of Jonathan and Mary, hairstyles and colours hinting at the era of each image.

Bhatta considered that Mary Ullenorth appeared deeply traumatised by recent events. He had seen her hysterical at the scene of the train crash and then defiantly protective when Jonathan had been discharged from hospital. On each occasion, it was due to her will to protect the husband who was the centre of her world. He knew that he had to be careful in the way he spoke to her and adopt a less forceful tone than he usually did. Although untrained, he aimed to emulate the communication style of police officers he had worked with previously, who were specially trained to deal with distressed victims. The key was to establish trust, keep the questions simple and explain why he was asking them.

"Mrs Ullenorth, I am trying to piece together an accurate timeline of events leading up to your husband's death. I know that you have already helped in that respect following the train crash. What I must ascertain now is the same for what happened after. Do you understand what I am trying to do?"

"Yes," she said breathlessly, "I get it. Go on."

"Tell me about him. What sort of a chap was he?"

"He was proud. Yes, proud. He had been an investment broker and he had worked hard at that. Built up his business. He had retired but was still a shareholder."

"What did he do with his retirement?"

"We have lived here in Eckscarfe for forty years. He served on the Parish Council for most of that. He was involved with the 'Friends of the School' group as well, at least, until the former Head stopped it. He was very public-spirited, you know? He has done a lot for this community. The hours he gave to help others, I can't count. Sometimes he would be out until after midnight, then get up to go to his office in Pendale early in the morning."

"What did he do to relax?" asked Bhatta, who felt that his visit was more for show than to gain any real insight.

"He has a – had a real passion for military history. He collected things. Books mainly, but he would get very excited about anything that had been used in war. He had some old uniforms, badges, flags, bayonets, that sort of thing."

"How would you describe Jonathan's manner? After the train crash, I mean."

"He was okay, considering, to begin with. He was lucky to be alive after the Village Hall collapsed on him and his friends. He had lost Fred and Len. That affected him. He was high and then low without warning. Normal, I suppose, if there is any normality in such circumstances. He was, erm, well, managing things, until the morning he went missing. He had been here all along. I heard the phone ring and I had tried to answer all calls up to then, but I was upstairs getting dressed. We have had reporters calling at the door as well, very annoying. When I heard it, Jonathan must have answered the phone. I heard him speak."

"Who was on the phone?" asked Bhatta.

"I don't know. I never will now."

She paused to compose herself again before continuing. Bhatta did not take any notes. He listened attentively.

"It was strange after that. He wouldn't leave the house, not even to his den, the room at the back of the garage. It's where he keeps his military stuff. He said that everything was okay when I called to him. I went out to the shops a little later. I didn't see him alive again."

She lurched forward and Bhatta sat up as though to catch her and prevent her from hitting the oak floor. She sat back to take in air then wailed loudly again. Bhatta was helpless to do anything useful to assist her. It was grief, pure undiluted grief, and it had to come out any way it could. He waited until it was humane to do so then he sought to change the atmosphere.

"Please may I see Jonathan's den?" he enquired. She nodded and stood up in a more composed manner.

She led him back through the hall and into the kitchen where she took a key from a row of hooks on the wall by the tall fridge. They went outside and to a door into the room behind the double garage. Mary Ullenorth paused and gasped in surprise.

"What is it?" asked Bhatta.

"The door, it's open. He would never leave it unlocked. He has things in there that should be, you know, kept safe."

Bhatta saw that the lock had been forced. The mechanism was hanging out.

"Is this the first time you have been to the den since . . .?"

"Yes. I haven't been here for about a week." She was, in an instant, fully composed and clear in her speech. She reached for the door but Bhatta stepped ahead of her.

"I'll go in, if you don't mind," he asserted.

She stepped back in a gesture of acceptance. Although it went unsaid, they both anticipated the possibility that an intruder may currently be inside. Bhatta was also considering the absence of the standard protective equipment usually at his disposal. He used the back of his hand to push open the door. Seeing the entrance area to be clear, he stepped inside and scanned the room. Light from a high, horizontal window and that from the open door allowed him to scan the room. It was the same width as the double garage at the front, but it was shorter. Cupboards and shelves surrounded the walls. Military regalia was on show across most of it. Regimental flags, propaganda posters, newspaper cuttings from war correspondents. He reached for the light switch and clicked on the strip light above. Books on tanks and aircraft, all carefully categorised, came into view. Once satisfied that there was nobody there, he called Mary Ullenorth inside.

"It's creepy. I only came in here to clean. It was always Jonathan's little man-cave, I suppose."

"Without touching anything," he urged her, "tell me if there is anything out of place or missing, please."

She moved around as though she was judging a flower show, stopping to dip down and inspect each new storage facility. She passed an empty area on what seemed to have been used as a desk. She gasped and put her palm over her mouth.

"What is it?" asked Bhatta.

"Jonathan's computer disks, they're gone. They sat here. There were about twenty disks. He had old war documentaries on them." She pointed to the space against the breeze-block wall. "And the drawers have been left open. He wouldn't have done that."

"What should be in them?"

"His military stuff. What he had collected over the years."

"Did he own a bullet-proof vest?"

"What? Erm, oh, yes, he did. I remember him getting it from some dealer years ago. He showed it to me. Why do you ask about that?"

"Because he was wearing one when he was found."

Bhatta stared intently at Mary's face, looking for something that might suggest some awareness of the reasons for her husband's demise. She gave away nothing but incredulity. When the revelation did compute with her, she said,

"Why would he put on a bullet-proof vest? Did he think someone wanted to shoot him? Why would he think that?" she started to get upset again. Bhatta tried to remain impassive but human.

"I can't answer that, not yet anyway. All I can do right now is find facts. The conclusions will come when we have enough of them. Now, please tell me what else should be here."

She regained sufficient composure to continue with her scan of the room. In a corner, she dipped down and pointed to a space under a table.

"The safe, it's wide open," she said in a bewildered whisper.

Bhatta also crouched to look inside. It was an old cast-iron strongbox with a hinged front. It was empty but for some squashed cardboard packets. Bhatta took out a pen and flicked them out onto the polished, concrete floor. The packaging was old and discoloured but there was printed labelling on them. This showed that the original contents had been .38 calibre ammunition. Thirty-six rounds in each box. He stood up at the same moment that Mary did.

"Bullets, Mrs Ullenorth. Does your husband's collection of militaria include bullets?" She swallowed hard before answering.

"I suppose it doesn't matter so much now, but he had some things that he should not have had." Her tone was part embarrassment at the indiscretion of illegal possession of such items and part relief at being able to speak about it. "I told him not to keep them. At least he kept it all to himself and didn't get me involved."

"What else did he have, Mrs Ullenorth?" probed Bhatta, taking a firmer line.

"There was a gun, an old wartime revolver. He kept it in the safe with the bullets."

*

"Is there any new information about the missing kitchen hand, Gregor?" asked Lane-Wright during her daily visit to the incident room. Mel Sharpe answered her question.

"No sightings since the day of the crash. All we know about him is that he turned up asking for work at the pub and the Grejznis took him on to work in the kitchen. About 5'4" or 5" tall, could speak some English but rarely spoke to anyone anyway. He was a slightly built chap but a good worker, by all accounts. They gave him a bed in a loft space behind the pub. Quite basic but he didn't complain. He got his meals and a tenner a day spending money. He worked twelve hours a day, which sounds a bit like slavery to me."

There was some raising of eyebrows in the Incident Room, many of the team were exceeding twelve hours work in a day. Sharpe continued.

"He had breaks in the afternoons and he went out for walks up the hills and around the lake. He didn't have much time to go anywhere further afield."

"Who saw him last?" asked the SIO.

"Sophia Grejzni, the landlady at the Barley Mow," answered Sharpe without looking at her notes. "Gregor left the kitchen after finishing the washing-up from lunchtime. That was at ten past four."

Lane-Wright was keen to probe Gregor's movements.

"Do we know his surname? Where he was before he came to Eckscarfe? What part of Poland he came from?" Sharpe had an answer to the last question.

"All we know is that when Marcus Grejzni, who was born in Gdansk in the north of Poland, said something to Gregor in Polish, Gregor didn't get it. He must have been from elsewhere. Poland is a vast country with many remote communities. They don't all speak the same dialect."

"Or maybe, like that bloke who was living rough in Pendale, the one we thought was Gregor, he wasn't Polish at all. He might have been saying that because he was another illegal," offered Lane-Wright, showing that her long absences from the Incident Room did not mean that her knowledge of the case was impaired.

Bhatta had listened intently. Gregor had been a thorn in his side throughout the investigation. The plain fact that he had disappeared since the derailment made him supremely suspicious. He put his thoughts into an order that made sense before sharing them with the team.

"I've been thinking about this Gregor fellow. He is a foreign national, arrives with no known background and goes when the devastation happens. Was he a terrorist? Did his actions have a political basis? If that was true, what was his cause? There would be little point in carrying out an atrocity like this if the world doesn't know what it was for."

There was some visible restlessness among the team. Nobody wanted what Bhatta was suggesting to be true, but they knew that they were in no position to dismiss it. Most coppers would prefer a straight-forward crime of greed or anger to one based on an ideology. Lane-Wright chose a course of action, which she hoped would appease Bhatta's concerns, although she privately had no faith in that possibility.

"Okay Inspector, let's get hold of the Special Branch and see if they can link this to any similar acts which have been linked to terrorist causes, shall we?"

The briefing went on to establish the next phase of enquiries to be addressed. Most were developments of existing avenues but some, including the Special Branch theory, were recorded as a new line of enquiry. Bhatta felt that he was a lone voice, devoid of any real backing. He had effectively and politely been fobbed off by Lane-Wright. In his mind, Gregor remained ever-present, an unscratched itch he was unable to reach. He tried to see Gregor in a new light. One nagging possibility that came to him, was that Gregor had witnessed something that day, something that had scared him into fleeing the village. Bhatta was determined to find him and uncover the evidence he could provide.

*

Whilst Sharpe was preparing to interview Liddle, Bhatta was at his desk reading completed T.I.E. actions when his phone rang.

"Incident Room, Inspector Bhatta."

"I want my fucking car back."

Although they had only met once, the deep, rasping, Mancunian voice was, to Bhatta, instantly recognisable.

"A big car takes longer to examine, Mr Maxlow. When the Forensic team have finished with it, you can have it back - providing that it was not purchased from the proceeds of crime, that is."

"I want it now, you little prick! I know how you bastards work. On the take, the whole stinking lot of you. How much is it going to cost me?"

Bhatta was initially taken aback by the suggestion that payments could be made and accepted in such matters. Did Maxlow really move in corrupt circles? He had no experience of this. Was this an attempt at bribery, or a set-up with a recorded call?

"Well?" said Maxlow with increasing impatience. "Do you understand what I am saying or are you too thick to get it?"

Bhatta's approach to this strain of conflict came from his time in the legal profession. When someone was getting heated in court, he had found that it was best to remain calm and resort to subtle sarcasm.

"There will be no need to pay any money, Mr Maxlow. We seize and examine vehicles without charge. It's all part of the service. Besides, I understand that you have another one, a BMW I believe. What a fortunate chap you are."

"You are messing with the wrong man." Maxlow's tone was lower but no less menacing. "I have connections that could make life very difficult for you."

"A threat, Mr Maxlow? How uncivilised. I would have thought that a respectable businessman like you would not stoop so low as to make threats. Anyway, I would love to chat but I have things to do. I will be speaking to you again. I have no doubt about that. Goodbye."

He resumed his paperwork as though no such conversation had taken place.

Tommy Liddle remained as belligerent as he had been before he was arrested. The interview at Pendale Police Station was not his first. He was of that mindset that allowed no room for himself to be wrong or anyone else to be right. His determined incivility was illustrated on his fat face and the only words he uttered were drenched in vitriolic contempt. Mel Sharpe was not going to be intimidated. Waving his right to legal representation, Liddle entered the interview room expecting to be interviewed by a male officer. He sneered at the 'little girl' seated opposite. She was diligently skim-reading her preparatory notes.

Sharpe had learned in her early days as a police officer that it was of optimum importance to maintain composure during an interview with a suspect. To stick to the plan, address all relevant issues, challenge denials with evidence not argument and do not allow the suspect to dictate what happens. When the suspect is Tommy Liddle, no amount of preparation was going to get him to answer any of her questions. He remained mute throughout the interview. Nothing was gained other than the time and space for the search of Liddle's yard to be carried out. When the interview ended, Liddle was released without charge.

His dogsbody, Nicholls, was at home on the family farm. He had been deployed by Liddle to clear some building rubble from a landscaping job at a country house, but having finished the work, he had sloped off home rather than return the yard to be given more work to do. When arrested on suspicion of causing criminal damage to the train line, he instantly made the link to the deaths of the occupants of the Village Hall. He panicked and burst into tears. Unable to wipe his face due to being handcuffed to the rear of his body, he dribbled and dripped all down his shirt in a most undignified fashion. Between sobs, he made an impassioned plea to his captors that he was innocent of any wrongdoing. The arresting officer recorded his reply when cautioned,

'I never did now't, I never broke the track, honest.'

The conversation flowed from Nicholls, in stark contrast to the interview with his boss. He vehemently denied any involvement in the rail crash, sticking to his earlier story about being in Pendale with Noel and Hugh at the time. He did acknowledge that the Yamaha quadbike in Liddle's yard was his and that he had managed to get it working. He had taken it out 'off road' but had more work to do before it was roadworthy.

Followed by Mel Sharpe, Bhatta entered his office within the incident room complex to find Ian Carraway waiting for him. As Crime Scene Manager, Carraway was in a position to co-ordinate all aspects of fingerprint and forensic submissions. His face carried a sternness beyond the gloom of the crime scenes he regularly managed. Bhatta sensed something was not right.

"Hello Ian. Got something for me?"

"Yes." He waved a buff folder across his chest then put it down on the desk. "Two submissions to tell you about, Sir. The first is the angle-grinder recovered from the Mercedes owned by Guy Maxlow. It was compared to the cuts in the rail-track and the results were inconclusive. It could have been that one or maybe it wasn't. It's like scissors cutting paper, it doesn't leave any clear mark. What we can confirm is that it does belong to Tommy Liddle."

"So Tommy Liddle's machine was in Maxlow's possession?"

"Yes."

"I wonder what the connection is between Liddle and Maxlow. Neither of them is likely to explain that to us if asked," said Sharpe.

"Maxlow's Mercedes is too wide to negotiate the path to the railway line," said Bhatta thinking aloud. "So our offender could have taken the cutter on the quadbike, then put it into Maxlow's car after? If so, why?"

Sharpe voiced the first possibility that she thought of.

"To hide the cutter somewhere out of Eckscarfe?" she offered. "I can't think of anyone else who left the village that night." Bhatta added his thoughts,

"Either Maxlow was in on this, or someone put it there to make it look as though he was."

Ian Carraway coughed to remind Bhatta and Sharpe that he had more information to impart.

"Sorry Ian," said Bhatta. "What's the second thing?"

Carraway leaned forward and pushed the door shut. He swallowed hard and disclosed what had been troubling him.

"The laptop recovered in the rubble of the Village Hall."

"Yes, I remember. We wanted to know which one of the Councillors owned it."

"That was what we were looking for, but we found something else on the disk that was in it."

"What was on it, Ian?"

"I'll warn you that it isn't pleasant. It is video footage but these are stills from it. The whole thing has been preserved for evidential viewing."

"Go on."

Ian Carraway flipped open the buff folder and produced three still photographs. They were grainy and of poor resolution, but the subject matter left no room for doubt. Bhatta put his hand over his mouth. From behind it he uttered,

"That . . . is . . . Oh! I feel sick."

CHAPTER SEVENTEEN

Eckscarfe Hall Special School came into being in the 1960s, although the building was early Victorian. It had been the country home of the landowning Linstope family and was, when compared to other early Nineteenth century mansions in the countryside of Northern England, a modest twelve bedroomed pile with ornate grounds and an estate of nine farms spanning across into the next valley. It also owned the lake and all of the fish swimming in it. The Linstope dynasty's ownership of the Hall ended in the early 1950s.

The house was discreetly put on the market by the estate's administrators. Whilst the farmland and most of the gardens were snapped up by well-placed investors, the house itself took longer to be reallocated. Eventually, after the National Trust had turned it down, the County Council assumed ownership and began the conversion process from home to school.

Whereas Eckscarfe already had a village primary school, the purpose of the new school was significantly different. It was a residential establishment with shared bedrooms for the children and individual rooms for the staff. The criteria for admission was initially for those orphaned and unable to be placed with foster families. Over the ensuing years, the service provided had expanded to address the needs of children with challenging behavioural difficulties. Severe autism, Asperger's Syndrome and many more conditions more difficult to diagnose and treat could be found on its student roll.

The old house was maintained on the County Council's budget and whilst the building remained functional, it had lost much of its earlier splendour. Stained-glass windows had been replaced by plastic versions. Artistic features such as plaster cornices and dado rails were taken down and the plain, magnolia emulsion of modern living had taken their place. Even though it could not be from the main road because of the overgrown trees, there were some among the district who felt the need to keep this jewel in the crown of local history in the style for which it had originally been intended. The Parish Council took a keen interest in the preservation of the building and the welfare of its residents, raising funds and applying for heritage grants to make it beautiful once more. School trips were arranged by the concerned few in the community and, where possible, the children were invited and included in village activities.

However, most of the activities of Eckscarfe Hall Special School were carried out away from the view of the public. Challenging behaviour was dealt with swiftly and with unmistakably clear parameters. Several rooms had been soundproofed so the summary punishments imposed within them could neither be heard nor imagined by those beyond. Most incidents went unreported to the police or education services, or if they were, nothing more than a cursory glance at the allegation would be carried out.

The school had been under repair for the past two years. Scaffolding was in place around much of the exterior and the regulation concerning listed buildings had contributed to the lack of progress. Prior to all that, there had been fifty-six pupils. The present roll totalled eighteen. The staff numbers had reduced in proportion. Several members of the Eckscarfe Parish Council had been instrumental in supporting the school for years. Graham Posner had served as the chair of Governors and Fred McAulden had acted as clerk at the meetings. Because of this, they had their own keys and unchallenged access to the buildings.

The school entrance was a grand affair – in stark contrast to the nearest building, which had been the Village Hall. Eckscarfe Hall had stood for nearly two hundred years, whilst the Village Hall had lasted less than two. Giant, grey, stone pillars adorned with ornate carvings of exotic fruit, holding up a pair of rusting wrought-iron gates, long overdue for restoration. The gates had been left permanently open, allowing access to the winding path through the woods up to the old house. Many of the trees had been crudely cut-back but there was still a dense expanse of pine forest on either side of the tarmacked path.

At the side and rear of the main building were the old servants' quarters. A housekeeper, a cook, a gardener and a gamekeeper had all lived in the tied cottages, which had been used as storage rooms for the sports and activity equipment purchased by local fundraising. Behind the cottages was more woodland. Through it led a broad and surprisingly well-made footpath. Bhatta and Sharpe approached the school on foot and were both in a degree of awe at the scale and opulence, albeit now faded into disrepair.

As they walked, Sharpe spoke of the footage found on the laptop in the rubble.

"How old do you think that lad in the film was, Sir?"

"About fifteen or so. It's hard to be sure when his face is all creased up in pain. What sort of evil bastards would do that to a child?"

Sharpe had not yet heard him say anything so emotive. His calm, measured manner of speaking had given way to anger and she saw him in a new light. He seemed energised and more determined than before.

"I believe it's more about power than it is about sex," she said.

"And a group of them doing that to a boy whilst filming it? What is that about?" he snapped.

She knew that his ire was not directed toward her.

At the main entrance, they stood under a pillared canopy and rang the bell. The noises from inside were difficult to identify. They could make out some raised voices but there was no anger in them. Furniture was dragged across floors and the occasional referees whistle was heard to sound.

The door was opened by a slim, young woman in a tracksuit with a whistle hanging on a strap around her neck.

"Hello!" she said with a look of curiosity in her eyes.

"Good Morning, I am Inspector Bhatta, this is Constable Sharpe. We are investigating the rail crash. May we come in?" He had managed to get his fury under control once again.

"Yes, of course," she said, as the door swung fully open to allow them to enter. "I am Janet, one of the physios. If you will come with me, I will take you to see a permanent member of staff. The Head should be in her office about now."

"Thank you," said Bhatta. "Do I take it that you are an occasional contributor, Janet?"

"Yes, that's right," she said as they ascended the once grand staircase edged with a balustrade bearing repairs, which fell far short of the original design. "I work for an agency and I come here two days a week. Hilary is the one to see."

The sounds of unseen human activity continued without giving any indication as to where they were coming from. Janet reached the open door to an office along a corridor with a threadbare carpet and entered after a token knock. "Hilary, the police are here."

"Oh, bring them in please," said a haughty and superior-sounding female voice. They were guided into the office, which was a thoroughly disorganised but pleasant-smelling room with a wide, curved window overlooking the woods. The oak desk was set in the bay and the light behind her made it difficult to see Hilary's face. When she stepped forward to greet her guests, and the wall was behind her, Bhatta and Sharpe could make out her features. She was a rotund and ruddy-faced woman of the countryside, unapologetic about herself and seemingly well-placed in that environment. A floral dress of thick cloth with a hessian cord around the middle and sensible, flat shoes resembling Cornish pasties was, by the standards of most senior teachers, informal – but Eckscarfe Hall was no normal educational establishment.

"Welcome to Eckscarfe Hall. Please be seated," she announced as though she owned the place and they were privileged to be there. "I am Hilary Thorne, Head-teacher – for my sins." She let out a short and awkward laugh to punctuate her own weak and tired joke. Bhatta and Sharpe produced I.D. and introduced themselves again before sitting on two upright wood and metal chairs, which were a size too small for adults.

"Ms Thorne - " he began, taking what he thought would be a neutral path.

"It's Miss," interrupted the head whilst still smiling and clearly not offended.

"Ah, excuse me, Miss Thorne. We are examining the circumstances of the recent train crash and the subsequent loss of life. We hope that you can fill in some of the gaps in our knowledge."

"Well, I am the Head-teacher, that's what we do, you know." She laughed aloud again. Bhatta glanced at Sharpe before continuing.

"I understand that some of the members of the Parish Council were regular contributors to the school."

"Oh yes." Hilary Thorne's tone became less jocular. "A terrible business. Thankfully, Mr Posner has survived but, oh those poor men. So sad for the families too."

She waxed lyrically about the devastating effects the loss of the Councillors would have on the village. Bhatta had to work hard to get the conversation back where he wanted it to be.

"I quite agree, Miss Thorne. Please tell me – and understand that we do consider every reasonable possibility – have there been any allegations of improper conduct made against any of the people who helped out at the school?"

Miss Thorne fell silent as her eyes hardened. She was no longer the convivial country school-marm. She was the scourge of the perpetrators of unacceptable behaviour in 'her' school. That it was being raised by the police made little difference.

"Miss Thorne?" he urged her to answer.

"If you are implying that there were some . . . irregularities in the conduct of this school, then you should make your case through the official channels." She began to shake and take on a complexion somewhat paler than before.

"Miss Thorne. My question is not a complaint. I merely seek to know about any complaints that may, or may not, have been made."

"Complaints about what!" she snapped. "The food was too hot? Hmm? The bath water was too cold? Perhaps the grass was too green?" She swept a dramatic hand toward the window and the outdoors beyond to emphasise her tirade of sarcasm. Bhatta remained calm.

"Complaints of abuse, Miss Thorne. Have there been any complaints of that nature?"

In the face of such composure and confidence, Hilary Thorne began to lose some of the intensity of her indignation. She let out a long breath before sucking in another one.

"Inspector. I understand that you are trying to get to the bottom of this sorry business but I fail to see – "

It was Bhatta's turn to interrupt.

"I have reason to believe that some abuse has taken place in Eckscarfe. What I want to know is who the victim was, and I need your help to establish that. It is also pertinent to my enquiries to find out if any complaints of abuse have been made here. Can you help me to do that, Miss Thorne?"

She pondered the issue in silence for a few seconds. "It should be a matter for the Governors," she suggested.

"Not if the allegations may concern one or more of the Governors," he asserted.

She gasped and covered her open mouth with her hands. "You don't mean . . . "

"There is nothing proven yet. It may not lead to anything, but I must pursue it. I'm sure you appreciate that."

She was beginning to accept his request, as she slowly understood the reasons for making it.

"I find it impossible to accept that any of our volunteers would . . . but I will cooperate with your enquiries. Let me tell you this, there have been several complaints, of all sorts, made by disgruntled families of those unfortunate young people who have come to us because of life's cruel twists. Most of them are made because they are angry at the blows that life has dealt their loved ones and not at their treatment here. We are an easy target for them, please remember that."

"Miss Thorne, we, the police, are also an easy target for spurious complaints. Please trust me to be thorough enough to be able to differentiate between the real and the imagined."

"I must point out that there have been no substantiated complaints against staff or volunteers during my tenure as Head."

"I will take that into account. Thank you."

He had found an accord in which they could cooperate. She stood and took a bunch of keys from the pocket of her cardigan. Unlocking an old green, metal filing cabinet. She pulled open the lowest drawer and flicked to the back of the folders. She pulled out a buff cardboard folder about two inches thick and brought it to her desk. Bhatta and Sharpe moved their chairs to be able to see it.

There were very few actual complaints recorded in the folder. Most of the volume of paper related to how complaints had been investigated and resolved. Some fell short due to lack of independent evidence, invariably one party's word against another. This was exacerbated by the absence of those family members who had made the complaint and the alleged victims' difficulties in expressing what had taken place. Miss Thorne had been in post for nearly three years. The reports went back to a time beyond her administration.

Sharpe pulled out a bundle of papers stapled together. She examined them in silence as Bhatta and the Head-teacher discussed the complaints in general.

Sharpe found something she wanted Bhatta to see. She placed that file in front of him on the desk. He read it and looked up at Miss Thorne.

"This refers to an allegation that a boy who was living here was abused by men. It doesn't name any of the alleged abusers, but the boy is named as Elliot Bathmont. Does this mean anything to you Miss Thorne?"

"I have not taught anyone by that name."

"The complaint was made by a family member, but it didn't get very far because no supporting evidence could be found. It suggests that the lad had a vivid imagination. Who wrote this part?" He passed the bundle to Miss Thorne who said,

"That was my predecessor, Ann Turmey. She died of cancer and I took the post soon after. I didn't get to meet her, unfortunately."

"Were you in post when the 'Friends of the School' group was disbanded or was it Ann Turmey?"

"That was Ann's decision," said Miss Thorne. "I don't know why, officially, but I am sure she had her reasons."

Bhatta stood up sharply. "Miss Thorne, I appreciate that this is your office and I am being terribly rude, but would you mind if I used you phone?"

"Certainly. I shall leave you to it. Dial '9' for an outside line."

"Thank you," he said, as she closed the door. He picked up the phone and called the Incident Room.

"Yes, I need you to do something quickly. Go to the store and get a copy of the footage found on the laptop in the Snooker Room at the Village Hall. Take a photo of the face of the victim but be careful to avoid any sexual aspects in the picture. Is that clear. Get it up to me ASAP. Eckscarfe Hall Special School, urgent please."

Bhatta emerged and asked Miss Thorne to identify any member of staff who had been at the school at the time Elliot Bathmont had been a resident. He also asked for, and received, Elliot's admission file, which contained the diagnosis of his condition. It outlined the various difficulties in function and stated that he was capable of coherent speech and understanding but had little emotional range. He was physically able but prone to self-imposed isolation. When the police car arrived with facial photographs of the boy in the video, Miss Thorne also reappeared with an older teacher who she introduced as Violet Weeks. Violet was told very little of the reasons for the police enquiries. She was simply asked to identify the lad in the photographs. She peered through bifocal spectacles attached to a chain around her neck.

"Why, that's Elliot. Elliot Bathmont. No doubt about it."

*

"Elliot Bathmont had left Eckscarfe Hall School at the age of seventeen. That was four years ago. According to school records, he went to live with family in London. There is an address in Harrow which needs to be visited," announced Lane-Wright as she waved a summary of the developments, hastily written by Mel Sharpe. "I will ask for the Met. to establish that the address is current before deploying someone to make that journey. We are now sure that he is the victim in that video found in the rubble of the Village Hall after the train crash. Whilst it shows Frederick McAulden and Leonard Hurlington abusing the boy, the only other people present can be seen but not heard.

There are four men in the footage. We believe that one of them was Graham Posner because of his size. Nobody else who is associated with McAulden and Hurlington carries so much body-weight. The fourth should, logically, be Jonathan Ullenorth. The four of them had uninterrupted access to the Snooker Room at the old Village Hall and that carried on to the new building. Ullenorth's death remains suspicious. There is insufficient evidence that it was homicidal. The fact that he was wearing a bullet-proof vest would suggest that he considered himself to be a target, even if the pathologist is unconvinced of that."

The small group of officers and support staff murmured between themselves conspiratorially before being called back to pay attention by the S.I.O.

"I think that we have to look at Graham Posner as a possible target now. Get someone up to the hospital to guard him."

"Erm, Ma'am, Posner was released from intensive care and moved to an ordinary ward this morning," uttered a timid voice from the back.

"What? Get someone out to him and do it now!" demanded Bhatta.

The urgency was expressed without the need for any repeat. The officer who had given the update on Posner darted from the room.

A new surge of energy flowed through the team. The initial shock gave rise to a form of euphoria, not at the gore and suffering, but at the challenge of getting to the core of the case, gaining answers to so many questions. Laborious and time-consuming lines of enquiry had served to level-out the enthusiasm across the various roles at work in and out of the incident room, endless house-to-house questionnaires, fruitless missions, red herrings and wild goose chases had taken their toll on the focus of the team, but now, there was a renewed impetus. Credible motives were being unearthed, tangible evidence was found, and its potential recognised and the previously unanswered questions were beginning to be matched to their answers.

Bhatta was in his glass-panelled office writing in his policy book when Lane-Wright entered. "Imran, we have had a reply from London."

"Just a sec, please Ma'am." He stood up and leaned out into the corridor. "Mel!" he called out to the enquiry team area. Mel Sharpe leaned back from her desk and saw him beckon her. "Mel is at the hub as well as me. It will save me retelling her."

"Yes, quite right," agreed the Superintendent. Mel entered the office and closed the door, without being asked.

"The Met. have been to the house at Harrow. The Bathmont family have moved away and there is another occupant. They couldn't tell us anything, but the neighbour did. It turns out that Elliot was found floating in the Thames last year. The inquest concluded that he took his own life."

"Oh shit!" exclaimed Bhatta. "That's our best chance of a witness. If he can't tell us who was carrying out the abuse, we will struggle to identify who the remaining targets are."

"Are you convinced that the train crash was an act of revenge?" asked the SIO.

"Yes, I am. The full picture is yet unclear, but at least one child was being sexually abuse in the Village Hall and possibly more. The 'Friends of the School' had unchallenged access to the kids for a prolonged period. Each one could be behind this. It is audacious, I accept, but it was a simple way to kill all of the offenders and not be there when it happened."

Mel was looking for some silver-lining amidst the disappointment of the Harrow enquiry. "Who identified the body?"

"What are you getting at Mel?" asked Bhatta.

"Just because Elliot is dead, the possibility remains that he could have told someone what had happened to him at Eckscarfe Hall School. They said he was able to speak and express himself."

"That is worth pursuing. Get back on to Miss Thorne at the School and find out who Elliot's friends were there and where they are now. As for his family, the Met. have done a thorough job for us so far, you must avoid any suggestion that we are picking fault so word your request carefully please."

"Will do, Sir. Before I do that, I have been reviewing the footage of the abuse. There is something that bothers me."

"Hardly surprising, it's child abuse," said Lane-Wright, stating the obvious. Mel ran to her desk and returned with her laptop, which was closed. She flipped up the screen and the image came back. It was the closing image of the footage, in still form. "Watch this bit please," she urged them convincingly.

She moved the curser back to let the footage run. It was only the last ten or fifteen seconds. They watched as she had asked. Sharpe explained her deductions.

"The filming of the abuse in the Village Hall snooker room ends with Hurlington appearing to signal to the camera operator to switch it off, see? He makes a 'cutting' hand-movement, but the camera operator leaves it running. Hurlington does this twice before heading toward the camera to end the filming himself. The rest of the footage shows a clear intention to avoid any of the faces of the abusers on the film. McAulden only moved into shot when he thought that the filming was over and Hurlington made the same mistake as he came to the camera. Why did whoever it was keep on filming? Did one of them want to implicate the others? Blackmail them maybe?"

"There is no direct link to the cutting of the track," said Bhatta, "The cameraman would have been able to punish them or profit from them without resorting to killing them. This might be a separate crime. If so, we have to keep our focus on the murders."

Lane-Wright gave her take.

"You are both right, in different ways. If your theory is right Imran, then the murders are related to child sexual abuse. If your idea is right, Mel, then the people who made – and are in that film, are either responsible for the murders or they were all the intended victims."

"Could Ullenorth have recorded it, or Posner?" asked Mel Sharpe. Her suggestion went unanswered as the phone rang on Bhatta's desk. He picked up the receiver.

"Inspector Bhatta . . . go on . . . okay. I'll come and see you there, thanks." He replaced the handset and took a silent moment to rationalise his thoughts. He looked up at Lane-Wright and Sharpe. His eyes told of bad news.

"What has happened, Sir?" asked Sharpe. He sighed and swallowed hard before answering

"That was the team we sent to the hospital. We were too late, Graham Posner died."

CHAPTER EIGHTEEN

When Bhatta and Sharpe arrived at the hospital ward where Posner had been treated since the rail crash, the press were already there in numbers. He saw the ever-present local reporters along with the national press pack. The usually composed and articulate Hugo Latimer was getting shouted down by his less-polite peers. Dan Delerouso had adopted a walking stick to aid his movement. He stood aside to avoid having his foot injured again in the melee. Marci Wicker was at the front but could not be heard at all as the elbowing descended into an undignified scramble for positions. Keith Marlin seemed to be getting the better of his rivals. Their questioning had become less composed than it had been before. It was more aggressive, even personal.

"How many more have to die before you resign, Inspector Bhatta?"

"Are you out of your depth, Inspector Bhatta?"

"Is there blood on your hands?"

Bhatta remained impassive. He left Sharpe to get the details of who was on duty and who had found Posner dead. He entered the individual room and was apprised of the events by a uniformed Sergeant who introduced the ward doctor, a thin fellow with the complexion of a sun-deprived teenager. He explained that the patient's age, existing state of health and the extent of his injuries had contributed to his weakened condition. Earlier that day, he had been moved from Intensive Care onto a male surgical ward and was being monitored every half hour. He had not regained consciousness since the Village Hall had collapsed on him. Bhatta thanked the doctor for his explanation. He looked at the lifeless form on the bed. Looking away and around the room, Bhatta saw a ceiling-mounted CCTV camera. Its dome was of dark blue glass and it emitted a faint light through it, barely noticeable in the ambient daylight.

"Is that camera recording, doctor?" he asked with evident haste.

"Erm, I think so," answered the doctor, who had more important things to consider in carrying out his duties.

"Sergeant, please check with the ward clerk if that camera works and preserve the footage if there is any."

"Yes, Sir," answered the Sergeant as he headed out of the room.

Bhatta slowed his breathing to calm himself before conducting a careful, visual examination of the room. He asked the doctor to remain, which he did. Bhatta's eyes rested on the monitoring equipment at the side of the bed. A drip-feed bag, of clear liquid, hung from a tall stand. The other end of the tube remained attached to the cannula in the back of Posner's hand. The bedding had been thrown to the foot of the bed and a pillow was discarded against the wall, a 'Call Nurse' button on a cable was curled up and hung on a hook and a trolley-mounted, heart-monitor display was now lying dormant. All appeared consistent with attempts to resuscitate a dying man.

"Doctor, was this equipment attached to the patient?" He pointed at the monitor.

"Yes, that keeps us aware of his heart-rate. It is clipped on a finger, normally."

"Was it there when he was found?"

"Erm, I can't be sure. I was more concerned with checking for vital signs. I don't use such equipment for that. It has to be done manually, so to speak."

"But it was definitely attached to his finger when he was last seen."

"Definitely. The times of visits are all here." He picked up the patient record on the clipboard at the end of the bed. Bhatta took possession of it as the Sergeant re-entered.

"Sir, can I borrow you a minute?" Bhatta nodded and followed him out of the room and, joined by Mel Sharpe, to the nursing station where a computer screen was showing a still image of the room where Posner had died.

"The CCTV is on a time lapse system. It takes a series of stills at three-second intervals, the Sergeant explained. "Watch this."

The stunted footage showed nothing of interest for ten seconds then the door beneath the camera was opened. The next picture showed the door closed again and a figure standing with their back to the camera and facing the bed. He wore a baggy, black coat with wide side pockets and a baseball cap. In the next image, the figure is leaning over Posner and their raised elbows and shoulders suggested some form of physical contact with him.

"Who the hell is that?" exclaimed Bhatta.

Sharpe had spotted something else. "Look! The heart monitor, the numbers have gone. There is just a line across the middle of the screen. They were there in the last picture."

"What is he doing to him?" asked Bhatta rhetorically.

Nobody tried to answer him. The final picture was of the intruder turning away to head out, throwing a pillow down under the bed as he walked away.

"The pillow! Posner was suffocated!" Bhatta turned from incredulous to angry. Posner had been murdered whilst in his care. He had failed to properly assess the risk to Posner's life and, paedophile or not, he should have been able to keep him alive. He turned to the wall of the ward office and punched it with the base of both clenched fists.

"Shit, shit, shit!" he took in a deep breath and let it out again slowly. Mel Sharpe stood up and said,

"I'll get the room sealed off as a crime scene. Sergeant, would you ensure any other CCTV in the hospital over the past week is not erased until we can get it all seized and examined, please."

"Will do," he said and, replacing his cap, he set off to do it.

"Sorry Mel. I lost it there," he sighed heavily.

"Come on, Sir. We have more evidence now. We are getting there."

"Right, yes, thanks." He turned to look at the screen again. "Mel, wind that back to that last image of that chap in the cap please." She tapped the buttons and produced the picture he wanted. The killer's face was not, at any stage, visible but the clothing had sparked something in his mind.

"That cap - and the black coat. I think that might be our missing kitchen hand." He leaned into the screen, "You haven't gone far have you, Gregor?"

*

"We have had another update from the Met. about Elliot Bathmont," announced Janette Lane-Wright. "They are trying to trace the family, as we discussed. Another neighbour says that his father left when he was a toddler and his mother died when he was ten. He went with his sister into foster care nearby but, due to his condition, they couldn't look after him, so he went to Eckscarfe Hall. When Elliot was found in the river, his body had to be identified by dental records. No family were traced."

"What about the sister, Ma'am?" asked Bhatta.

"She was older than Elliot. Last heard of going off to University, somewhere in London, eight or nine years ago. I know, there are loads of Universities in London."

"Yes. I went to one," said Bhatta gloomily anticipating a 'needle in an urban haystack' line of enquiry on the off-chance that the sister knew something about historic child abuse on someone else three hundred miles away.

He had been advised during his secondment to the CID as a Sergeant, that any investigation should be likened to a tree and whatever branch you are on, you should always keep the trunk in sight. The trawling of University records in London for Elliot Bathmont's sister seemed, at that moment, to belong on one of the thinnest branches of that investigation tree. Nevertheless. He deployed Mel Sharpe to begin that process.

The Incident Room staff were re-assembled to bring all up to speed with developments. Bhatta gathered his composure before speaking.

"The post-mortem examination of the remains of Graham Posner revealed that he had been manually asphyxiated. There was no sign of any digital contact on his throat and traces of cotton lint, consistent in form to that of the bed linen used at Pendale Hospital, were found in his windpipe. This indicated that the pillow had been used to cover his face and deny him air. The pillow on the floor had traces of Posner's DNA on it but this proved inconsequential because it had been his own pillow for several hours before his murder. So, we are now looking at four suspicious deaths. Hurlington and McAulden were murdered by whoever cut through the rail track. There was, at first, insufficient evidence to establish that the intended victims of the derailment were those men of the Parish Council. Ullenorth, having survived the collapse of the Village Hall, went on to equip himself with a bullet-proof vest which he was still wearing when he turned up in the lake.

"Mrs Ullenorth says that her husband kept a collection of war memorabilia in his man-cave. This included a firearm and bullets. If he knew the gun was missing, does that explain the need for him to start wearing a bullet-proof vest? If someone steals a gun in a burglary, what would make the victim think that they were going to come back and use it on him?"

"The disks," offered Mel Sharpe. "It wasn't just the gun that he was worried about. The computer disks were also missing."

"Weren't they full of war footage, documentaries and that sort of thing?" asked Lane-Wright.

"Mrs Ullenorth believes them to be just that," added Bhatta. Sharpe had found a gap in their thinking.

"Okay, Mrs Ullenorth rarely goes in that room behind the garage, right? She has no interest in his obsession with old war relics, she just dusts the room and leaves. We have footage of several people abusing a child in the snooker room and, although some of them are not seen, the ones who do appear are close associates of Ullenorth."

The penny was beginning to drop around the room. She pressed on,

"Where best for Ullenorth to watch the porn they had made than in that room? He was with the others in the snooker room at the time of the train crash. Were they watching it on the laptop when the roof caved in? Perhaps he was there when the child porn was filmed as well."

Muttering among the team grew into an excited clamour. Lane-Wright called for order like the speaker of the House of Commons.

"Thank you, thank you." She lowered her voice once order had been restored. She turned to Mel Sharpe.

"That is a credible timeline of events, well worked out. Now, assuming that the burglary at the Ullenorth house was solely to seek evidence of child abuse and the intruder gained the same footage as that found in the snooker room after the crash, they would have known Hurlington and McAulden to be guilty but they wanted to find out who else was there. The taking of the gun and ammunition could be the prime reason for breaking in, or a lucky find once in there. Either way, we should be acutely aware that there is someone out there with a loaded gun."

"I've remembered something else that may be relevant," said Bhatta, "Before the crash, Peter Keld was investigating an attempted burglary at Leonard Hurlington's house. Burglaries in Eckscarfe are rare enough but at the homes of two people so closely associated? Beyond coincidence, I'd say."

*

Peter Keld was about to finish for the night. He had parked his car at his police-owned home and set off on foot to make some visits and check his vulnerable or high value properties. This was old fashioned, preventative, police activity which usually went unnoticed. He was aware that the invisible Councillor Pamela Hazeldene was away, and she had asked him to keep an eye on her house during her absence. Her vacations tended to be lengthy and her return dates could be anytime over the suggested date. It was never earlier.

Councillor Hazeldene and her husband Alan had discovered the delights afforded by cruise-liner holidays. The Mediterranean, The Caribbean, The Baltic, Northern Lights were all on the list of their leisure adventures. They had been known to add land-based holidays to their planned cruises. Loretta Rokestone's observations on Pam Hazeldene's absenteeism in Council activities was well-founded.

Their home was a white, detached bungalow in a garden of shaped trees and raised flowerbeds. From the road, only a glimpse of the house could be gained. The white, ranch-style gates and a post box built into the concrete gatepost alleviated the need for anyone to enter in the absence of the occupants. Keld, however, had due reason to check the property, front, back, top and bottom. A break-in would have proved highly embarrassing to him personally. As the illumination from the streetlamps was rendered inadequate by the high bushes, Keld reached for his torch.

Before he had switched it on, he saw something. It made him stop and focus his concentration. In the house, he spotted a light. It was not a steady, constant light, as would have come from a ceiling fitting or a table lamp. It was the flash of a narrow beam, a thin search-light scanning inside the house.

Keld squatted down to watch it as he tried to calculate the possibilities. Had the Hazeldenes returned home without letting him know that they were back? Were they unable to get the electricity working? Were they using a torch to facilitate the repair? As he watched with his radio volume turned down, a figure came into view in the lounge of the bungalow. Keld was unable to see his face, but he was sure that it was a man and that he was wearing a head-torch. He knew that the only male occupant was Alan Hazeldene. The man momentarily stood upright, and the light was trained downwards into the lounge. At that moment, Keld knew that what he was seeing was not right. All of his suspicions had been confirmed because he knew Alan, and he knew that he was 5' 3" tall. The man in the house was far taller.

Keld whispered a message into his radio asking for some back-up, knowing that the Pendale patrols, even at speed, would take some time to get there. He moved along the path, crouching and unseen, trying to identify the point at which the intruder had gained entry to the house. As the rear of the house came into his view, although obscured by darkness, he could make out that a window, large enough to climb through, was wide open. He moved behind a garden shed and maintained his vigil on the open window. He ran through the best, case scenario in his head. The Pendale patrols would arrive, switching off any sirens long before, surround the house and peacefully extract the trespasser who would have no option but to surrender himself into custody. He knew that the real outcome would be something less efficient than that. It always was.

When the light from the head of the man came to the window, Keld realised that the time for him to act, and act alone, had come. He saw the light go out then the shape emerged from the window, dropping a bag onto the patio outside, then following it out before gently closing the window behind him. As he began to walk around to the driveway near to the shed where Keld was waiting, the Eckscarfe community policeman leapt out and dived at him, hitting the man with his shoulder into his lower back. Keld followed through and kept his grip around the torso as the man was knocked to the ground. With the air suddenly expelled from his body, there was no resistance and Keld used this to secure him, by feeling for his arms, he managed to get handcuffs on his prisoner. The light was insufficient for any enquiries to be initiated about who the man was or what he was doing there. He raised the man to his feet and walked him to the gate. He put up no protest. As they reached the road, the patrol car from Pendale arrived. PC Helen Quinn and PC Gary Watts stepped out.

In the improved illumination, they looked at the man and tried to remember if they had seen him before. As they opened the rear door of the police car, Keld spoke to his prisoner.

"Okay, we will talk about what you are doing here once we get to the police station. But, for now, who are you?"

The man did not answer the question. Keld was relieved at having avoided a prolonged physical contest. He was not fit enough for such exertions. At that moment, he was not in any frame of mind for grilling the man verbally either. He searched the detainee's pockets as Helen Quinn searched the bag he had been carrying. In his back, trouser pocket there was a wallet. The manacled prisoner let out an audible and exaggerated sigh of defeat when he saw that his wallet was being examined. When his driving licence, with his picture on it, was taken from the wallet by Keld, his refusal to say who he was seemed pointless. Keld announced his identity.

"We usually like to welcome visitors to Eckscarfe, but not when they break into houses. Do you understand that, Mr Andrew Fentley from Manchester?"

*

Fentley was taken to Pendale and placed in a cell. His presence in the computerised custody system was matched to the Incident Room database, which alerted the rail crash investigation team. Although Bhatta had already gone home, he was called and he came back to try to determine the reasons for Fentley's presence in the village. Wherever Fentley was, Maxlow must have something to do with it.

A CSI examination of the Hazeldenes' bungalow found that the window had been forced by a chisel-type implement and the striation marks matched a tool found in Fentley's bag. Inside the house, nothing had been stolen, although this could only be confirmed or denied by Pam and Alan when they returned. What was suspicious was the doors and top of the bureau in the lounge lying open and the paper contents strewn all over the floor. Ian Carraway had offered the view that the intruder was looking for something specific. The absence of any documents, or any apparatus for copying documents, in Fentley's possession would suggest that he did not find what he had been looking for. Bhatta wanted to know what it was.

The interview with Fentley was to wait until the morning. This would allow for the CSI to finish at the bungalow, the Hazeldenes to be contacted and the Fentley's chosen solicitor to travel from Manchester to Pendale. Bhatta went home again to get some sleep.

He slipped into bed in the near darkness. Sunila turned over to wrap an arm around his chest and nestle her face under his stubbly chin. He felt the abrasion on her and apologised.

"Sorry, I haven't shaved."

"It's alright," she assured him with a kiss on his cheek, "I like the 'rugged' thing occasionally." She made him laugh.

She had that ability to lighten a tense mood through mild humour. She was what he needed her to be and, when he became insular and serious, she spotted it and understood the reasons why - even though her own job carried with it stresses that most people could not grasp.

"Want to talk about it, Imran?" she uttered.

"No, it's fine. Go to sleep," he said. She kissed him again then turned back to settle down to sleep. He could see her face in silhouette. He thought about the support that she gave him, freely and constantly. On the occasions when he had done, or not done, something she felt important, she would not shy away from confronting him about it, but she usually was right, and the matter was closed promptly. Through his police career, he had heard his colleagues complaining about their wives or husbands. He had no such complaints to express. He wouldn't change anything about her.

*

At the two-bedroomed flat in Pendale which was home to Mel Sharpe, she woke in the night with a dry mouth and a need to use the toilet. She had no clue as to the time other than that the sun was yet to rise. She left the toilet and headed for the fridge where a jug of tap water awaited her claim on its contents. She drained a glass and allowed it to bring a shiver to her body. Objective achieved. Mel slipped back into the Egyptian cotton sheets and let out a long breath in preparation to going back to sleep.

"You were talking in your sleep again," whispered Claire.

"Oh, did I wake you?" said Mel, aware that Claire had work to go to as well as her.

Claire taught P.E. at a high school and had a thirty-mile daily commute. Although her working day was long, it was largely predictable and she was able to maintain a regular sleeping pattern. Mel had never, as long as she had known her, kept regular hours. Claire had always admired Mel for her work ethic and that she did not bring her work problems home to unburden those issues on her. Lately, however, Mel had been at home so little that Claire had felt lonely. A conversation about what Mel had been doing which had kept her away for so long would have been appreciated. She was also in a profession which required confidentiality and could be trusted with sensitive information. Claire was more concerned about the pressure on Mel than about her own curiosity. Any conversation would be good. Perhaps that would improve when the rail crash case was finished, or at least the stage in which Mel was working so hard.

"No, I wasn't asleep really," Claire reassured her.

"Was I saying any actual words?" asked Mel.

"Some. No sentences but you did say: 'village' and, erm, what was the other one? 'Gregory?' Yes, you were talking to someone called Gregory."

"Ah!" said Mel smiling, "We are looking for a bloke called Gregor, a foreign chap. It must be praying on my mind. Sorry."

"No need. If you want to talk about it, I'm here. Wake me if you need to."

"Thank you." Mel leaned up onto her elbow and kissed Claire. "I should work on something I 'can' get my head round. Maybe I could tell better stories in my sleep. This case, well, it doesn't get any clearer. We aren't eliminating any suspects - we just keep getting new ones. Anyone could have done these things, killed these people."

"What about your boss? Is he putting pressure on you?"

"No. The pressure is all on him. He's a bit snappy sometimes but it's not surprising considering what he is up against. He is in a temporary post just like me, but higher profile and more is expected. He has the Press all over him as well. I wish I could do more to help him."

"You are working sixteen-hour days as it is. You couldn't do more without making yourself ill." Claire reassured her. "Anyway, stop talking whilst you are awake. Go to sleep, I want to hear the next instalment."

*

At breakfast, Ali was already in position at the head of the table. The clean-shaven Imran was not normally concerned with such patriarchal customs, but he knew that Ali was well aware of them. It took place in his house all of the time. It reminded Imran of TV wildlife programmes with gorillas claiming the Alpha-male status over the others. It was a game which he had no intention of playing.

"Good morning!" he said to all around the table. Sunila and Lania returned the greeting. Ali read a newspaper. Lania was interested in the case Imran was working on, or at least she was trying to show an interest.

"It must be fascinating, Imran. We have seen the news on the television. It must be like trying to find a needle in a haystack."

"It is like that in some ways," he said, "but it feels like we have to look at every piece of hay and decide if it is the needle."

Ali looked up from his paper and rolled his eyes in silent disapproval. Imran considered overlooking that snub, but this was his house and he was not going to let it go.

"Imagine that Ali, in your profession, you have to rule out what the patient is not suffering from before you can treat the real problem. That is right isn't it?"

Sunila was keen to head off a full-blown argument. "Yes, it is similar."

"Hmmm," grunted Ali, returning to his newspaper. "That is a matter of opinion."

*

At Pendale Police Station, Bhatta was updated about the burglary scene at the Hazeldene residence. Contact had been made with the globetrotting pair who had confirmed that nobody had been given permission to enter in their absence. Reassurances had been offered that the situation was under control and that there was no urgent need for them to curtail their travels. On that premise, they chose to stay where they were.

The CSI examination of the papers found scattered on the lounge floor revealed that they were mainly financial. Bank statements, investment letters, lease agreements for properties they owned and let to students out of the area. Fentley had been looking for something which was not accessible by legitimate means. This meant that Maxlow was behind it. Why would Guy Maxlow want access to the private financial records of Pam and Alan Hazeldene? Pondered Bhatta. The only thing that came to mind was that Pam was an elected member of the Eckscarfe Parish Council who had, collectively, denied Maxlow permission to build houses in the village. Was the burglary an act of revenge, or one of intimidation?

When the solicitor arrived, Fentley had a private consultation with her before his formal interview. Once the tapes were rolling, he offered 'No Comment' to all questions put to him, including to confirm his name. His fingerprints had been scanned and a match had been found to those taken after an earlier arrest. There was no doubt that he was Andrew Fentley. The address on his driving licence turned out to be out-of-date. As he had refused to reveal his current address, he was declared to be of no fixed abode. This allowed the custody officer to authorise his detention to go straight to Pendale Magistrates Court the following day.

Alone in his cell and without the lawyer, Fentley began to think for himself about his predicament. He activated his cell buzzer and asked the jailer if Inspector Bhatta was available. A message was sent to the Incident Room and Bhatta came to Fentley's cell to speak with him. As Fentley had already been charged with burglary, the custody officer allowed the visit to go ahead.

"You want to speak to me, Andrew?"

Fentley was dishevelled and pitiful. His hair hung limply over his brow and the swagger and grooming he had displayed when they had met previously was gone.

"I don't really want to, but I have to."

"I'm listening." Bhatta knew that asking questions of a charged person without his solicitor was only permitted in dire circumstances. He was, however, allowed to hear what a detainee had to say.

"I was sent. I knew it was a bad idea, but I was ordered to do it, by Guy Maxlow. You've met him, you know what he's like. There aren't many who can stand up to him, I know I can't. He wanted me to find some dirt on that Councillor, the woman whose house I was in. She was lucky, I suppose. If anyone gets in his way, he just tramples all over them."

"So, he wanted some dirt on Councillor Hazeldene and he sent you to get it."

"Yeah. He wants to build all these big houses in that village and the Council lot said 'No.' He wants to get rid of them and get a new Council, put in people who will do what he wants. He will threaten people, with violence or expose their secrets. There's nothing he won't do to get his way."

"Including killing people?"

"I haven't been a party to any of that, but I wouldn't put anything past him." Fentley moved awkwardly on the bench-bed of the cell. He took a deep breath and looked into Bhatta's eyes. "I know I'm in trouble for the burglary, but I want to do a deal."

"A deal?"

"I know all about Maxlow, what he's done, the stunts he has pulled, the taxes he has dodged. It's millions. I can give you all that - if my case is dropped."

"I am investigating the rail crash murders. High-level corruption and fraud are someone else's responsibility. I will speak to someone about it. Meanwhile, tell me again what you did on the night of the crash."

*

Mel Sharpe was dispatched to London to make enquiries at the main Universities. Intending to catch up on her record-keeping during the train journey, she had used her laptop to update the reports she was due to submit. Due to encryption, she was unable to access the internet, but she could complete template documents already saved onto her disk for that purpose. She caught up on her work for the first hour of the journey. As the train left Warrington Bank Quay Station, her eyes began to droop and the mythical 'Arms of Morpheus' gently but firmly wrapped around her.

Just a few minutes, a power nap. The rhythm of the train on the tracks gave soothing, backing music to her slumber, like a lapping tide on a peaceful shore. Dreamless, and hopefully without an accompanying monologue, her body slowly replenished as she headed South with a handful of silent strangers for company. It felt warm and comforting to be semi-conscious, then fully unconscious. The journey would take another two hours. She wouldn't need to be out of it for more than a few minutes. That was all she needed. All was well as long as the train stayed on the track.

"Ahhhh!" she awoke with an unearthly shout of panic. Her head shot backwards and her knees lifted involuntarily, hitting the underside of the table. Her dreamless state had been a lie. She had felt the train leave the rails and she had been thrown around the anchorless carriage. She shook herself to full consciousness. Embarrassed in front of strangers, nobody seemed to acknowledge that she had screamed in terror as she had been ripped from the sleeping world and blasted into reality.

"Are ya alright, Hen?" asked a matronly refreshment-trolley attendant with a Scottish accent. "Can I get ya a drink a' water?"

Mel shook her head and thanked the lady. The remainder of the journey was spent awake and fuelled by caffeine.

She knew that her task would be affected by confidentiality issues, and that she was unlikely to be able to gain any usable information by asking and showing a warrant card. What she hoped to achieve was to narrow the field and establish which University Elliot Bathmont's unnamed sister had attended before seeking the relevant authority to have her questions answered. She had a list of five educational establishments to begin with but before she did so, she called Bhatta as she had been asked to.

"Ah Mel, have you arrived in 'The Smoke?'"

"Yes, and its charming, thank you Sir."

"I have lived there, and I know that it isn't," he corrected her.

He summarised the developments regarding Fentley and told her what he had said in his cell.

"It's not exactly 'Watergate' but Maxlow has got some explaining to do," he concluded. "It does explain some of his actions. His visit to Loretta Rokestone when she wouldn't talk to us about it, and his association with Tommy Liddle."

"Why Liddle?" asked Sharpe.

"Because he is recruiting compliant or corruptible people to stand for the Parish Council so that he can control it and the decisions they make about his housing development. That is why he came here after the planning application had been rejected. He wanted the Council in his pocket before he made a new application."

"Killing half of the Parish Council in a train crash would make that easier to do," offered Sharpe.

"Exactly," he concurred with her suspicion. "Anyway, all other lines of enquiry are still current, and I want to talk to you about yours."

"Okay." She awaited his directions.

"I've had an idea. Feel free to rule it out if you wish but it might work. Universities are bound by the Data Protection Act but, the Alumni offices may prove more productive. If you speak to them, they are keen to highlight the achievements and career prospects of past students. I'm not advocating lying to them, just a different path to reach the same destination, okay?"

"I think I understand, Sir. Thanks."

She trawled the internet and called the Alumni office of the first institution on her list.

"Oh Hi, my name's Melanie Sharpe I am a police officer. Nothing to be concerned about. I am making enquiries about a past student at your University. Nobody's in trouble or anything, it is to do with the death of a relative of hers."

She winced at her own ability to misrepresent and hoped that it sounded plausible. To her surprise, the Alumni officer checked their computer records and confirmed that they had entertained no student by the name Bathmont in the last fifteen years.

Once fluent, she carried out the same ritual on the other entries on her list. At the fourth attempt, the administrator confirmed that there was a female student called Francesca Bathmont who had graduated and left three years ago. Mel asked to meet the clerk in person, which was agreed. She took two tube trains and arrived at the reception desk. The Alumni officer, who was herself a past student, showed her up to a tiny office on the sixth floor. She wore a name badge, which read 'Suzi.'

"An unusual name, Bathmont. That helps when you have thousands on your records," said Suzi, signalling for Mel to sit down.

"Is there a current address for Francesca, please? It's very important that we contact her," asked Mel. Suzi typed in more details and brought up the records.

"Ah, here we are. Sorry, no forwarding address. No information about career highlights recorded either."

"What did she study, Suzi?" asked Mel, in a manner that made her think that she was beginning to sound like Imran Bhatta.

"Erm, Media Studies, yeah," pondered Suzi, who was just pleased to be speaking to a real person as opposed to answering faceless emails.

"Is there anything else, anything that might help me find Francesca?"

"Graduation photos, perhaps?" suggested Suzi. I have them all here, if I can find them." Her speech slowed down as her concentration shifted to the search for computer-held photographs. "They don't all have individual ones, they are expensive, but there is always a full class picture taken, even if nobody buys it."

She fell silent in deep and intense scrutiny at the screen. Finally, she found the right class picture. Fifty-eight smiling young people, formed in four rows, all sporting black caps and gowns with pale blue trim. Detailed beneath was a schedule of corresponding names. Suzi leaned back to allow Mel to read them. On the third row, two from the right, was the name Francesca Bathmont. Mel scanned the image above to find her. She saw a slim, young woman, pretty but with no significant defining features. There was something memorable about her, but she could not identify what it was.

"That's her then?" she said to Suzi who was very pleased that she had managed to do something useful.

"Sorry I couldn't be of more help," she said, not meaning it. "Can I do anything else for you?"

"Please can I have a screen print of that class photo, Suzi, with the names on it?"

"No sooner said . . ."

Suzi tapped two keys and the printer on the table behind her clicked and hummed into life. She snatched the print from the tray and handed it to Mel Sharpe. She examined that face again briefly without registering where she had seen it before. She slipped the photograph into her bag, thanked Suzi and headed out.

She set off to Euston Station to catch the train back to the North. Once in her seat, she took out that picture again. Mel had not studied at University, but she had appeared on a similar, although less formal, picture at her local college. Maybe it was that experience that the picture in front of her was reminding her of. It also made her recall the photo of her class when she had completed police training. Either way, it reminded her of something.

*

Bhatta was at his desk when Sharpe arrived back in the Incident Room. She summarised the London enquiries and showed him the class picture, pointing out Francesca Bathmont in the third row. He put the print down on the desk and looked up at her.

"And there's no current location for Francesca?"

"No. The Alumni records have nothing about her since she graduated. I can't explain this, but I think I've seen her before. I can't make a link and it's been bugging me all day."

"There was a picture in one of the houses we visited. Where were we?" he tapped his temples with his fingertips until that memory came back to him. "Got it! Victor Leshman's house. There was an individual graduation picture of a young woman on the table in the hall."

"I'll go and check," she said, turning on her heels. "If this woman is linked to the Leshmans, where might that take us?"

"I don't know," he pondered, "other than finding a current location for Francesca."

Sharpe went alone to Eckscarfe. She parked outside the Leshman house and walked up the path. From inside she heard a woman's scream. She sprinted to the door and tried the handle. It was locked. She ran along the side and to the back door as another cry of pain and fear came from within. Fumbling for her radio in her bag, she interrupted another transmission to call for back-up. The back door was unlocked, and she ran into an empty kitchen.

"Police!" she called out, but her words were drowned out by another scream. This time she could get a bearing on where it had come from. In the largest bedroom Victor Leshman, scarred and disfigured was standing bent over Nadine who was cowering in a ball in the corner by the chimney breast. Victor raised his hand to strike her again saying,

"You bitch, you evil bitch!"

Mel Sharpe grabbed his elevated hand and pulled it hard, making him fall backwards onto the floor by the nearest of two single beds. His burned skin felt strangely cold. She kept hold of his wrist and turned it inwards causing instant pain, it was his turn to feel it.

"Ahhh! Get off. I'll kill you, get off!"

Sharpe reached for her handcuffs and snapped them onto one wrist. Leshman was lying on the other wrist so she twisted the metal into his skin to get him to comply. His damaged skin seemed not to respond as she had expected so she had to physically pull his other arm free to be able to cuff both hands behind his back. Nadine was crying into her hands, too distressed to watch what was happening. Sharpe had to shout to her to get any response.

"Nadine . . . Nadine! Are you alright? Do you have any injuries?"

Nadine Leshman shook her head and remained curled up.

"Nadine, listen to me. I need you to go and let the police officers in through the front door. They will be here any minute. Nadine, go now."

Nadine managed to compose herself sufficiently to do what Sharpe had said. Victor had begun crying too. He was offering no resistance to his incarceration. The next voice Sharpe heard was that of Peter Keld. He hurried up the stairs and came to her aid. Together, they got Victor to his feet and took him to Keld's police car where he was placed in the back seat to await a van from Pendale. Sharpe returned to find Nadine sitting at the dining-table holding a handkerchief over her mouth. Sharpe carefully edged it away and saw that Nadine was bleeding from her mouth and the skin around her eye was beginning to swell.

"He can't help himself. He never used to get so angry but after what happened to him, he gets frustrated," she sobbed.

"It doesn't mean he has a right to take it out on you. You haven't done anything to deserve this."

"Oh, haven't I?" she said, somewhat suggestively.

"No!" insisted Sharpe. "You haven't."

"But I have. It's all my fault. I can't leave him. Look at the state he is in. It would finish him if I left. I can't do that. Please don't put him in jail, he couldn't handle it."

"Can you handle it if we don't?" asked Sharpe. Nadine did not answer that. "Nadine, it's up to you if you make a statement. What I saw is enough to charge Victor with assault on you. What we need to look at is what happens from now on. If you aren't safe with him around, we have to keep him away."

"Please don't do that. I'll be okay here. He won't do it again. It will be different now."

"What sparked his temper today?"

"I, Oh God, I told him . . . that I had somebody else in my life. It's not, you know, anything sordid. I just got close to somebody. He thinks I'm going to leave him. That's why he flipped. He said he was going to tell the whole village."

"This 'somebody' you are close to. Does he live in the village?"

"Ha!" she scoffed with evident yet unexplained cynicism, "You are making assumptions there."

"Someone away from here then?"

"No, you don't get it. You could never understand. Please, I can't say who it is."

Sharpe paused before asking questions of a different nature.

"On the night of the rail crash, Nadine, you were not at home, were you?"

"Not all evening, no."

"Did you go to see your 'friend?'"

"Yes. I left Victor on his own for two hours."

"So, the alibi you gave him was not true, was it, Nadine?"

"No."

"We will speak to Victor about what he did that day after we have asked him about assaulting you. I understand your reasons but lying to the police in a murder investigation could get you in a heap of trouble. You get that, don't you?"

"I get it, yes."

"We will need to speak to your friend in order to confirm your movements that night," explained Sharpe. Nadine darted a piercing look at her.

"I will not . . . cannot do that. It would do so much harm. I'm sorry."

"I can assure you that we will act with as much discretion as the law allows. Why can't you tell us who you were with?"

Sharpe looked into Nadine Leshman's eyes with renewed intensity. She saw something she had not spotted before - a hint, an attitude, an unspoken cry of frustration. Sharpe recalled where Nadine had popped up earlier in the investigation. She was a player in another person's secret. Sharpe realised then what might be troubling Nadine.

"Nadine, tell me it's none of my business, but your 'friend' isn't a 'he.' That's right, isn't it?"

Nadine reacted with widened but defeated eyes. That silence she had strived so consistently to maintain was weakening. Her eyelids waned and wilted in acceptance. Sharpe had worked it out.

"How, how did you know?" she mumbled whilst turning her face away. When she turned back to look at the police officer who had stopped the beating she had been taking, she saw a different attitude on her face.

"I worked it out from your movements recently. I also have personal knowledge of such things. It was different for me," said Sharpe. "I always knew. In many ways it's easier these days."

"You? You are, erm?" she stumbled in realisation.

"Yes, Nadine. I am gay. There is no need to be shy about it."

"But you don't live in this village, do you?" said Nadine, getting another wave of tearfulness, "and you don't have a husband who is suffering like Vic is."

"No, I don't have to deal with those things. I have to deal with a murder enquiry. I need to know what you did, where you went and who you were with on the night of the train crash."

CHAPTER NINETEEN

"Two things," began Mel Sharpe in Bhatta's office, "The picture in the Leshmans' hall is not the student in the class picture, there is no link to the Bathmont family. Secondly, Nadine Leshman cannot give Victor an alibi because she was out seeing her secret lover at the time of the rail crash."

"Didn't she go to see Councillor Rokestone when she was upset?" he asked.

"Yes. Nadine is in a secret relationship with Loretta Rokestone?"

Bhatta said nothing as he digested this revelation. He thought about the sighting of Nadine at Loretta's house the day before. Two middle-aged women in a small community, keeping their secret from the world. He had no wish to expose them, unless it had something to do with the murders.

"Okay. I didn't see that coming. It confirms what we suspected earlier. Vic Leshman has no alibi. Someone from the Domestic Violence Unit is interviewing him right now. He is ours after that."

Sharpe and Bhatta went to the custody office to prepare for the interview. They spoke to the officer who had interviewed Leshman for assaulting his wife, who said that Victor was full of remorse for his violence. He would not explain what it was that had made him erupt in that way.

In the interview room, Vic Leshman looked like a cartoon villain in a fantasy story. The scars, which swathed his face and the side of his head, were disturbing to look at. The gloomy, defeated expression on the parts of his face which could express emotion, told of an emptiness where life had previously existed. His eyes told his story more clearly than any words. Once the preliminaries were observed, Bhatta assumed the 'driver's' seat.

"Mr Leshman, we spoke to you about your movements at the time of the rail crash. Now, we understand that the full circumstances didn't come to light at the time. Would you care to tell us what you did on that evening?"

"I was at home. I don't know anything about it, nothing to do with me." He folded his arms to gesture the end of his contribution to their enquiry. Bhatta was just getting started.

"Your wife said that she was at home with you at the time."

"That's right."

"We understand that she was not at home. She went out, leaving you alone in the house."

Leshman said nothing.

"You used to work on the railway, didn't you?" Leshman leaned forward with a snarling expression.

"I didn't get this in my bed." He pointed to his missing ear.

"And you left your employment after an industrial accident which involved acetylene cutting equipment."

"It was welding equipment." Leshman corrected him sardonically.

"You know how to cut through metal, through railway tracks, don't you?"

"And that makes you think I did it?"

"You tried to sue the railway company after your accident, claiming that they were responsible for what had happened to you." Leshman did not respond. Bhatta continued, "A tribunal decided that it was your fault and you were not compensated for your injuries and inability to work. Is that the case?" Again, Leshman did not speak. "You are now living off benefits, aren't you, Mr Leshman? That must have been disappointing."

Leshman narrowed his eyes and ground his teeth. He was boiling up inside, but Bhatta spoke to him as though he was chatting about the weather.

"You have a reason to be resentful toward your former employer, you have the skills to be able to cut a railway track, it happened a short distance from your home, you have a propensity toward high levels of anger and violence and, now, your alibi has been proven false. That is what makes me think you did it."

Leshman held his shaking frame for a few seconds then his shoulders dropped, and his head dipped into his hands. He shook all over once more but this time by sobbing and not in seething fury.

"I had a life!" he finally blubbed, "I had a job, a good job. My wife loved me – and now I look like this! She can't look at me, I am disgusting to her now. That's why she has got somebody else."

Sharpe looked at Bhatta and dipped her eyes to express a request. It could only mean one thing and Bhatta nodded his assent. She adopted a softer approach.

"Victor, I have spoken to Nadine today. I'm not going to pretend that your marriage isn't in trouble, but I can assure you that she doesn't think about you in that way. We want to know about what you did on the day of the crash. If you didn't do it, tell us how we can prove that. Until then, you remain under suspicion. Help us please Victor."

Leshman responded by looking up at her. He stopped crying in stages and gave her his recollection of the day.

"I went out in the late afternoon. I was on my own, walking, just walking."

"Did you see or meet anyone who could confirm this?"

"No, I avoid people. I can't stand how they look at me. At least the children have the honesty to say what they are thinking. 'What's that on the man's face, Mummy?' You know what I mean? I don't want anyone to see me. I've become good at that."

"Cast your mind back to that day, your walk. Who did you see and avoid?" asked Sharpe, whose tone was more supportive than inquisitorial.

"There was nobody around, really. Nobody I can remember."

Bhatta and Sharpe exchanged another look. Sharpe turned to Leshman,

"Okay, thank you Victor. We will end the interview there – " she reached for the off switch but Leshman stopped her.

"Just a minute, I saw somebody, in a car. I was on my way home about eight o'clock. It was a Mercedes, a big one, like a wedding car. I couldn't see who was in it, tinted windows. It went into Tommy Liddle's yard."

Bhatta remembered the forensic report presented by Ian Carraway. It had included that the angle-grinder found in Maxlow's Mercedes had belonged to Tommy Liddle. The link had already been established but the reason for it remained a mystery.

*

The low, buzzing sound, ever-present in the head of Inspector Imran Bhatta had grown in volume into a cacophony. He placed his hands on the side of his head and closed his eyes tightly. He felt unable to breathe freely.

"Are you alright, Sir?" asked Mel Sharpe standing in the doorway of his office.

Her eyes showed all of the fatigue that he was experiencing too. He felt like throwing everything away and starting the entire investigation again. There was a mountain of facts, evidence, unanswered questions, suspicions, intelligence, actions to be worked through and every atom of it seemed to be shouting simultaneously in his head. Bhatta let out a long slow breath. He thought that he would never breathe in properly again.

"Are we getting anywhere with this job, really?" he said, slightly light-headed through an impaired flow of oxygen to his brain. Mel closed the door.

"We are getting there, slowly, Sir." The issue she had intended to discuss when she had entered the room now seemed unimportant. He had been under pressure, they all had. This was the first time he had shown the strain he was feeling. "I can hold the fort here Sir, if you need some time, you know?"

Bhatta came around quickly. His subordinate was stepping into the gap he had created. Was he being unprofessional? Was he out of his depth? Mel Sharpe's expression was not judgemental. It was a team ethic, stepping in when needed. He had chosen her to participate because of her competence, enthusiasm and ambition. What was on display in front of him was also her loyalty. He had to look at things differently, he was missing too many things of value, both in the case and in his own team.

"I'm going out for a couple of hours, Mel."

"Okay, Sir."

He left the office, passing the staff at their computer screens, through the door and down the ceramic walled stairs. He got into his car and drove, with a pop music station on the radio. With the windows down, he drove to Eckscarfe.

As he passed the road sign bearing the name, he saw a huddle of four people at the side of the road. One was holding a shoulder-mounted TV camera and another held a boom-mike over their heads. As Bhatta slowly passed them, he saw that they were conducting an interview with the redoubtable Mrs Barbara Hunter.

She was stretching her time in the limelight as far as she could take it. Attired somewhat more respectably than when he had first seen her, Barbara leaned on her crutch and waved her free hand around in dramatic gestures whilst relating her ordeal for the camera. With a purposeful thrust of her arm, she signalled across the field toward the section of the West-coast line where her fame had begun.

Bhatta parked at the Barley Mow, where the pushy reporter from the Daily Start was standing in the doorway smoking a cigarette whilst speaking animatedly into his mobile phone. He seemed not to have noticed Bhatta's arrival. Through the window of the pub, he saw Markus Grejzni collecting plates and glassware from the tables. The other members of the omni-present press-pack were also in there at the bar. The well-spoken bloke from The Times was in deep conversation with the young freelancer with the big eyelashes.

Bhatta walked through the village aimlessly. He was not looking for anything in particular. He passed Tommy Liddle's house and yard. Gary Nicholls was standing on the path at the side with Noel Keld and Hugh Barron. Nicholls looked up at him then turned away. Bhatta continued along the main street, past the end of the lane leading to Kingfisher Cottage. He paused there and looked across to the flats where Hilda White lived.

A car came past him. It was an old Astra with a different coloured door. It turned into The View where Wayne Crewgard's arrest had taken place. At the gate of the primary school, two of The Proles were killing time whilst their instruments were inaccessible. Freddie Parr and Adrian Hallimond played frisbee on the school field. Bhatta walked on, past the police house where there was no sign of activity. He imagined the frustration Peter Keld must have been experiencing.

At a kissing gate beneath a pointer sign on a wooden post, he passed through and began to negotiate a path between the houses. Despite his unsuitable shoes, he continued through the overhanging branches and out across an open field. The path rose gradually. He ascended the hillside of grey scree and wild grasses, stopping occasionally to regain his breath and admire the constantly improving view. The path took a sharp turn to help walkers to negotiate the gradient then another until a zig-zag route had formed. The open sky beckoned as the fell-top came into view. Bhatta had taken off his jacket and was carrying it. His brow was oozing beads of sweat, which he wiped with a handkerchief. At the top of the fell was a flat stone platform with a circular, brass plate indicating the names and heights of the neighbouring peaks. Bhatta sat on the plate and took off his shoes.

The sun's heat came through the thin, wispy cloud sitting high in the sky. There was no breeze to speak of, so the cloud sat undisturbed above. The vapour trails from aircraft made white graffiti across the rich, blue expanse.

Bhatta looked around at the valley below. He had no real purpose other than to try to see things differently, from a new angle, to open his closed mind. He could see the quarry from an elevated position. The vastness of that chasm became clearer. The buildings at Wilson's Aggregates were tiny, as were the quarry trucks that he knew to be huge at close quarters. The vast scar caused by centuries of quarrying resembled a dormant volcano and the thin swirls of dust rising from it added to that effect. His view panned to the railway line, the point of ignition for the fire that burned relentlessly beneath his skin.

A speeding train came into open view from behind the distant trees. It was the first one he had seen, or perhaps noticed, since the crash. Further down the track, at the point of the derailment, some of the machinery of repair remained in place. Equipment containers sat track-side awaiting removal, and the twin cranes resembled giraffes in courtship.

Beyond that he saw the rapid traffic of the motorway. Nobody was going to Eckscarfe but everybody was going past it. He saw the spire of St Jed's church standing out over the rooftops of the village. It should serve as a beacon of righteousness, something for the people in its shadow to be in awe of, but there was scant evidence of that here.

Among the trees, he could see the roof turrets of Eckscarfe Hall. What abominations had been inflicted on those who had dwelled under that roof? What suffering of innocents had that place facilitated? He put his shoes back on and stood on the brass plate. Before he embarked on the return leg, he again scanned the vista. The answer to what plagued him was there, right in front of him. He had to open that place up and be ready to seize the moment when the gaps appeared. Whoever had killed here was still here, he was completely certain of that.

*

Sharpe returned to the office where Bhatta was already busy at his desk. He was staring intently at the screen of his computer terminal. The rest of the room was dark, the light from the screen showed the lines of strain on his face. Sharpe went to her desk and wrote the summary of the interview with Victor Leshman.

When she had finished, she went to speak to Bhatta. His office door was open. She stood in the doorway and waited for him to see her. He did not look up.

"Ahem," she coughed in gesture only. He darted a glance at her then looked back at the screen.

"We have missed something, Mel. What are we not seeing?"

She stepped into the office. "What are you looking at Sir?"

"I am watching the video again, Elliot Bathmont's abuse footage. The end bit bothers me. Come and see." She moved behind his desk and leaned toward the screen. The scene was frozen at the point that Len Hurlington and Fred McAulden's faces came into view. "You have spotted this already but there is something else. Watch what Hurlington does with his hand. It's a scissor action with his fingers. You try that."

Sharpe stood upright and replicated the actions in the footage. "Stop there!" snapped Bhatta. Sharpe froze in position. "You have done it with your thumb raised and I did the same. Hurlington's thumb is wrapped around his palm, why?"

"I don't know," she said, "He's signalling for the filming to stop, like a director shouting 'cut' I suppose."

"If you were to do that, how would you do it?" asked Bhatta. Sharpe flicked a flat hand across her throat twice.

"Like that," she added.

"Yes, I would too. So why does he do that?"

"He was one who volunteered at Eckscarfe Hall wasn't he?"

"Yes, he did," confirmed Bhatta.

"So, kids there have disabilities. If they are deaf, it would be something the staff would have to learn." Sharpe was making sense, but neither were making progress.

"Are you suggesting that the filming is being done by one of the kids from the Special School?" Bhatta was trying to maintain rational thinking, despite feeling that it was leading to another blind alley.

"Either that, or it was somebody who also communicates by sign language," she said.

"It can't be Ullenorth or Posner, they have to be the ones in the footage as well." Bhatta looked back at the screen as he spoke.

"I wasn't thinking of them. Why make the gesture to cut like that unless it was for someone who couldn't hear?" Sharpe was thinking a step ahead of him.

"Deaf?" he uttered, doing more thinking than speaking.

"Yes. Whoever is filming this might be deaf." Sharpe's mind was racing ahead of her ability to express it. "Wayne Crewgard is deaf, it nearly got him shot by the firearms team."

"Hold on, Mel. Crewgard has not been deaf for long and this was over three years ago. Remember, he is still learning to lip-read and do sign language."

"And it's Alastair Sackler who has been teaching him. Sackler used to do odd jobs at the old Village

Hall. He would have been there when the abuse was happening." Her eyes widened as she made the link and considered its consequences. Bhatta jumped from his chair.

"Come on, Sackler could be the next victim."

They headed out of the room and across the main office floor.

"There was something I wanted to tell you about that photo from the University in London, but it will keep until after we find Sackler," she said as they descended the concrete stairs of Pendale Police Station.

"What about it? I thought you had drawn a blank there."

"I did too until I saw something else in the picture. There's a name under the photo."

"There are lots of names under the photo." He corrected her vagueness and urged her to get to the point.

"The name is familiar, but I don't recognise the face," she said

"Who is it?" he snapped.

"I have run an internet search and, well, it doesn't make sense. She is currently in New Zealand working for a newspaper."

"New Zealand? That can't have any relevance here, can it?" pondered Bhatta.

"I know, that's what I feel about it. The photo is from a few years ago but that face doesn't bring any memory to mind."

"Have you got it with you?" he asked as they crossed the car park. She wrestled the print from her bag and handed it to him.

"Her," she pointed out. He slowed his pace to examine it then handed it back.

"Nope, nothing. Which one is Elliot Bathmont's sister again?" She indicated the appropriate face among the assembly. He stopped walking and squinted closely at it. "Yes, I've got that feeling you have. She is familiar. It's the eyes. Where have I seen you before?" he said to the face in the photo. He shook off the distraction and walked on to the car.

On the way to Eckscarfe, both Bhatta and Sharpe were quietly thoughtful, mulling over the images they had seen and trying to make some sense of them. Bhatta realised that Sharpe was probably thinking the same thought as he was.

"Come on Mel, share please."

She sighed and offered him her disjointed thoughts.

"When Sackler used to do his odd jobs in the old Village Hall, he could have been in the building when the abuse was going on. Maybe he got involved just by being there, initially anyway."

"He's not exactly in the same social circle as the Parish Councillors, so that would explain it," mused Bhatta. "There is no other clear link. What about that picture? There's something in that. Something important."

Alastair Sackler's house was another of the cheaply built wartime constructions, which should have been demolished in the 1950s but wasn't. Semi-detached with an unkempt front garden, it had been shored-up and pebble-dashed, but it still looked shabby. The unmarked police car arrived in evident haste to which the tyres gave audible testimony.

Bhatta was not prepared to wait for backup before entering. The front door was unlocked so he pushed it open and gave Sharpe a flick of the head to indicate that the back of the house should be covered. She ran around the side and he headed inside.

He had to juggle the need to secure evidence and prevent its destruction by announcing his presence. He needed to avoid being mistaken for a burglar and sustaining an attack from a terrified and justified householder. Once he could see Sharpe through the window at the back, he closed the front door and locked it with the chain. Any attempt from Sackler to escape could be delayed at least. He peered into the lounge. It was an untidy and neglected room with only an armchair and television appearing to be in current use. He passed through to a kitchen/dining room where he could see Sharpe outside the back door. He unbolted it and let her enter.

Wordlessly, they approached the stairs and crept up to the landing. The single curtain was closed, shrouding a gloom across the doors. One door was wide open, but no additional light emanated from it. A look behind the other doors revealed nothing but the open one suggested that something, or someone, would be found there. Bhatta flicked on the light and they went inside.

The room was in stark contrast to the dysfunctional mess downstairs. The dresser displayed a range of male toiletries, all lined up in triangles on either side of a vanity mirror. On the mirror was a message, a single word that said far more. It was spelled correctly and written in lipstick.

'Paedophile!'

CHAPTER TWENTY

Sharpe opened the curtain a little. The rest of the room revealed nothing out of the ordinary.

"It looks like we aren't the only ones who suspect Sackler of participating in child abuse," she said.

Bhatta remained silent and continued to scan the room. He seemed to have been holding his breath. When he finally let it out his mood changed. He saw that Sharpe was looking intently at the lipstick on the mirror.

"What is it, Mel?"

"This is a very deep red, maroon almost. Not many women are so daring in their choices."

"We can't assume that it was a woman. A man could have done that just as easily." He dipped to look more closely at it saying, "He isn't likely to have written this himself." He stood upright, turned and stepped past Sharpe and looked out of the window.

"His car, the old, grey Astra with the blue door, it's not here. Get on the radio and circulate that car."

They left the house after sending for a Crime Scene Investigator to deal with the lipstick message.

A visit to the nearest neighbours turned up no recent sightings of Sackler or anyone else at his home. He lived alone, that much was clear from the interior of the house. As the CSI vehicle arrived, Bhatta and Sharpe returned to the house. A radio message came through which Sharpe responded to.

"The Astra has been seen. Ten minutes ago on Shipley Road."

They leapt into their car and Bhatta sped away. He weaved through the narrow main road of the village and accelerated onto the country lane linking Eckscarfe to the Shipley Road. Behind them was Peter Keld in his own car approved for patrolling his beat. He would undoubtedly have heard the same radio message, although he was not to know why it was so urgent that Sackler be found. It occurred to Bhatta that many interested parties could be tuning in on police radio frequencies and that could include the press pack. They could also turn up as well at any moment. He reminded Sharpe about the likelihood of that happening.

"The hacks will be around for this. You wait and see."

"The press?" exclaimed Sharpe who fell silent to process her thoughts. "The press, there's a young woman, the freelancer. Her name is Wicker. The girl in the graduation class photo, there's a Wicker."

She scrambled in her bag and produced the printed image. Marcia Wicker is on this picture. She's reporting on the rail crash. It can't be her. Oh my God. I know who she is."

On the Shipley Road bridge stood the grey Vauxhall Astra. The passenger door was open. Bhatta stopped the car and jumped out as Sharpe climbed out more carefully. She had spotted something.

"Sir, look!" she pointed to the bridge parapet where a human form was standing over the track. It was Alastair Sackler and he was fixed to the spot. Standing beyond him, also on the raised platform, was another person.

"It's her," uttered Sharpe. "that's Marcia Wicker."

Wicker saw them approaching and they saw her kick Sackler's ankle to get his attention. Sackler seemed to be in a daze. He slowly turned his head to look at her. She gestured something in sign language and his head sank to his chest in response.

"Marcia Wicker," called Bhatta, "Step away from him, now please."

His voice was authoritative but in a higher pitch than usual. Sharpe moved aside to let him see better. Wicker saw her move and sensed that they meant to interrupt her plans.

"It looks like I'm talking him down doesn't it, Inspector? Well, you know I don't want that to happen."

"We know you mean that. We understand what you are trying to do. We get it. You are Francesca Bathmont, aren't you?"

A smile came across her face. "The hacks all thought you were out of your depth. They were all too busy preening themselves to notice. You worked it out, due respect for that."

"We know what happened to your brother," Bhatta began to reason with her.

Sackler's life hung in the balance, and, at a moment's notice, Bhatta's words could tip that in either direction.

"Do you?" The breeze wafted her hair across her face. She made no effort to move it away. "Do you really know how these evil predators used boys from the school for their own depraved pleasure? Do you get how they tormented my brother when they should have been caring for him? How he tortured himself afterwards and took his own life? Well, you can't know, you just can't."

Bhatta moved a step towards her. She swept a hand behind her and produced a handgun. It was an old, military revolver – as described by the widow of Jonathan Ullenorth.

"Stop there. I've nothing to lose. I've killed four of these bastards and I won't be denied the fifth one. This piece of shit was operating the camera on that video of my brother, tied to a snooker table whilst they took turns to rape him. I wanted to take them all out at once in the train crash but two of them survived and this one wasn't there."

"Ullenorth drowned in the lake," said Bhatta.

"Because I took him there, at the point of his own gun." She waved the gun barrel around to emphasise the point. "I made him row the boat too. He pleaded, crying like a baby. Did Elliot plead for mercy from these bastards? Did he? He didn't get any." She turned the barrel of the gun back toward the ribs of Sackler. "And that other one," she spat out her words with unbridled venom, "The fat whale in the hospital? I had to bring Gregor back to get my second go at killing him."

"You? You were Gregor?" said Sharpe in disbelief.

"I had to invent him. I had to work it all out, how to put everything in place, without raising suspicion, you know?"

"Francesca, you have killed these people, but it must stop, now," appealed Bhatta. He doesn't have to die. We have evidence that will convict him of his part in what happened to Elliot. He will go to jail for what he did, for a very long time."

"And that is alright with you, is it Inspector? You think that's the same as what I have in mind?"

Sharpe moved one foot. Francesca Bathmont, alias her University classmate Marci Wicker, turned the barrel of the gun on her. "No, no, no. You will stay where you are," she said, in full control of the situation.

Sackler seemed to realise the gravity of his predicament. He looked at Bhatta with plaintive desperation in his eyes. His expression was a silent plea for his life to be spared. With it was an acceptance that he was at the mercy of all of the parties present. At least the police would let him live.

"All that remains to be seen is how I do it," said Francesca Bathmont. "Anytime now," she pondered as though revealing a parlour trick. Bhatta heard the faint zipping sound from the overhead cables. He turned to Peter Keld and shouted,

"Stop the trains, get them to stop the trains."

"Too late," called Francesca Bathmont as she shuffled her feet to the edge of the parapet, the gun trained unerringly on the hapless deaf man. "There's nothing left for me. My brother was my only family. At least they won't be able to abuse any more kids like Elliot."

"Stop!" appealed Bhatta, "Nobody else has to die."

The sound of the oncoming electric train grew louder. Sackler began to sob, not for the first time that day. Bhatta and Sharpe both threw caution to the wind and dashed forward. Sackler was going to die and she was prepared to die with him. The gun barrel was pressed against Alastair Sackler's throat. Bhatta was within six feet of them. Sackler had a moment of absolute desperation. He knew that he was going to die. It no longer mattered how. He grabbed the gun and tried to wrestle it away. His tormentor kept her grip on the trigger and her aim true at his vital organs. The fizzing and crackling of the overhead cables reached a pitch of fevered intensity and the ground-shaking rumble of three-hundred-tons of unstoppable machinery hurtled into the void beneath the Shipley Road.

There was a moment, a hiatus, a minuscule pocket of suspended time where there was no sound. Bhatta reached out and touched the cloth on Sackler's trousers but could not grip anything. His fingers cramped and snatched again, grasping nothing. Sackler and Francesca Bathmont tipped over the parapet and disappeared.

CHAPTER TWENTY-ONE

Bhatta squeezed his eyes tightly shut. The train powered through and pierced the still air on the other side. The bridge shook from the thunder beneath. Sharpe stood with her body pressed against the metal parapet of the bridge. She too had suspended breathing. A shudder of cold raced through her body. She was the first to regain some composure. She shook Bhatta by the arm before climbing onto the parapet. He climbed up after her as Peter Keld ran to the narrow road leading down to the side of the line. As the rear of the train came into view, the air was polluted by a strong, burning smell. It was a mixed aroma of burning cloth and flesh. At the side of the track was a body. A human form curled up and smouldering from its contact with the high-voltage overhead cable. Between the drifts of dark-grey smoke, they could see that it was Alastair Sackler.

The chances of him having survived that impact were all-but nil. Bhatta and Sharpe saw Peter Keld approach from the grass slope of the cutting. He ran to the spot and slowed down as he got near enough to see it in detail. They watched Keld tentatively lean over the stone chippings on which a human being had landed after huge trauma. Keld swiftly placed his hand over his nose and mouth as the flesh of Sackler gathered in combustion. Flames began to appear around him. Keld was unable to tell if Sackler was dead or alive. He had to err on the side of life. He rapidly removed his body armour and began smothering the flames, denying the fire the oxygen it needed to effectively consume Sackler.

Keld was joined by other uniformed cops. One had a fire extinguisher from their police van. A few blasts of the light-grey cloud put out the fire, but it was too hot to examine. Bhatta drew an imaginary line in his mind. Sackler was dead or nearly dead, but where was Francesca Bathmont. Sharpe was thinking the same thoughts.

"Where did she go?" she asked as she scanned the immediate area. There was no sign of her on either side. The overhead cable was intact and contained no surplus debris.

"You don't suppose," began Bhatta, who was slow to regain his powers of speech, "that she hit the train?"

"And was stuck to it, do you mean?" Mel shuddered again. "Oh God, no. What if she is splattered across the front of it?"

"Somehow I doubt that," said Bhatta. He leaned over the edge of the bridge and saw that there was a ledge five feet below. It was wide enough for a person to walk along and it led to the sloping grass edge of the cutting.

"She didn't jump. She pushed Sackler but she didn't jump. Come on, she has a head start but she has to be nearby."

The trees and bushes surrounding the bridge restricted the view of where she might have gone. A radio message alerted the patrols in that area. There was a partial view across the fields beyond that and the church spire of St. Jed's and chimney pots of Eckscarfe could be seen nestling in the valley.

"Set up road checks on all routes with vehicular access within a one-mile radius," ordered Bhatta over the radio.

The controller organised personnel to get into position. Bhatta went to the dirt track as Peter Keld emerged. His face said it all, but he spoke to confirm.

"We need a paramedic to pronounce it officially but he's a gonner, Sir."

Bhatta was not surprised at that. His first rational thought was that he would be unable to get an account from Sackler, who may have been able to implicate other members of the paedophile ring. He shook that away and looked over Keld's shoulder at the lane behind him. He had not been down there before, but he knew it from a map in the Incident Room. He also knew that the lane continued to the village but, was there anywhere to hide along there? Francesca Bathmont, whilst first posing as Gregor the kitchen porter, then as freelance journalist Marci Wicker, must have used that path to get to the bridge on that stolen quadbike, then to the point where she cut the track. It was a route she knew.

Sharpe reminded Bhatta that the only building on the track was the cottage occupied by Rodney

Brickshaw, whom she had visited during the house-to-house phase. Bhatta was acutely aware that the fugitive was armed and had killed five people in a week. He deployed a firearms officer to join him and Sharpe in the visit to Rodney's house.

Leaving the police car near to the Shipley Road bridge, they walked the hundred and fifty yards to the single-story house. Rodney's well-cleaned Fiat was in its usual position beneath a lean-to at the side. A healthy stack of firewood logs lined the wall. The front door was under a canopy adorned with colourful flowers, which gave it a feel of time standing still. Bhatta knocked and waited. He knocked again. The door latch clicked up and the door came open only a few inches. Rodney peered out, through his crudely repaired spectacles, and focussed on the unexpected visitors.

"Mr Brickshaw, I am Inspector Bhatta. PC Sharpe here came to see you a few days ago, remember?"

Rodney seemed to be struggling to make sense of what was being said to him. He glanced at Mel Sharpe and mumbled that he did recall their previous meeting. Bhatta explained the current reason for calling.

"We are looking for a young woman in connection with the rail crash. She was in this area within the last fifteen minutes. She is about five-foot-five, dark brown hair, in her twenties. Wore a blue suit?"

"Not seen anyone," said Rodney, who was now fully participating in the conversation."

"Well, if you do see her, please don't approach her. She is armed and dangerous. We have roadblocks and the area is in lockdown until we catch up with her.

If you see anything, please stay at a safe distance and call us on 999, okay?"

"Aye, I'll do that, alright," said Rodney, who closed the door effectively ending the visit. Bhatta turned to Sharpe and expressed a shrug at the abruptness of the old farm hand. Sharpe added some encouragement,

"He is quite an observant sort, Sir. He'll call us if he sees anything."

"Okay." Bhatta accepted that and headed back along the track.

Behind the old, oak door, Rodney felt the barrel of the revolver in the side of his ribcage. Emerging from concealment under the hanging coats, Francesca Bathmont stared into the old and frozen eyes of her hostage.

"You and me are going for a little drive."

*

There had been no further train activity since Sackler's demise. The forensic team had to work fast. In most other crime scenes, the examiners would have all the time they wanted to gather evidence. However, a closed main line, especially so soon after the crash, would not be tolerated for long by the rail company or its indignant passengers. Bhatta's thoughts moved on to other, more pressing matters.

"Francesca Bathmont has no ties in this area. As Gregor she had the Barley Mow and as Marci she was surrounded by the press pack. As herself, she has nobody. What would you do to get away if you were her, assuming she has no more people to kill?"

"A car would be the obvious choice," offered Sharpe.

"Does she have a car? She must have had transport to be able to get around, this past week. She went to Pendale Hospital to suffocate Graham Posner too."

"We can't ask the other hacks about her, can we?"

"We would be opening a can of worms if we did. On the other hand, she's killed five and she's on the run with a gun. How can we keep that to ourselves? If she shoots someone, we get strung up for not warning the world, and if we do, it can cause panic and that's our fault too. I have to speak to the S.I.O."

They reached Shipley Road and Bhatta took out his phone to call the boss. He explained the events and that the number one priority was to find Francesca Bathmont before she killed again, not that they knew of any further targets.

As Bhatta paced the grassy edge of the road, Sharpe spoke to Ian Carraway who had arrived to direct operations in the pursuit of forensic evidence. They were discussing the events leading up to the death of Alastair Sackler when a car emerged from the narrow lane by the bridge. It was Rodney Brickshaw's old but immaculate Fiat. Rodney was at the wheel. She waved an acknowledgement at him, but Rodney stared back impassively, as abrupt as he had been earlier. No surprise. He remained still, staring, for no apparent reason before pulling slowly away. He turned right, away from the gathering of investigators on the bridge. Mel Sharpe watched him drive away and was distracted from her conversation with Ian Carraway as she did so. Carraway continued to talk but she had ceased listening.

"Sorry, Ian. Excuse me." She hurried to where Bhatta was speaking animatedly to Lane-Wright on the phone. He saw the concern in her eyes and paused the call.

"Sorry, Ma'am. Hold on please. Mel what is it?"

"Rodney Brickshaw just drove out in his car."

"So, he can do that if he wants."

"He only uses it at weekends. Why now? It's odd."

Bhatta made the link.

"She could be in it, come on."

They leapt into their car and spun around to pursue the Fiat. Sharpe activated the emergency channel to summon help from firearms officers and marked patrol cars. The staff at the checkpoints were also alerted. Accelerating through the gears, Bhatta negotiated the bends in hope that there was nothing coming the other way. On the straight sections, he saw no traffic and sped up to catch sight of the Fiat. A radio message informed them that the main road checkpoints had not seen the car.

Meanwhile, in the Fiat, Rodney was driving with trembling hands and a sweating brow. Lying across the back seat and concealed under a tartan travel rug, Francesca Bathmont held the revolver close to her chest with the barrel trained at the back of Rodney's seat.

"Where am I going?" he said with his voice cracking in evident distress.

"The police are looking for me. You have to avoid them and get me out of here. I will kill you if you don't. You should be in no doubt about that."

Rodney had not been in any doubt. Her manner was as serious and desperate as he had ever encountered. The life-threatening experiences of his early adulthood came back into his mind. Images of Malaya flashed by and the harsh memories of it returned to him with hurricane-force. The fear of death he had known then had revisited him in the guise of a desperate and dangerous young woman. She had further instructions for him.

"That cop said that there were roadblocks. You have to avoid them. Find a way out of here and you get to go home in one piece," she said.

Rodney knew the area as well as anyone. As well as the roads, he knew the lanes, footpaths, bridle paths and any other lines of travel. Getting a car out of the area was not going to be easy and he didn't believe that she would spare his life if he did comply with her demands. The more he thought about it, the clearer his predicament became in his mind. He was at gunpoint, that was in no doubt, one finger movement and he was dead. The only advantages he had were that he was okay as long as he kept driving and that only he could see out of the car. His captor stayed under the tartan rug, unable to know where he was taking them.

Rodney also knew that a police roadblock could be the tipping point. Should she decide to shoot her way out, he would probably be the first in the firing line. He already was. He became aware that she was peeping out through the side window. He didn't want that. He wanted her unable to see what he could see.

"I see a roadblock," he said. "over 'field." She dipped back down out of sight, unaware that there was no roadblock.

"Keep clear of it. Turn around if you have to," she ordered from beneath the cloth.

Rodney drove on in the hope of getting some help from somewhere. A car flashed past going the other way. It passed too quickly for him to have made any signal to the driver. Eventually, he spotted a real police checkpoint. He approached it and saw that the uniformed cops were speaking to the drivers. There was a queue of four cars waiting for the front one to be searched. Rodney drove toward it and, maintaining a steady speed so as not to raise the suspicions of his passenger, he drove at the gap to the side of the line of stationery vehicles. PC Gary Watts was the cop in the path of the Fiat. He saw it at the last second and he had to dive over the bonnet of another car in order to avoid being mowed down. Rodney was in no mind to harm Watts, but he had to get their attention somehow. Watts shouted his objection as the Fiat was leaving the scene. Bathmont heard the shriek.

"What was that?" she snapped.

"Cyclist," answered the customarily abrupt Rodney.

Unable to contest that and convinced by Rodney's manner, she accepted his explanation, unaware that the police patrols had initiated a pursuit of the car which had failed to stop for the checkpoint and nearly wiped out one of their own. In the distance, a faint sound of a siren was heard. It grew louder and more consistent.

"Is that the police?" she said.

"I don't know, can't see it," answered Rodney, who had learned, as a young soldier, to think and lie quickly but never thought he would need to again.

The wailing siren reached a deafening rate. Rodney was thinking of where to take the pursuing police cars. A junction ahead gave him two options: either head into the village or up the hill to the quarry. He chose the quarry.

Spinning hard left, the little Fiat straightened out into the minor road. Rodney regained balance and revved hard to ascend the hill up to Wilson's Aggregates.

"It's the police, don't lie to me," she demanded. She emerged from the concealment of the rug and looked behind at the oncoming blue lights. "Shit. Where does this go? Tell me now."

"Quarry, past there you can't take cars. It's your only chance now."

Rodney was more confident but tried hard not to show it. On the straight sections, both Rodney and Francesca could see the line of cars behind the pursuing marked police cars. Among them was Bhatta and Sharpe. As the gradient levelled out, they reached the entrance to Wilsons' Aggregates. It was otherwise a dead end. She gave Rodney his orders.

"Go in there, through the gate, don't slow down."

Rodney complied. The ground beneath them became rough and uneven. Dust was kicked up in thick clouds, frustrating the chasing pack. Francesca took encouragement from that.

"Keep going, they can't see us," she said as though Rodney was a willing contributor to her cause.

The Fiat continued through the quarry, rising up the grey, dusty track normally navigated by tall-tyred trucks, its suspension straining at every bump and dip. The chase was temporarily curtailed due to poor visibility. The pursuing fleet were unable to see anything ahead. Every advantage was sought by the fugitive to put distance between her and her pursuers. The car continued to go uphill. Rodney noticed that she was looking backwards as frequently as she was looking forward. An idea came to him, and in the absence of any better one, he decided to put it into action.

At the top of that path the incline of the road tailed off and the full vista of the gargantuan chasm of the quarry came into view. Centuries of human excavation had forged that vast void in front of them. The crest of the path had been reached and the nose of the car began to dip down toward the edge. Rodney had only one chance and that was a slim one.

He slammed on the brakes at the same time as he squeezed the seat-release lever below his seat. As the car stopped suddenly, Rodney's seat was thrust forward, crushing his chest against the steering wheel. He was ready for that and had braced himself for the impact, mitigating the pain of the compression. Francesca was not ready for it. She was cast into the foot-well behind Rodney's seat. She was unable to control any of her movements, including that of the pointing of the gun. Before she could do so, Rodney put the second part of his plan into action.

Still gripping the seat lever tightly, he straightened his legs and thrust the seat backwards pinning his tormentor between the front and back seats. Francesca Bathmont let out a scream of intense pain. Her ribcage was crushed, her breathing inhibited and Jonathan Ullenorth's revolver was pressed into her body.

Rodney opened the door and rolled out onto the ground. As he landed, the pain he had sustained in his chest and arm shot through him with an additional surge. He scrambled, lizard-like, across the ground through the drifting quarry dust, tearing the cloth and skin covering his knees and elbows as he went. Through the haze, he heard other cars coming to a halt. In relief and exhaustion, Rodney stopped crawling and fell to the ground. As the dust cleared, Bhatta and Sharpe saw him and darted to his aid.

"Where is she? Where is she?" appealed Bhatta, not realising Rodney's state of incapacity. Rodney was unable to speak. He tipped his head to the side indicating that she was where he had just come from. The dust swirls were lessening, and visibility returned. The Fiat sat on the crest of the quarry path, its drivers' door wide open but nobody was emerging from it.

"Rodney, is she in the car? Tell me!" demanded Bhatta.

"Yes . . . behind . . . seat . . . gun."

Bhatta turned to the firearms officers who were out, armed and ready.

"She is in the car, behind the front seat. Still armed." The car was approached by the four armed cops. They dipped at the knees and spread out in a semi-circle, edging toward the Fiat.

"Armed police!" called out the team leader. "Throw the gun out of the car and step out with your hands raised."

There was no movement from inside the car. After nodding their agreement for their next move, they edged nearer in short steps. Bhatta and Sharpe stayed with Rodney and watched with bated breath as the firearms team did what they do best. A faint sound was coming from the car. A low moan, a breathless cry of desperation. Bhatta turned to Rodney.

"What has happened here?"

"She is behind the drivers' seat. She can't get out," explained Rodney, gradually regaining his power of speech but still shivering in shock.

Bhatta wanted to tell the armed officers why Francesca Bathmont was remaining in the car. As he called out to the firearms team, he heard a creak and felt a moment of impending doom, a sinking lead-weight in his already churning stomach. The tyres of the Fiat moved one inch, then the car moved again. It began rolling forward, gathering speed as it went. It had passed the apex of the hill and was slowly heading down the other side.

"Shit!" exclaimed Sharpe. "The handbrake's off, it's going!" Sharpe ran forward and Bhatta followed. The Fiat headed toward the cliff edge. Faster it rolled, the firearms team lowered their weapons, unsure of the change in threat level. The Fiat moved faster and as Sharpe touched the passenger-side rear window with both hands. She saw the terror in the eyes of Francesca Bathmont, pinned between the seats and unable to reach the lever to release the front one. The barrel of the revolver was sticking out, but it was pointing at Francesca's own chin. Sharpe called out,

"She's stuck!"

She dropped back before sprinting ahead toward the driver's door, which was flapping open. The car continued to gather speed as it neared the quarry edge. Sharpe had only one thought, to stop the car and get her out alive. Bhatta was five yards behind. He could see things differently.

"Mel! Stop! Let it go, let it go."

Sharpe was in a red mist. She did not hear him. She grabbed for the drivers' door, but its erratic movement meant that she could not get a grip of it, tipping the door edge with her fingertips. As she finally got hold of the door, she was about to push it aside for her to climb in when another irresistible force yanked her away from the car and pulled her down to the dusty ground. Sharpe saw everything in painfully slow motion. The driver's door of the Fiat remained open as the car reached the edge of the cliff and dipped over the precipice. The back of the car disappeared, as did any hope of saving the life of the trapped and troubled soul inside it. Sharpe's heart sank and tears came into her eyes.

CHAPTER TWENTY-TWO

The sound of the explosion was muffled due to it being so far down the sheer rock face. There was no doubt what had blown up and what it had meant. The weapons of the armed police officers were lowered in a gesture which reflected the end of the threat and the end of a life.

She turned to see that the decision to let the car go had been taken away from her by Imran Bhatta. He had tackled her to the ground and was still holding her as though any release would endanger her once again. When Sharpe's tears subsided, she saw that the edge of the cliff was only seven yards from where they lay on the ground.

"You tried Mel, but you would have gone over with it. I had to stop you."

The gravity of the situation became clearer to her. The silent appeal for help displayed in Francesca Bathmont's eyes had overwhelmed her and rendered her blind to the mortal danger she had been in. When the realisation came over her, she creased her eyes and tried to stifle a high wave of tears. Bhatta got to his feet and helped her to hers. Helping her back along the path to their police car, he sat her inside and went back to collect Rodney Brickshaw.

The crime scene examiners together with Forensic Service staff took over from the Fire and Rescue crews. Janette Lane-Wright spoke to TV cameras at the entrance to the quarry, obliging Neville Allerton by keeping the Wilson's company logo out of shot.

"The people of Eckscarfe have been through a series of traumatic events. It now comes clear that they were all connected. The derailment of the train and subsequent loss of life in the Village Hall was an act of premeditated criminality and the subsequent deaths all emanated from that. The Coroner will oversee what remains of this as a criminal investigation, although, unless evidence emerges to indicate otherwise, there will be no prosecution."

Dan Delerouso interrupted with a question aimed at goading an unwise response from the SIO.

"Was the death at the quarry an execution carried out by the police?"

It provoked some sharp intakes of breath among the assembly. Even the other journalists thought that Delerouso's question was below the belt. Nevertheless, it halted all other questions as they eagerly awaited an answer. Lane-Wright chose to answer in her own way.

"I wish to say that the investigating officers have worked doggedly, and with immense integrity throughout this challenging case. They have acted above and beyond their duties. I shall be recommending that commendations will be appropriate. It is also right and proper for one of my officers to be commended separately for risking her life whilst trying to save the life of another person. Keeping the community safe - all of the community, safe, has been the top priority of my team. I am not taking questions. Now, if you will excuse me, I have pressing matters and I will hold a further press conference tomorrow."

Bhatta and Sharpe had reports to write. Once their accounts had been committed to the Incident Room I.T. system, Lane-Wright told them to go home and get some rest. The strain of the case had become visible and, as there was no suspect alive to interview, it was the Coroner's file which required work and not a prosecution file which came with tighter deadlines.

A visit from the Fraud Squad to the Incident Room allowed Bhatta to brief them about the activities of Guy Maxlow. There was sufficient evidence to initiate an investigation into bribery, blackmail and conspiracy to commit burglary. Tommy Liddle was also to be questioned as part of that investigation. Andrew Fentley was to be the subject of a witness protection intervention.

Sharpe prepared a summary of those who had fallen under suspicion during the case. Whilst no apologies were offered, Victor Leshman, Wayne Crewgard, Clive O'Flindall, Perry Vanaugh and Noel Keld were among those named on that schedule. She suggested that each one be seen and informed of the outcome of the case. She also added that it might bring some closure to Simon Butters, whose suffering had been as uniquely acute.

Mel Sharpe arrived home to where Claire had prepared a candlelit dinner of fish pie and green vegetables accompanied by soft music and expensive wine. She listened as Mel relayed the events of the day. Watching two people die in separate but linked incidents had brought on the symptoms of delayed trauma. Claire held Mel as the tears flowed.

"You have been through so much Babe, I am so proud of you," said Claire as she cradled Mel in her arms on the sofa. Mel wiped her eyes and nestled on Claire's lap.

"I have seen dead bodies, but I haven't seen anyone die before, then there are two in an hour. It feels surreal, you know? That woman, she had murdered five people and injured dozens, but, when she was there, in front of me, about to go over the edge of the quarry, that didn't matter. I was *this* close to saving her life."

"I can't imagine what you have been through, but you are home now, you're safe."

They stayed in that embrace for a few minutes whilst the soothing lounge-music played. Claire stroked Mel's hair until she fell asleep. The fish pie would keep for later.

Imran Bhatta's return home coincided with his in-laws preparing to set off to return to London. As Lania hugged the children, Ali placed the suitcase in the back of the Jaguar. Lania hugged Imran and congratulated him on the closure of the case. Ali returned to the kitchen where Imran was leaning on the sink panel and drinking a glass of chilled water.

"Spare me another lecture, Ali," he said in a voice drained of energy. "I know your opinion and we will just have to accept that we disagree on some things."

"No, no lectures, Imran. I heard on the news about what happened," said Ali. "Colleagues in London have called me about it. It is big news all over the country. You caught a serial killer, Imran. You succeeded, and you can look those who judge you in the eye. I take off my hat to you. I have saved many lives, always one at a time. You have achieved something big here. I cannot fully appreciate it, not as you do anyway, but you make a difference. Perhaps this place needs what you bring to them." He shook Imran's hand and went out to the car.

Imran sat at the kitchen table and rested his head on his folded arms. By the time Sunila and the children came back into the kitchen, he too was asleep.

**

Other titles by Barry Lees;

This City of Lies

It is 1959 and war veteran turned San Francisco private eye Kerrigan takes on a routine matrimonial case in which those involved are not what they appear to be. Events take a dangerous turn when he finds that he too has become a target, but for who? When he witnesses a murder, his instinct to survive takes over. Alone and struggling with the memories of his war experiences, Kerrigan must find the killer before the killer finds him.

The Governor's Man

It is the Fall of 1959 and San Francisco Private Investigator Kerrigan is hired to find a missing person. A name from the past evokes painful memories, which force him to challenge his own judgement and question his loyalties. Cast into a complex web of deceit, politics, religion, theft and murder, he has to investigate and eliminate many suspects, each with equally compelling motives, to uncover the truth, catch a killer and put right an old injustice.

By Sword and Feather

It is 1960 and San Francisco Private Investigator Kerrigan reluctantly accepts a job as a bodyguard to foil a kidnap plot. Whilst trying to avert a diplomatic incident, he becomes involved in an investigation into a murder with a bizarre yet familiar modus operandi. Made to relive old traumas of the Burmese jungle, he is driven by the need to avenge the death of an old friend.

Exiles from a Torn Province

Belfast 1978. Catholic James falls in love with Protestant Lizzie. Knowing the risks, they keep their identities secret from each other. When both suffer the loss of a family member in violent circumstances, their respective communities whisk each of them to safety overseas - but to different countries, whilst Darry, an ambitious I.R.A. operative, is caught, and jailed for one of the killings. Although neither knows it, all three are set on a collision course. The clash of peace against violence is taken to the extreme. The result is an audacious, terror-plot aimed at the heart of the U.K. establishment.

Wasps Among the Ivy

When a sting operation to catch Manchester's most notorious drug dealer goes wrong with fatal consequences, detective Russell Warren gets the blame and is sent back to uniform in disgrace to work a beat that nobody wants. Stretched to its limits and dangerously under resourced, Heavem Hospital is home to the mentally ill, the handicapped, the addicted, the troubled, the vulnerable, the suicidal and the criminally insane. It is described to Warren as 'a disaster waiting to happen.' When it does, and with devastating consequences, it is up to Warren to keep the innocent safe from the murderous.

The Blue, the Green and the Dead.

When a company fracking for shale gas are found to have caused earthquakes, the community forms a strong objection and large-scale protests follow. Amidst the protesters, one of them has a secret. An agent of a powerful player is trying to inhibit the fracking operation, but for different reasons. Highly trained, ruthless and a seasoned killer, he will stop at nothing to achieve his aims. Among the police lines is another secret, a cop with a past and the skills to equalise this situation.

Violence and rancour grows and deaths soon follow. When the anti-fracking campaign takes a dramatic and catastrophic twist, it creates a flashpoint that really does shake the ground beneath.

Printed in Great Britain
by Amazon